LEARNING
TO SWEAR
IN AMERICA

LEARNING TO SWEAR IN AMERICA

KATIE KENNEDY

BLOOMSBURY

NEW YORK LONDON OXFORD NEW DELHI SYDNEY

First published in the United States of America in July 2016
by Bloomsbury Children's Books
www.bloomsbury.com

Bloomsbury is a registered trademark of Bloomsbury Publishing Plc

For information about permission to reproduce selections from this book, write to
Permissions, Bloomsbury Children's Books, 1385 Broadway, New York, New York 10018
Bloomsbury books may be purchased for business or promotional use. For information on
bulk purchases please contact Macmillan Corporate and Premium Sales Department at
specialmarkets@macmillan.com

Library of Congress Cataloging-in-Publication Data
Names: Kennedy, Katie.
Title: Learning to swear in America / by Katie Kennedy.
Description: New York : Bloomsbury Children's Books, 2016.
Summary: Brought over from Russia to help NASA prevent an asteroid from colliding with Earth,
seventeen-year-old physics genius Yuri feels awkward and alone until he meets free-spirited Dovie.
Identifiers: LCCN 2015025454
ISBN 978-1-61963-909-6 (hardcover) • ISBN 978-1-61963-910-2 (e-book)
Subjects: | CYAC: Asteroids—Fiction. | Survival—Fiction. | Genius—Fiction. | Love—Fiction. |
Russians—United States—Fiction. | Science fiction. | BISAC: JUVENILE FICTION / Social Issues /
New Experience. | JUVENILE FICTION / Science Fiction. | JUVENILE FICTION / Love & Romance. |
JUVENILE FICTION / Action & Adventure / Survival Stories.
Classification: LCC PZ7.1.K505 Le 2016 | DDC [Fic]—dc23
LC record available at http://lccn.loc.gov/2015025454

Book design by Colleen Andrews
Typeset by RefineCatch Limited, Bungay, Suffolk
Printed and bound in the U.S.A. by Berryville Graphics Inc., Berryville, Virginia
2 4 6 8 10 9 7 5 3

All papers used by Bloomsbury Publishing, Inc., are natural, recyclable products
made from wood grown in well-managed forests. The manufacturing processes
conform to the environmental regulations of the country of origin.

To my family

CHAPTER 1

NO NEED TO PANIC

Because there's no air in space, the asteroid hurtled toward Earth in absolute silence. Of the two objects headed toward North America—the BR1019 asteroid and Yuri Strelnikov's flight from Moscow—only his plane made a sound. The thought made Yuri smile faintly as the American military plane descended, engines roaring.

The aircraft touched down and taxied, and a moment later the pilot opened the door for its lone passenger. Yuri stepped to the top of the airstair and surveyed the sun-drenched airport. Then he trotted down, carrying a single suitcase and a book bag looped over his shoulder, and headed to a waiting helicopter.

Yuri dragged his suitcase with one hand, felt the bite of the book bag's strap and the heat of the sun on his shoulders. He rolled up the sleeves of his dress shirt with his free hand as he walked. He'd grown an inch in the past six months, and while the sleeves were long enough now, they might not be in a couple of weeks.

How would he get a new shirt here? Better to roll the sleeves up from the start, so people were used to it.

An American officer stepped forward to open the helicopter door. He got in after Yuri and nodded to the pilot. Yuri took the headphones he offered, and a moment later the man's voice crackled through. "NASA's Near Earth Object Program is housed at the Jet Propulsion Laboratory in Pasadena. I'll point it out as we get close."

Then the pilot lifted off, and once again the ground fell away below Yuri. The pilot threw the throttle open and the craft shuddered and then responded. Yuri laid his cheek against the glass and gazed into the blue arcing over America. He wouldn't see the asteroid. He knew that. By the time you could see it, it was too late. Because, although it was still in the dark reaches of space, the asteroid was traveling at 159,000 miles per hour.

Yuri sat in the back of the helicopter, his headphones muting the *whomp* of the rotors, and looked down at this dry city, lower and brighter than Moscow. He didn't know what he thought of it yet. It was just . . . different. Yuri glanced at the officer and tried not to fidget. He could see people in white-and-glass buildings watching their descent as the pilot banked and landed. As they climbed out, the officer shouted at Yuri to keep his head down, and put a heavy hand on his neck to make sure he avoided the slowing rotor blades. He ushered Yuri inside one of the buildings and said, "Good luck."

Yuri started to say, "You, too," but realized it wasn't appropriate, and was still searching for a response as the man left. Yuri stood for a moment, fingering the strap of his book bag, wishing he didn't have the suitcase with him. Who brings a suitcase to an office building? An air-conditioning vent blasted ripples through his blond hair.

A security guard walked over to him and said, "Follow me," then turned and led Yuri to a door off a large conference room. "You're supposed to wait in here." He jerked his head toward the door and walked off, and Yuri went in. The room was very small. It had two chairs on the right wall, two on the left, a tiny table with a pile of old magazines against the far wall. A boy of maybe five or six sat in a chair to the left. Yuri unslung his book bag and sat down opposite him.

The boy fingered the handle of a plastic tote bag as though Yuri might steal it. "Who are you?"

"Yuri Strelnikov. Who are you?"

"I'm not supposed to talk to strangers."

"Oh."

They were quiet for a moment.

"I'm Tim." The kid flopped across both chairs, with his head hanging off the end. He rolled to his side and pointed at Yuri's bags.

"What's in there?"

"Clothes mostly."

"I've got blocks in mine."

Tim opened his bag and dumped a pile of blocks on the floor. He began to build a tower, one block on top of another.

"Your base needs to be wider. See how it leans?" Yuri pointed. "It's already maybe eight degrees off vertical."

Yuri got on the floor beside him and snapped two long blocks onto the bottom of the tower. "See? This will increase your structural integrity."

Tim grabbed more blocks and widened the base of his tower again, so that it was four blocks wide at the bottom.

The door opened. A tall man peered in at them. He was bald and had piercing blue eyes below a forehead that rose like a crown. "Dr. Strelnikov?"

Yuri rose. "Yes?"

The man flushed, then stepped forward and threw out his hand. "I'm Karl Fletcher, director of NASA's Near Earth Object Program. Nice to have you aboard."

He led Yuri out of the room. "Sorry about the confusion. The boy is the grandson of one of our support people. He's waiting for her."

"Oh."

Fletcher cleared his throat. "You're seventeen, right?"

"Yes."

Fletcher shrugged apologetically, and then Yuri got it. *Oh*. The security guard thought Yuri was the grandson. And the director had walked in to see two kids on the floor playing with blocks. It could not be more humiliating. Yuri felt his face flame and knew that just made it worse. Fletcher pulled him into a large conference room, mostly open, with tables holding coffee decanters and doughnuts pushed against a far wall. The suitcase still embarrassed Yuri, and he pushed it under a table with his foot. The director introduced him to a half-dozen people—the local caffeine addicts, probably—and Yuri slowly relaxed. They wore name tags emblazoned with "NASA" and the agency's symbol, an orbit and wing in mid-century style.

Fletcher handed him a name tag, and Yuri looked at it and smiled. He had seen his name spelled in English before, but it still looked funny, English requiring a *y* and a *u* to make one Russian letter. He pinned the name tag on his shirt.

"I don't know what you've heard about this rock," Fletcher said. "Since you're gonna help us stop it, let me bring you up to speed. BR1019"—he said it like "Bee Are Ten Nineteen"—"isn't from the asteroid belt—it came from way out. We don't know if it's swung close by Earth before—it could have an orbit in the thousands of years. Or it might have hit some piece of space junk that altered its orbit."

Yuri nodded. Happened all the time.

"It's dim, so we were late picking it up—and of course it's coming out of the sun. Makes it harder." Fletcher snagged a doughnut off the table. "It was an amateur who found it."

Yuri shrugged. "Not so embarrassing as it sounds. You were looking at places where asteroids come from, yes? And this one is in retrograde orbit."

"Not what we were expecting," Fletcher admitted. "We haven't had a chance to do everything yet. Shape, spectral analysis—we had to concentrate first on calculating the orbit, and once we realized it'll be a direct hit, we've had to calculate speed . . ."

"So we know how long we've got," Yuri said.

"Right."

Against the wall, the coffee decanter was doing steady business as people filtered in and out of the room, feet soundless on the light blue carpet.

"So what exactly do you want me to do?"

A man with rimless glasses and thinning hair approached the table, but he wasn't looking at the decanters. There was something in his stride that made Yuri stiffen, and he shifted to conceal his suitcase. The man cocked his head to the side and as Fletcher gestured toward Yuri, starting an introduction, he spoke. "Russia's boy wonder. Huh." Yuri wasn't sure how to answer that, or even if it was a question, but he felt the room stir around him. People were watching. "I'm Zach Simons."

"Zach is your team leader," Fletcher said. "Zach, this is . . ."

"Yeah, I know who he is, I just don't know why he's here. I got a question for you, Dr. Strelnikov. Do you shave yet?"

"On formal occasions," Yuri said, keeping his eyes on Simons. "I shaved for night I accepted Wolf Prize, for example."

Simons reddened as an appreciative murmur rose from the other scientists in the conference room.

"Okay," Fletcher said. "Nice that you guys met." He led Yuri to the far side of the conference room, away from Simons. "Obviously nudging it off course would be the first choice," Fletcher said, getting back on topic. "It's too late for that, so we're going to try to shoot it down. Send weapons into it, try to blow it into several pieces, and hope they're small enough to burn up in our atmosphere. We already know our best window will come when the 1019 is very close."

Yuri shifted impatiently. He already knew this. Everyone already knew this.

"Essentially we're making one giant mathematical computer model. I've divided it into twenty-three different sections." Fletcher finished off the doughnut and licked his fingers. "We have that many teams, each working on one part of the problem."

Fletcher motioned him back to the other side of the room, and Yuri sheepishly retrieved his suitcase and lugged it over to Fletcher. Because being a third the age of everyone else didn't make him stick out enough.

"You're Team Eleven, working with the charming Zach Simons and Bruce Pirkola, who's the sonofabitch over there swallowing a bottle of Tylenol. See, in the corner? Because he chose this particular week to get a goddamn kidney stone." Fletcher stared into Yuri's eyes. "I trust you're too young to have a kidney stone?"

"Yes, sir."

"Good." He thrust a thick printout with a black binder clip at Yuri. "This is an overview of the model. Your section is highlighted. You and Simons and Pirkola figure out what goes in it."

"What weapons are we using? We'll need to know mass, speed . . ."

"Yeah." Fletcher rolled his jaw side to side. "We've got people working on that. You don't need access to the weapons list."

Yuri stared at him. "This is critical information. To calculate our section . . ."

"Your team doesn't have to know this," Fletcher said.

Yuri picked at his bag strap with his thumbnail. "How can you possibly keep information from some of people working . . ."

"Not some people," Fletcher said, smiling tightly. "Just you. Look, if you really need something, if you think weapon specs will change your calculations, ask Simons. He's your group leader. He can talk to me, and I'll figure it out."

He led the way upstairs and to a small office off a hall to the right, brushing powdered sugar from his shirt as he walked. "This is yours for the duration. And we got you a hotel room. A car service will take you over there tonight. There's a cafeteria downstairs. You don't need money, just take what you want. We've . . ."

"But won't we be working all night? I mean, is critical situation."

"Of course not," Fletcher said. "This is going to take days. You know impact is June ninth, right?"

Yuri nodded.

"We're all going to work our asses off, but we'll get it done. The last thing I want is a bunch of sleep-deprived zombies making critical decisions."

He opened the door to Yuri's office. Yuri unslung his book bag from his shoulder and rested it on his foot.

"If you need something, just hit '1' on your phone. The person who answers isn't a secretary; she's one of us. You can talk physics to her, explain what you need, who you have to get hold of."

Yuri ran a hand through his hair and looked at this pale blue office half a world from home.

"We have to avoid group think," Fletcher said. "Make your

own calculations, and then the three of you hash it out. Pray you come up with the same damn thing. You have to agree, because whatever your group comes up with is what we're going to enter. Then we'll embed the equations in the computer model they'll use to program the weapons. Got it?"

Yuri nodded.

"Now get the hell to work. You're already behind everybody else." Fletcher started back down the corridor.

"Sir? Dr. Fletcher?"

He turned. "Yeah?"

"Am I the only one who's not American?"

"No, we got a Chinese guy, too. He arrived four hours ago." He stared for a moment at Yuri's blue eyes, his tousle of blond hair. "Your work on antimatter? Blew us away. If we survive this, you're gonna be the youngest person to win a Nobel." He shook his head, then waved his hand toward the office as though sweeping Yuri inside, and started back toward the conference room.

Yuri licked his lips and called after him. "Dr. Fletcher? What they're saying, that if this doesn't work, asteroid will explode over Los Angeles with enough force to devastate whole city? Is that true?"

Fletcher took a breath, then answered flatly.

"That's what Moscow's saying? It isn't true. If we have impact, it'll lay waste to the whole region. A tsunami may take out Japan."

Yuri stared at him.

"But," Fletcher said, "I guess they didn't see any need to panic people."

CHAPTER 2

ONE PIECE OF TAPE ON

Yuri walked into the pale blue office, found a roll of masking tape, and wrote his name on it in marker, copying from his name tag so he couldn't misspell it. He ripped the piece of tape off, enjoying the faint rubbery scent, and smoothed it on the wall outside his door: *Strelnikov, Y.A.*

Then he sat at the desk and pulled his calculator out of his book bag, and a hockey puck signed by Moscow Team Dynamo's captain. When he left Russia, the authorities had given him twenty minutes to pack. He'd thrown clothes in his suitcase, tossed in a couple of reference books, but was stumped when it came to keepsakes. He didn't get where he was, as young as he was, without giving up a lot of things—that meant he didn't have a shoe box stuffed with ticket stubs and photos with friends.

So with a driver standing at the door, tapping his foot, Yuri had tucked in a photo of his dissertation advisor—Dr. Kryukov, a wonderful old man with extravagant eyebrows—and the puck, his one true keepsake. The photo wasn't framed, so he kept it in his bag. It was enough knowing it was there. He rolled the puck under his palm, released it, and let it clatter to a rest. Then he spread the printout of the work and scanned it, trying to get his bearings. He should get some idea of what he was doing, and then talk to his team members.

But Fletcher's words ran in an endless loop inside his skull, like a bird he'd once seen trapped in a library dome. It flew in faster and faster circles and finally dropped, dead before it hit the floor. *If we survive this.* Because Yuri had just put himself in the path of the asteroid.

There was time to do the math, to make the computer model to guide the missiles. It would be hard work, but there was time, enough that Fletcher wanted them to sleep well, even unwind a little. Yuri would do his work; Simons and Pirkola would calculate their solutions. They would compare, and because they all knew what they were doing, they would get the same result. They would give Fletcher their part, and the Americans would shoot down the asteroid. He would go home, exaggerate his role, and maybe get laid.

And if it didn't work?

He was seventeen and he would be dead in three weeks.

Who would mourn him? Gregor Kryukov. And his mother, of course. They'd probably put a memo on her desk, and she'd read it when she had time. But he wouldn't be like all those regular dead kids who had a park bench with their name on a plaque. He wouldn't get a bench, but he didn't want one, either. He wanted a Nobel.

No—after his group worked out their part of the math, he was just going to have to fly home to Moscow. It would be painful explaining to Fletcher that he was leaving them, that he'd done his best, and if it didn't work, well, Yuri didn't want to be in Pasadena when it hit. But it wouldn't be the *most* socially awkward moment he'd ever had.

He flexed his hands, stood his puck on its edge for luck, and started reading. An elevator down the hall rumbled, or maybe it was a drink cart going past. Did they do that? And then the puck rolled to the end of his desk, paused, and rolled the other direction. He stared at it. Yuri had studied with brilliant people at one of the best institutions in the world. He understood laws of motion. He didn't understand this. A body at rest . . . flew off the edge of the desk. And then the books were shaking, inching forward on the shelves, and falling off, splaying open on the carpet, and he could feel the vibration through his feet, all the way up to his knees. *Earthquake.*

He ran from the room. The hall was filled with people standing calmly in their doorways. "Is earthquake, I think!" he shouted, running down the hall. A few doors were closed and he beat on them as he ran by. "Earthquake!" He paused at the elevator and imagined the car swaying on its cable, and he plunged into the east stairwell.

The shuddering stopped, but he grabbed the railing with both hands and crabbed down sideways, not convinced that the ground wouldn't move beneath him again. It looked ridiculous to hold on like that, but it beat being buried in rubble for three days and having to drink his own urine. At the bottom he looked up and saw a dozen faces on each of the stairwells above, looking down at him. Idiots. They were all going to die, and he was going to have to stop the asteroid by himself. The ground gave another jolt. He threw his arms up and shook his hands and shouted, "Earthquake!" over the rumble. Then he ran out the stairwell doors and into the lobby.

He could see the coffee decanters in the conference room bouncing across the table, as though containing that much caffeine had finally gotten to them. A lamp swung overhead, reminding him of Galileo's pendulum experiments, but, with the unsteady rippling of the earth, the time the light took to complete its arc was not constant. And that was so, so wrong.

"Help me, Galileo," he muttered. It was as close to praying as he was going to come. He started for the front door, but it was glass, and he should stay away from glass, right? So he stood in the lobby, hands out at his sides, palms down, as though to calm the earth.

"Hey." It was Karl Fletcher, the director. The ground quieted.

"Is earthquake, I think."

"Yeah, we get these."

"We need to evacuate building. I banged on doors upstairs and shouted to people, but maybe nobody heard."

"Seriously? Okay, let's get you outside." He gripped Yuri's upper arm and pulled him through the plate glass door, down the steps, and into the middle of the street. "Better?"

Yuri watched the street suspiciously. The rumbling was over, and the pavement was still. Inside, the lamp would be describing normal arcs again, and then be stationary. He took a breath. "Nobody else came out."

"Nah, this wasn't too bad. Enough to get your attention, though, right?"

Yuri flushed and glanced up. The windows were lined with people looking out into the street. "Perhaps I overreacted?" The director laughed and slapped him between his shoulder blades. "I didn't want to have to drink my urine," Yuri said.

Fletcher was silent for a moment. "We do have beverage alternatives. There's a vending machine downstairs."

Yuri barked a laugh.

Fletcher led him back upstairs to his office, one hand on Yuri's arm, the other angrily waving gawkers away.

"We have asteroid coming in very fast. Would be nice if Earth stayed in same place for little while."

"It would be nicer if it moved the hell out of the way," Fletcher said. He smacked Yuri on the back. "Show's over. Get to work." He shut the door and left.

Yuri picked up the fallen books while his stomach settled, then restored the puck to his desk, sat down, and got to work. It was simple, in a sense, to arrange a killing strike at the asteroid. Getting it right was what made it hard. They had to account for the rotation of Earth, the speed and rotation of the incoming body, the gravitational pull of the moon, for solar flares, for mass and speed and Earth's tilt on its axis. He didn't think the asteroid would pass one of the points of Lagrange, but it would be a pretty good idea to check. Even the Coriolis effect would slightly alter the missiles' trajectory if they were leaving from Earth. Did the Americans have missiles stationed in space? Someone had to choose the weaponry, and the angle of fire, and the exact moment of launch.

And the calculation had to be precise, because although the asteroid was big for space junk, it had to be struck in the right spots or the wreckage would be too big to burn on entry into Earth's atmosphere. And then there would be multiple points of impact.

And it was moving so fast.

Yuri read the whole problem through, front to back, twice. No time for a misunderstanding—there would be no second chance. His group had a small but complex calculation to make. There were multiple variables and no ability to experiment. He was a theoretical physicist, anyway—a math guy, not a lab rat, but it was the kind of problem that would normally take him a couple of hours to write out. A semester to solve. What they were doing here was more like working a crossword puzzle. Jot some things in, and hope that last word would fit.

He set to work, and when he glanced up and saw the round institutional clock on the opposite wall, he was shocked at how much time had passed. He stretched and walked down to the conference room and its beverages and pastries. At least the decanters were standing still.

Yuri poured himself a cup of tea. A woman nodded to him.

She had to be seventy, her steel-gray hair pulled back in a neat bun.

Yuri poured a coffee for her.

She smiled faintly and took the cup from his hand. "Dr. Strelnikov, you're not a waiter. Do what you do best." She inclined her head and walked off.

A girl walked into the room. Yuri gaped at her, his hand tightening on the decanter he still held. She clearly didn't belong here, but she didn't seem to know it. Or maybe she just didn't care. She was about his age, shorter than average and not a thin girl. Her bangs were yellow, not blond, against dark hair and they stuck straight up. He had a sudden certainty that in an algebra equation, she would be the unknown x.

Her dark eyes took him in, standing at the refreshment table, and as she smiled and started toward him, he felt a moment of irrational panic. She was wearing a sundress and those shoes with just a V of plastic between your toes, and long, dangly earrings that swung when she walked. He didn't know anything about jewelry, but he was pretty sure there should be no dangling in a NASA building.

Yuri's genius did not extend to social relations in the best of times. This girl—he'd never seen anything like her. How did one talk to American girls? And she was walking straight toward him.

A guard cut over and intercepted her.

"Miss? You have business here?" He was curt.

"Um, I'm waiting for my father."

"He work here?"

"Yeah."

"What's his name?"

"John Collum."

Yuri shifted so he could see her past the guard.

"Where's his office?"

"Um. He's a janitor."

"Not in this building." The man said it as though pronouncing a prison sentence.

"No, he's down in . . ."

"Why don't you wait outside, miss?"

He didn't say it as a question, and he took a step forward. It wasn't a threat, exactly, but Yuri felt a flash of anger. If the guard had to keep her out, he could have been . . . nicer. The girl turned and went outside, her shoes flapping as she walked. Yuri put the decanter down and stepped forward so he could see out the conference room door. She walked down the steps and sat on the edge of a planter in front of the building. Where janitors' daughters could sit, apparently.

Yuri went back to the table and, using napkins for sanitation, grabbed three doughnuts. He ripped off a box lid and laid them inside, tossed in sugar packets and powdered creamer. He balanced the box lid on his arm and held her coffee in one hand, his tea in the other. When he got to the door, he realized he didn't have a hand to open it.

"Excuse me. Security? Can you open door, please?" Yuri enjoyed making the guard walk back across the lobby.

The man opened the inner door for him, and Yuri stood in the lobby and waited for him to open the outer door, too. The heat smacked him in the face. He was walking down the steps when he realized that he'd been afraid of the girl when she was coming at him. Now he was going to her? He thought about turning around, but if the guard was still there, it would be too embarrassing. The girl was fiddling with her phone, but she saw him and her face lit up and she smiled. He sighed and walked up to her.

"I thought maybe you wanted pastry," he said, holding out the box, trying not to stare at the green glitter above her eyes.

"I did! There were so many on the table I thought I could sneak one." She laid her phone on the planter and pulled out a chocolate-glazed cream-filled doughnut. Her rings, a different-colored one on every finger, caught the bright California sunlight.

Yuri held out the coffee and she took it, then scooted over and gestured toward the planter. He hesitated, then sat beside her. Only his toes touched the ground, so he inched forward so that his feet were down flat. It left him half leaning awkwardly on the planter. At least he wouldn't look like a kid. The girl's feet hung in the air, and as she rolled her toes under, her plastic shoes smacked against her heels.

"You won't get in trouble for being out here?" she said.

"Pardon?" Then he realized she couldn't see his name tag, and thought he was in food service. He laughed. The woman inside, who'd told him not to act like a waiter, would not have been pleased.

"You have a nice laugh."

"No, I don't."

"Are you contradicting me?" She gave him a severe look that was undercut by the chocolate on her lip.

"Yes."

"Why?"

"Because you're wrong. My laugh sounds funny." Why had he confessed that he didn't like its sound?

"Well, I like it. But you probably don't get a chance to practice it with those self-important jerks in there."

Yuri flushed. Must be the combination of tea and sun, because what did he care what she thought?

"They're doing important work," he said.

"Yeah. But they could be nicer while they do it."

He didn't say anything, because she was right. He sipped his tea and tried desperately to think of something to say. The problem with conversations was that you had to know something about the other person—what would interest them. And how did you know that until you'd had the conversation?

"Are you in school?" she asked.

He wanted to congratulate her for thinking of something to say, but maybe it wasn't as hard for her. "No, I finished."

"Drop out or graduate?"

"Oh. Um, I graduated."

"That's good. Then you can go to college if you decide to."

He just nodded. They were silent for a moment.

"I wish I was done with school," she said.

"Why?"

She stared into her coffee cup. "I kinda hate my math teacher."

He recoiled. "Seriously?"

"Yeah. Why? You like math?"

"Very much. It's language of universe."

She blew air out sharply. "Then the universe is swearing at me."

He thought about explaining math's beauty to her, the elegance of an equation, the simplicity within the complexity. The thrill of touching truth and knowing it as ancient and unassailable, as permanent and profound. But he was a math guy—he didn't have the words to do it—not in English. Probably not in Russian, either.

"I don't like algebra," she said, "but it's mostly the teacher. I mean, he could spend his life searching for x without being such an a-hole, you know?"

Yuri nodded carefully. He was talking to a pretty American girl about math. Life wasn't likely to get better than this—but he didn't know how to proceed. He gave his cuffs a quick check, glad that he'd rolled them up. The shirt still seemed to fit. At least his arms hadn't chosen today to shoot out longer.

His tea sloshed in the cup, and then he heard the rumble. "Is another earthquake, I think." He set his cup on the ledge and moved to the street, hands out to his sides, looking up at the buildings.

"Yeah, it's an aftershock," she said. "The Cal Tech seismologists said we'd probably get a couple."

"A couple? More than one?"

She shrugged. "You never know."

"You need to stand in street." He waved her over. "Is safer. In case glass falls."

"We should be okay." Her tongue scraped over the cream filling in her doughnut.

"No," Yuri said. "I must insist." He walked over to the planter, his stride wide for balance.

"Howdy, pardner," the girl said.

He didn't have time to find out what she meant, because he was taking her coffee and wanting his fingers to brush hers, but they didn't. He set the cup on the planter and led her into the street.

"I think is okay now," he said, eyeing the buildings around them.

"We're going to get run over."

"Is earthquake! Doesn't traffic stop?"

"Not for this." She started to say something, then stopped and said, "That's my dad. Thanks for the doughnut."

"Take one for him."

She smiled at him and his stomach made a final flip, even though the rumbling underfoot was stopping. She ran back to the pastry box and picked up a cruller with her fingers. He winced at the lack of sanitation. Then she ran across the street and interlaced her fingers with those of the man walking there, as though it was the most natural thing in the world. She turned to wave as they walked away holding hands, the man eating his cruller. Yuri retrieved his tea and held it, watching her until she was lost to sight.

When he turned to go back into the building, he saw her phone lying on the planter. He retrieved it and brought the screen up. He got into her contacts and found a number listed under "home," but who would he ask for? It really only made sense to look through her social media sites so he could find out her name. Just so he could return the phone properly. It wasn't spying; it was chivalry.

There were photos at a picnic with a girl identified as Mary, and selfies at an art museum. And then he heard the *slap slap* of her plastic soles and looked up, and she was around the corner and running back toward him, her sundress a spot of color between the white buildings. He used his thumb to get out of her sites as he walked toward her. She smiled and he held the phone out.

"Thanks. I can't believe I left it." And then she was gone again.

Yuri stood watching her go a second time, then turned back to the planter to clear away the box. At least he had her phone number, even if he didn't know her name. He had the phone number of a pretty American girl who might need help with math. He stuffed the box in a garbage can outside the building and smiled as he walked into the lobby.

Then he stood stock-still. He didn't remember it. The number beside "home." He couldn't remember what it was. It was the greatest failure in the history of mathematics.

CHAPTER 3

ONE PIECE OF TAPE OFF

Jet lag had finally caught him and Yuri was sitting upright at his desk, dozing, when a soft kick at the door startled him awake.

"It's Simons and Pirkola. You're on our team."

"Oh." How did Americans give permission to come into a room? "Enter freely." There. That sounded good.

Simons was smiling as he walked into the office, carrying two plates. He had bottles of water tucked in his armpits. Pirkola trailed, ashen, his hands wrapped around a glass bowl of applesauce covered with cellophane. What was left of Pirkola's hair was dark, and he had serious biceps exposed under a navy polo. He must log significant gym time. Yuri was vaguely disappointed that they hadn't all been issued matching shirts. He'd never been on a sports team. This was his best chance to be part of a group, and it wasn't an unreasonable idea. The cosmonauts had matching shirts. Someone at NEO should have thought of this.

"Thought we'd have a late dinner in here. It'll give us a chance to talk." Simons handed him a plate.

"I'm not good for much," Pirkola said. "Damn kidney stone."

"Can't they perform laser technique at hospital?" Yuri said.

"I don't want to waste the time until we've got our part figured out." Pirkola took the cellophane off his applesauce and stared at it. The sweat on the plastic matched his upper lip. "What have you been doing so far?"

"Uh . . . just getting . . . adjusted. Looking at what we're doing." He wondered if Simons would make another boy-genius crack, but he seemed to have come in peace.

"We should have found this thing sooner," Simons said, taking a pull on his water bottle. "I can't quite let go of that."

Yuri shrugged. "BR1019 is from out of solar system, with orbit sharply off plane. There was some attention to L4 and L5 of Sun-Jupiter system, but as far out as 1019's orbit goes, and with budget cuts in Russia and here? Nobody was looking."

"I know," Simons said glumly.

"There's about a hundred people in the world who look for these things," Pirkola said, fingering his spoon. "And it's a big sky."

They ate without attention to the food, leaning together, talking. After an hour a loudspeaker crackled on, and a woman's voice said, "The sun is setting."

"Sun is setting? They make announcement?"

Simons nodded. "There's a good view from the west lobby. Come on."

Yuri followed the older man down the hall to a three-story stairwell with a glass wall. Scientists lined the stairs and spread across the upper hall, gripping the railing, watching the sun set. It was beautiful, Yuri thought, pink and purple streaks across an orange sky, brighter than at home. Stronger colors.

"Seventeen left," someone murmured. One guy walked over to horizontal strips of colored duct tape stuck on the wall beside the window. There was an orange piece, and below it a purple, then a pink, repeating downward. The guy ripped off the top strip and balled it in his hand, working it with nervous fingers. It left seventeen strips. Then Yuri got it—seventeen sunsets. One strip for every day left.

It was unsettling to see their lives displayed in duct tape—and to hear a day rip away. Yuri was suddenly tired. He yawned, and Pirkola *thunked* him on the back.

"If you call '1' from your office, they'll get you a ride to your hotel."

Yuri nodded but stayed behind to watch the last orange glow. Then he explored the lower corridor. Cafeteria, storage rooms, and, farther down the hall, voices. He followed them: baritones talking over one another, laughing, and as he got closer, Yuri heard the flip of cards and clink of poker chips on a table. Decibels rose and waned, and he saw the undulations as they would look if graphed. The science of social life. He wanted to listen, was drawn toward the voices just as, on evening walks in Moscow, he looked through undraped windows into homes where people gathered over food or games, caught glimpses of girls turning to smile at people who were not him, men opening bottles of vodka, then holding them aloft as people clapped. Family, friends. He would stand outside, light spilling onto the street, almost to his feet.

He turned the corner, intending to loiter nearby, but the voices floated from a staff lounge with its door thrown wide, and he was standing in front of it. Four men in janitorial gray looked up at him, smiles fading slowly as they saw him. They sat on mismatched chairs around a small table covered with poker chips. Two of the men were black, one Hispanic, one white. The poker chips were red, white, and blue. The whole scene looked almost comically American.

"You lost?" one of the men called.

"Uh—no. Just exploring." Yuri started to move on, embarrassed, though he couldn't have said why.

"We're on break," the older black guy said, rocking back in his chair, his cards fanned across his chest.

Yuri shrugged. Not his business.

"You're NASA?" the guy said. "You an intern or something?"

Yuri flushed. "No. I'm physicist."

The men exchanged glances.

"You working with them? You a genius or something?"

"Well, yeah."

That made them laugh, and Yuri flushed again, not sure if he was being mocked.

The older guy patted a crate filled with procedural manuals, and Yuri walked over and sat. It was the kids' table in a janitor's lounge, but he was happy to be there. The men finished their hand, and the Hispanic guy facing Yuri grinned and raked the chips toward him while the others howled.

"So up there," the older man said, gathering the cards, "are you the smartest guy in the room?"

"Sure as hell is down here," the white guy said, and they all laughed.

Yuri thought for a moment. "No, probably not. But it's impressive room."

They nodded. The older guy shuffled. "Lemme ask you something." Instead of asking, he dealt the cards, one down, then one up. Thick, calloused fingers moved stacks of chips to the center of the table. "So if this thing hits us," he said, sliding a card to another man as he tapped his knuckle on the table, "what's it going to be like?"

They kept playing, none of them looking at Yuri.

He wondered suddenly what it must be like for them, being in the NEO building, swabbing floors, and not really knowing what was happening. How many experts had they passed that week, these men in uniforms that made them invisible? He'd spent a few years being ignored, too, because he was young—and he guessed his age was the reason they were talking to him now. It made him the only approachable physicist in the place.

He told them the truth. It was an issue of respect. "If it hits, there will be concussion—shock waves—not when it hits Earth, but when it enters atmosphere. That will kill people in California. It's because leading edge will get hotter than trailing edge. So it explodes in air, you understand? If there's any rock left—and there probably will be—impact on surface will raise dust cloud with global effects and regional calamity. And then tsunami may follow."

"Jesus," the white guy said. "Is it gonna be like the one that killed the dinosaurs?"

"No," Yuri said. "It's not Earth-killer. Worst case is we lose western United States, and maybe in hundred years some plants can get foothold here again, start over. But, that's Plan B. Plan A is we stop asteroid, and everybody lives."

"I like Plan A," one of the men said, and the others muttered agreement.

"You have another problem, too," Yuri said, standing to go. He nodded to the Hispanic guy. "I can count cards, and I think you have one too many jacks in your hand."

He was around the corner before the janitors understood. He smiled as he heard three of them howl, and one start rapidly explaining about a faulty deck.

One day closer to impact.

CHAPTER 4

IT WASN'T EGO

Time became a blur of work and paper and numbers. By the second day Yuri had his shoes and socks off and his hair stood on end like haystacks, the result of holding it in his fist as he bent, elbow on the table, over his work.

The math became life. He could see it when he shut his eyes. He dreamed once, sitting at his desk, of the calculations stretching out from Earth to the asteroid, the rock hitting the far number, hesitating, then hurtling downward, splintering exponents and integers, their shards flying into space. He jerked awake and walked to the conference room for a cup of tepid tea.

He drank half the cup and pitched it, then walked into the front office to see the woman who answered when he dialed "1." She had a no-nonsense look, but she smiled when he walked in. "Dr. Strelnikov. What can I do for you?" They hadn't been introduced, but of course she knew him. People always knew which one he was. He wondered if he'd miss that when he was forty.

"I want to set up Skype call . . . to Russia," he said.

"Sure. When do you want to call?" she asked.

He thought for a moment. It would be evening in Russia, late enough that his mother should be home from the hospital, early enough that she probably hadn't been called back in yet. Probably.

"Can I do it now?"

"I think so." She smiled again, and he was glad she hadn't asked who he wanted to talk to. There was nothing wrong with it, skyping with his mother, and he hadn't let her know he'd arrived safely. He should rectify that.

Fifteen minutes later Yuri was sitting in his office chair, staring into his computer. The Dial 1 woman was standing by the door. She'd said she'd leave as soon as she was sure the call had gone through. Yuri waited, gently kicking a desk leg with the side of his foot, and then his mother's face appeared on the screen. She had short blond hair and the blue eyes she'd given him. She looked tired and didn't have makeup on.

"Yuri?"

He smiled. "Hi," he said in Russian.

"What's going on?" Her tone was sharp. "I got a phone call from an American setting this up." She waved her hand vaguely at the computer. "Why is some American calling me?"

"Um." He was conscious of the woman in the corner. Did she speak Russian? His mother spoke English. They'd probably set it up that way. "I wanted to let you know I'm okay."

She was silent for a moment.

"Well, good. But why wouldn't you be?"

The blood rose in Yuri's face. Guess his mother hadn't been worried about plane crashes after all.

"Yuri? Where are you? Did they repaint your office?"

He blinked. His office? Had he not told her? Had he not told his mother he was going to America? And then he realized he hadn't. It had been so sudden, and he'd had to pack. He made sure the physics department knew, and his colleagues . . .

"Um, no. I'm in someone else's office."

They were silent for a moment.

"Do you need something?"

"No. I guess I don't."

He should at least tell her where he was. He didn't know why he didn't. "You probably have to get up early."

"Yeah, at four thirty." She didn't say anything else.

"Um, well. Good night, then."

"Good night." And she clicked her computer off, and the screen went blank.

The Dial 1 woman rushed forward. "Oh, shoot. We lost it. I think I can . . ."

"No," Yuri said, his face flaming. "That was all."

The woman was silent for a moment. "Oh. Okay, then." She slipped quietly out of the room.

He stayed in his office for the rest of the afternoon, working. When he needed a break he ran in place, instead of walking to the conference room for another cup of crappy tea. At dinner time

Simons came to Yuri's office by himself. Pirkola was in the hospital, having his kidney stone exploded with a laser. Waiting hadn't worked.

Yuri speared a green bean and twirled his fork, but didn't eat it.

Simons took a bite of his chicken, then spoke with his mouth full. "You look worried." He swallowed.

"Of course I'm worried." He wasn't—he was thinking about the girl with the sparkly green eye shadow. Not something he cared to admit.

"We'll get the equation done, give the weapons team the targeting they need, and before you know it, you'll be back to skateboarding."

Yuri's head snapped up. "Skateboarding?"

"You know." Simons's hand swooped in the chilled office air. "Whatever it is you do with your free time."

Yuri stared at him. *Skateboarding? Is that what they thought he did?*

"I talked with Pirkola before he left. We're on the same page—making progress, and we're thinking the same way."

"Good," Yuri said, still visualizing himself skateboarding through the corridors of Moscow State University, where he had earned a doctorate in physics the previous year, at age sixteen. He'd never stepped on a skateboard, but he was pretty sure if he ever tried, he'd kill himself. Then he imagined speeding down the hall past Gregor Kryukov, his advisor, and his anger dissolved into amusement. Kryukov would raise those eyebrows—he must have the strongest forehead muscles in Russia to lift those things—and say . . . what would he say? Something funny, and then they'd walk together to the little restaurant where Kryukov had been taking him for years, a run-down place with wobbly tables but the best borscht in Moscow, and that's saying something.

Simons wiped his mouth with a paper napkin, crumpled it, and tossed it into Yuri's wastebasket. For a moment it looked like a blob of sour cream in the soup, then Yuri lost the image of Gregor Kryukov and the restaurant, and felt a sudden stab of homesickness. Even though he'd always wanted to travel. And he'd only been gone a couple days. *Pathetic.*

"Let me show you what we've got so far," Simons said.

Yuri shrugged and stood by his desk as Simons slapped down a paper. Yuri read it, eventually forgetting about the older man standing there. He skimmed at first. Their line of thought matched his own work, but then it began to diverge. He frowned slightly, backtracking, reading more carefully. He put his forefinger on the page to keep his place, scanning back and forth.

"What?" Simons said.

"Surely you're going to use antimatter," Yuri said.

"We don't know anything about antimatter."

"I do. We reduce asteroid's size, and then you pulverize what's left." He shrugged. "That's most effective strategy."

"Nobody knows how to contain antimatter, let alone keep it concentrated over the kind of distance . . ."

"*I* know," Yuri said. "I have unpublished work on this. Is what I was working on before, in Moscow. Before this."

Simons jutted his head forward. "Has it been published?"

"No. That's typical of unpublished work."

Payback for the skateboard comment.

"So no peer review? No evaluation by others in the field?"

Yuri flushed. "My dissertation advisor has seen it, and he thinks it's promising."

"Your dissertation advisor? God, you're young." Simons shook his head.

"Russian engineering company is already developing prototype for energy production, way to . . ."

Simons rapped his knuckles on the paper. "This is no time to play with new theories. You know it's at half an AU now? That damn rock is halfway between us and the sun."

That made Yuri pause for a moment, because at the speed the asteroid was traveling, half an astronomical unit meant it was entering the neighborhood. He squeezed his eyes shut and focused. "Is not new theory. I just did math, that's all."

"Can you prove it will work? In space conditions, over several kilometers? Because a high-flux antimatter accelerator would have to be that far away."

"Point isn't proving it. Point is if it's right," Yuri said, slapping his own work on top of Simons's. He stubbed his forefinger onto the point where the work diverged. "It's right."

Simons read the critical part of the math.

"Tell you what," he said. "Get back on track. Stick to known quantities. We don't have time to run experiments and collate data and figure out if you know what you're doing. Then . . ."

"I know what I'm doing," Yuri said, louder than he'd meant to.

"Sure. It's just that I don't think there's another physicist in the world who would agree with the direction you're going here."

"Then every other physicist is wrong!" Yuri immediately felt foolish. Young. His words hung in the air, as though gravity didn't apply to stupid remarks. Simons appraised him soberly.

"This is not about ego. We can't afford to mess up because some teenager wants to prove he's a big shot."

Yuri felt the heat in his face as Simons rolled his paper and tapped the desk with it.

"It's seventeen days till impact," Simons said. "*Seventeen days*. We have time to get this done. We don't have time to screw up." Simons exhaled sharply. "Look it over again, see if you don't change your mind. But if you don't, it doesn't matter—it's two to one, and I'm senior to you, anyway. Whatever results you come up with, there's no way I'm submitting them if you used that process."

His eyes flicked over Yuri, and around the office.

"You're a long way from home, and you're still a kid. It's a lot of pressure to handle." He smiled tightly and left.

Yuri stood beside his desk, hands balled. He didn't feel like a kid. He couldn't remember the last time he'd felt like a kid, or been treated like one. And the professors at home hadn't patronized him like this since he was a twelve-year-old freshman.

But Simons was right—it wasn't about ego. It was about saving Los Angeles, and that came down to the math. If he submitted the result he was working toward, Simons would override him. And if Yuri went along with Simons's result, part of a continent would be destroyed.

It wasn't ego. It was just that he knew he was right.

CHAPTER 5

THINGS DON'T SQUEAK AT NASA

"Fire Eye-24s."

Yuri dropped his pencil and padded, barefoot, to his closed office door. Someone had been talking about Fire Eye missiles by the coffeepots that morning and had stopped when he walked in. It piqued his curiosity.

"They've decided?" another voice in the hall said.

"Yeah. A bank of Fire Eyes. They're targeting each one to explode in front of the previous one . . ."

"They'll still hit farther back on the asteroid because it's going so fast."

"Yeah."

"You talking about the weapons?" It was a woman's voice. No answer. Someone must have nodded. Yuri shifted beside the door, his ear at the hinge. "No air in space," she said. "We can't rely on the concussion. The nose cones will have to touch cold rock."

The speakers walked off, talking quietly about plasma fields and transfer of energy. Yuri stood behind his door, thinking. They'd already decided to use the Fire Eye-24s, then. But what were they? Nukes, surely. Or did the Americans have something else, something he didn't know about? He wasn't a weapons guy and it was ridiculous for him to have to guess. The asteroid was hurtling toward their city, not his.

Suddenly he was angry. They'd brought him here to have an antimatter expert—there was no other explanation for his presence. So clearly Fletcher thought they might need antimatter, or at least wanted the option of considering it. And they'd already discarded the idea without talking to him?

What if the weapons' specs *did* make a difference in the calculations? Why should he take their word that he didn't need to know the details when they hadn't even had a conversation about it? They were dismissing him. When he got his Nobel he was going to put it on a string and wear it around his neck, so he could wave it in the faces of the gray old men of physics. He snorted softly and gripped the carpet with his toes. He was going to wear it *to bed*.

Yuri would make his own determination of what he did and didn't need to see. He stalked to Fletcher's office, ready to demand a look at the list.

Fletcher's office was in the back hall, but as Yuri rounded the corner he saw the director's back disappearing into the men's room a few doors down. He hesitated for a moment, wondering how much damage it would do to his case if he pleaded it by a urinal.

And then he realized that Fletcher's office should be empty. Yuri valued honesty—but not nearly as much as he valued results.

Yuri glanced over his shoulder, saw no one, and walked quickly toward the director's office. He was almost there when a door opened down the hall and a man emerged. Yuri recognized him— he was an expert in cosmic dust working with Team Eight. Yuri kept walking past the director's office, put his hand out to the bathroom door, grasped the silver handle, and gently pushed.

It was a pull door and he knew it, but it looked like he was going into the men's room. The man down the hall shuffled a stack of file folders to his left hand, opened another door, and disappeared. Yuri took his hand off the bathroom handle, glanced behind him, and backtracked to Fletcher's office.

The entry had a number pad beside it, but the door was ajar. Yuri slipped inside, ready to ask where Fletcher was if anyone was there, but the office was empty. He glanced around.

Any chance the director would have a copy of the list out? He stepped behind the desk, gently lifting the papers spread across the top. No luck.

All in all, it was a clean desk.

Guys with clean desks kept things in file cabinets.

There were two file cabinets behind Fletcher's desk. Yuri moved to them, putting his back to the door. Four drawers each, eight drawers total, all labeled. Nothing that read "BR1019," or "Asteroid," or "Boom."

Yuri's eyes dropped to a cardboard box for temporary file storage. He lifted the lid with the toe of his shoe—work relating to long-period comets. Which meant that files had been moved to make room. He tried the top left cabinet drawer, the one labeled "Long-Period Comets," the one whose usual contents were now in the box on the floor. The drawer was locked.

Yuri exhaled sharply and turned in a circle. It was a sturdy file cabinet—heavy grade—but the lock was small. Most people wouldn't put the key on a ring. Yuri opened Fletcher's middle desk drawer. The guy had a secret candy stash but no key. Yuri glanced at the door and slid the top right drawer out. Pens, a laser pointer—and a small, unmarked key on a circular ring.

Yuri unlocked the cabinet.

The metal drawer was empty except for five inches of files relating to the BR1019 asteroid. Not much there—testament to the surprise the asteroid had provided when it appeared, dim and heading the wrong direction. The files were organized in alphabetical order, chronological thereunder. Good system. In the back folder, Yuri found a list of United States weaponry in a folder with dark green stripes and a top secret security designation.

He flipped it open and whistled. The packet listed every type of armament in the American arsenal, with full details—number available and locations, explosive power, range, targeting system, system vulnerabilities—everything. It even listed tanks. He visualized a Bradley sitting on the Space Station, firing at the asteroid as it flew past.

He glanced toward the door, wondering for a moment how long it would take Fletcher to use the bathroom. Would Yuri be able to hear water running in the sink?

He flipped back through the list and got a paper cut on the side of his finger. He sucked on it while he scanned the packet, looking for the Fire Eye-24 missiles. Every paragraph had a margin note marking it as top secret. Seemed like overkill after the cover on the thing. He found the right page and looked through the specs. It was a little too much to memorize, so he pulled his cell phone from his pants pocket and turned it on while he scanned the data. He was good at this, at focusing on the task at hand, blotting out other stimuli. Always had been. Which is why he didn't hear the whisper of the hinges on the bathroom door. Things didn't creak at NASA.

He didn't notice the door swing inward until Director Karl Fletcher was in his office. Yuri was standing behind Fletcher's desk, the top file cabinet hanging open, the armaments list in his hand. Ready to click a photo with his cell phone.

"What the hell?"

Yuri turned, looked at Fletcher, conscious of the weight of the spreadsheet, the smooth case of the phone in his hand. He thought for a moment, wildly, of some reason he could be here, some excuse, and realized he would have to settle for honesty. But he saw Fletcher register his mental calculation.

"You're photographing documents?"

"No—I'm sorry. I just needed to see weapons specs. To be able to visualize whole thing."

Fletcher moved in, standing in the path between the desk and the wall.

"You're photographing it?" Fletcher said, and his voice sounded like air escaping from a tire. "Damn it. Do you know how much trouble ... How did you get into that, anyway?" He continued without waiting for an answer, his forefinger jutting in emphasis. "There's only one little piece that you have to figure out. You are not responsible for the whole thing."

"Yes, but ..."

"I told you specifically that you do not have access to this information. That you don't need it."

"I'm sorry." And he was.

"You have violated my trust, and you have violated my office." Fletcher held out his hand for the phone.

Yuri hesitated, then handed it over and stood, miserable, while the director flipped through his photos. What was the last one? He didn't take a lot of pictures. His stomach twisted when he remembered the last set he'd shot. He was a celebrity judge at a science high school's project fair, and Larissa Smirnova had stopped by to hand the medals out. Yuri didn't like her brand of pop music, but she was stunning and he'd elbowed in with the students to snap shots of her. Now Fletcher was scrolling through two dozen photos of a pop princess, with her bodyguards blocking parts of the foreground. It was acutely embarrassing. He stared at his feet, realized he was shoeless, and squinched his eyes shut.

"Get out."

Yuri paused, looking at his phone in Fletcher's hand, then took a step toward the path beside the desk. The director didn't move over to give him room, and then Yuri realized he still held the weaponry folder in his hand—the one with the green bands, marked "top secret." A tiny drop of his blood was smeared on the front, from the paper cut. He paused, wanting to refile the folder. It would be the thing to do, but his back would be to Fletcher, and his hands reaching to the rear of the file cabinet would illustrate the extent of his trespass. He carefully laid the folder on the desk, then squeezed past Fletcher and left.

Yuri stayed in his office during the call for sunset. He wasn't sure how much trouble he was in. Would Fletcher say anything to Russian officials? A dour man with limp hair had lectured Yuri in the car on the way to Domodedovo Airport with one message—obey the rules. Do what the Americans tell you. Yuri had gripped his suitcase handle, thrilled to travel, to be wanted in America. He thought of that now, of Limp Hair lecturing him, and him nodding randomly while he watched Moscow's blocky apartment buildings stream past. It occurred to him now to wonder why Limp Hair had made such a thing of it. And he wondered, for the first time, why Fletcher had denied him access to the list.

He had a dull, pounding headache, and left as soon as the car service could take him back to his hotel.

He thought coffee might help the pain, so he stopped at the hotel breakfast area off the lobby. It was deserted. The doughnuts and cups of waffle batter from the morning were gone, but the coffeepot was still plugged in. He pulled a cup off the stack, reopening his paper cut, and stopped.

There was a rustling at the floor. Floors didn't rustle.

He slid slowly sideways, peering around the end of the counter. In the corner made by the cabinet and wall, a little brown mouse sat, gnawing a Froot Loop in its paws. Yuri lifted his hand in greeting.

"You're not where you're supposed to be, either," he said softly.

He took a green Froot Loop from the cereal dispenser, put it in his cup, and slowly crouched between the rodent and the lobby. He lowered the cup sideways to the ground, but the mouse was busy with the food it already had.

"You find that mouse?" the lobby clerk called. "Don't tell anybody, okay?" She started toward the breakfast area, then backtracked. "Try to trap it, will you? I'll get a broom." She disappeared through a door behind the counter.

Yuri snagged a second cup and moved it slowly toward the mouse with his left hand. It continued to nibble on its cereal until the cup was in front of it, then it darted sideways, away from the counter. Yuri slammed the other cup over it.

"Out-thought you, Myshka."

He grabbed a plate and slid it under the cup, then slipped into the stairwell before the clerk emerged with her broom.

In his room, he lowered the mouse into the ice bucket and fed it a package of crackers he'd pocketed from the cafeteria. When it stopped nibbling, he gently lifted it, surprised not to be bitten, and took it to the bathtub. He closed the drain and ran a little cool water. The mouse drank, then washed its paws and ears with the water.

Yuri pulled the tube out of the toilet paper roll and placed it upright in the back of the tub, away from the little lake. The mouse tried to climb it, toppled it over, then crawled into the tube. Yuri smiled. He'd always wanted a pet, but there'd never been time. There'd never been time for a lot of things.

"Did you know that when he was young, Isaac Newton made little wheel that would grind wheat into flour? And for power he used little mouse, just like you." The mouse stuck its nose out the end of the tube and wriggled its whiskers. Yuri laughed.

Finally he dumped the complimentary toiletries off a plastic tray on the bathroom vanity, placed it on the bedside table, and put the little brown mouse down. It started to scamper off, but Yuri lowered the ice bucket over it.

"Good night, Myshka."

He had a friend.

Yuri woke in the night. He walked out to the little balcony and stood in his pajama pants, staring at the sky. The constellations were shifted from the Russian sky, but they were the same stars— he could see Ursa Minor and Major before him, Hercules running to the east. There were other things out there, a million unnamed asteroids, black holes and supernovas and unknowable things, and the BR1019, hurtling straight toward him. The monster under the bed turned out to be on the ceiling, an unexpected attack from an unexpected direction.

He tried to imagine what it would be like if they failed. How many people lived on the Pacific Rim? How many school-children? But the picture in his brain was of the mouse's sinewy paws curled in death, its soft brown body limp as the earth convulsed.

Did that make him a bad person?

He lay back down, lying on his side so he could see the ice bucket covering his small friend. He wanted to cry. It was okay to cry, he told himself. It was work-related, and men could cry because of job stress. But his cheeks were dry as he fell asleep.

CHAPTER 6

SPAGHETTIFICATION

The next day Karl Fletcher was civil. There was no public calling out, no remonstrance for Yuri's trespass of the previous day. Okay, he shouldn't have gone into the director's office, shouldn't have looked at the weapons specs. Fletcher had been right—it didn't tell him anything new, but he hadn't known that until he'd seen the printout. And the jerk had kept his phone.

He'd given the mouse food and water and let it run in the bathtub in the morning, then put it in a dresser drawer, covered by the ice bucket. He calculated the air volume and oxygen concentration first. The mouse would be fine.

But Yuri wasn't sure that he was fine. The day passed like the others, consumed by work until evening, but his thoughts were derailed by a gnawing unease that perhaps Fletcher had a reason for keeping him from the weapons list.

Finally Yuri sighed. He rolled his neck, let his chin hang a moment against his chest, then pushed away from the desk. He walked to the director's office, hands thrust in his pockets, hesitated a moment at the closed door, and knocked. There was no answer. He raised a hand to rap again when a woman stepped out of an open office down the hall.

"Looking for Karl?"

"Um, yeah."

"He went downstairs a couple of minutes ago," she said, tipping her head toward the end of the hall, toward the west stairwell.

"Thanks."

Yuri slipped past her, aware suddenly of his bare feet. Maybe some people could do complex mathematics with their socks on, but he wasn't one of them. He hurried to the west stairwell and paused a moment, looking out the huge glass panes at the scrubby California vegetation and creviced hills beyond. The railing was cool under his wrists. He had eaten early with Simons and Pirkola, and the scientists working at NEO wouldn't gather here to watch the sunset for another hour. Palms fringing the parking lot sent spiked shadows toward him, and quiet voices rose in the stairwell from people talking on the floor below. He recognized Fletcher's voice and had one foot on the first step, the other hanging in the air, when he heard what the director was saying.

"No, he doesn't know. Christ, no."

"He seems on edge." It was Simons. "I thought maybe you'd told him."

Yuri took a silent step backward onto the landing.

"Why would I?" Fletcher said. "It would only distract him. We need him working right now."

There was silence for a moment, a shuffling, then the rattling of an empty soda can tossed in a recycling bin.

"Did anyone tell the Russians that we're keeping him?" Simons asked.

Yuri felt like he was falling into a black hole, being pulled by a gravitational tidal force into a strand of his component parts, each atom in his body extruded one at a time. Spaghettification, they called it. It started with being snapped in two. And that's exactly what had just happened to him.

"No. They'd probably try to extract him, even with that thing bearing down on us. They're incredibly territorial. And it's not aimed at them."

"You could make the argument that we're being territorial, worrying about him knowing too much. You know, given the situation."

"It's national security," Fletcher said. "First we save the continent, then the kid defects, whether he likes it or not." Another soda can rattled into the bin. "After he's seen that list, with our hardware laid out like that? Trying to photograph it? No way he's going home. That's from higher up."

Yuri took another step backward and his spine pressed against the stairwell wall.

"The Russians insisted he not see that list, and we promised we'd limit his access. They knew we wouldn't send him back if he saw it." Fletcher hissed in frustration. "They said they told him to behave. We did, too. It's his own damn fault."

"That's the problem with having a teenager in a place like this," Simons said. "What about the Chinese guy? Liu?"

"Lin. He's wanted to come here for a long time. We've had covert contact before. He knows he's defecting."

Distant footsteps came from below. The men rustled, breaking off their talk.

"Keep your mouth shut," Fletcher said. "Nobody else knows about this. We don't need the distraction while we're still working."

Yuri stood in the darkening stairwell. He would have stayed there for hours, staring west, away from home, but he heard a man's shoe slap against the bottom stair below him. He slipped out of the stairwell and hurried down the hall to his office. He shut the door silently and sat on the floor, leaning against his desk, until it was well and fully night.

The asteroid filled his mind, pulsing in his brain, making his head hurt. Because whatever results his team came up with, whether the asteroid slammed into Earth or not, life as he knew it was over. His life was in two pieces. He was being spaghettified.

That night he lay sleepless in his strange bed in his featureless hotel room. He'd brought half a dozen different foods home for the mouse to try. The mouse ate all of them, then urinated in Yuri's hand. That was the day's highlight.

Yuri thought he could probably get another cell phone. He could even borrow one from an unsuspecting colleague, or from one of the janitors. He wasn't sure how to call Russia from the United States—there'd be an international code, and he didn't know what it was—but he could find a way to call someone. His mother. Kryukov, his advisor. Someone in Russia—anyone.

But what would he say? Because if he left, the math would be wrong. The asteroid would hit North America. People would die. The asteroid should blow up when it entered the atmosphere, like the one over Siberia in 1908. No huge dust cloud to cover the planet, block the sun, wipe out the crops. But some impact on Russia, surely. Trade would be disrupted, the balance of power thrown off. It could hurt his country, too. It could endanger his wobbly table and bowl of dark borscht, and across from him the craggy, understanding face of Gregor Kryukov.

He had to stay to save these people who were willing to sacrifice him. He had to get home to Moscow, too.

So he had two problems. He had to save the world, and he had to save himself.

CHAPTER 7

SEATS

When the car service deposited him at the NEO building the next morning, Yuri had circles under his eyes.

In his office, he pulled out a fresh pad of paper and began to calculate the problem. He chewed slowly on a pencil eraser, and as he came to the point of divergence from Simon and Pirkola's work, his hand hesitated a moment, hovering. Then he brought it down decisively, scrawling longhand the same symbols he had used previously, following the same line of thought. The most logical approach was to reduce the asteroid with antimatter before they blew it up. And he knew how to do it.

He leaned forward, occasionally punching a calculator with his left hand, keeping his right hand moving over the paper. He was going to do the math his way. The right way. When he was done, he would explain it to Simons and Pirkola, make them understand.

An hour later he took a break to check his e-mail. He thought there might be a message from his mother, but there wasn't. There were several from people he knew at Moscow State. He had just gotten his doctorate and been made an assistant professor in the physics department, a colleague to his professors. He saved the message from his advisor until last. It said, "Возвращайся к работе. Get back to work." He laughed.

Then he exited his e-mail and pulled up airline flight schedules. It was late May. The asteroid would hit Earth's atmosphere on June 9, which stunk because he was going to miss the hockey playoffs by working sixteen-hour days, and Team Dynamo would be out early.

He needed to persuade Simons and Pirkola to his view as soon as possible. Yuri tapped on his keyboard, clicking "print" repeatedly. Giving himself hard copies of flight schedules for the next couple of weeks. If he could get his teammates to accept his approach, he could slip out early. Take a cab to the airport in the middle of the night, maybe, and be in Tokyo by the time he was missed. But if Simons was sticking with his own approach, Yuri had to be here, at the Jet Propulsion Lab, being very, very persuasive.

He folded the printouts and stuck them in the bottom of his book bag. Something to look at before bed.

A few minutes later, Karl Fletcher rapped on his door, opening it as he knocked. Yuri had a pencil sticking out of his mouth and looked up blankly, his mind still lost in his calculations.

"How you doing?" Fletcher said.

"Um, okay."

"You printed off some flight schedules."

Yuri stared at him. Were there cameras? Fletcher smiled.

"The computers are all connected, so we can troubleshoot."

"Oh."

"Why the flight schedules?"

Yuri flushed.

"Um . . . my flight home. I thought I should look. Like good luck, you know?"

"Ah. The airports will still be here, huh? Well, don't worry now about your flight. We'll take care of all that when the time comes."

"Okay." Yuri flushed again and wished his circulatory system had voluntary muscle control.

Fletcher pulled Yuri's cell phone out of his pocket and handed it to him.

"Don't make any calls in the US," he said. "It'll cost you an arm and a leg." He looked at Yuri for a moment, then left his office, hitting the doorframe with the side of his fist as he went by.

Yuri had trouble focusing the rest of the morning. He looked around casually, trying to locate cameras. He didn't think there'd be any—he didn't see the point in them—but once it occurred to him, the skin on his neck crawled. He tried to think what disgusting personal habits he might have displayed, and wondered if he'd given the Americans access to his e-mail by opening it on this computer. He'd have to be sure not to open it on his cell phone— no way they hadn't put some kind of spyware on it.

When his office phone rang a half hour later, he jumped. He

hit a button to answer on speaker so his hands were free to keep working, finishing his thought. Simons's voice echoed.

"Yuri? Let's meet in the cafeteria for lunch. I'm having dinner with Karl Fletcher tonight. Bring any notes you want to go over and we'll touch base, okay?" He went on without waiting for a response. "Noon."

"Um, okay." Touch base? Was this a baseball reference? Surely they wouldn't make him play.

Yuri opened a new tab. If the asteroid hit, there was a good chance it was because he'd spent too much time looking up American idioms.

He lost himself in work again, and it was already twelve when he glanced at the clock.

He hurried down to the cafeteria and lifted a hand to Simons and Pirkola as he got in the food line. It was a decent place, with tables big enough to accommodate laptops. It was almost full.

"Sorry I'm late."

"I just got here, too," Simons said, then went back to talking with Pirkola about some point in their work. Yuri made minimal eye contact, chewed on a leathery Salisbury steak, and thought that if an asteroid had to hit Earth, Salisbury might be a good spot to take out.

"You think about what we talked about the other night? About sticking with established work?" Simons said.

"Yeah, it's stupid."

Simons and Pirkola both moved their heads back slightly, as though an axle connected them at the neck.

Yuri leaned forward. "This is desperate situation, right?"

"We have enough time," Pirkola said. "In theory, we ought to be able . . ."

"Is big *chertovskii*—" He paused, wishing he knew how to swear in English, and started over. "Is big, bad asteroid coming toward Earth, to smash your country? Then maybe we should do it right, yes?"

"We intend to do it right," Simons said, his voice clipped.

"No, you intend to do it safe. You have how many years old? A hundred?"

Simons flushed. He was fifty-six.

"And still you have to do things like everyone else. Be all alike. You . . ."

"This isn't about peer pressure," Simons snapped. "It's about science."

"Then *look* at science," Yuri said, tapping the table. "We want to destroy asteroid, but it's very big. We can make it smaller with antimatter bursts and greatly increase chance of success—of debris burning in atmosphere."

"You know you're not the only guy who's ever looked at this, right? You're not the only physicist in the world."

"That's not point."

"That *is* point."

Yuri flushed. Russian didn't have articles, and while he knew that English was full of them, he was never quite sure when to use which. Easier just to skip "the" and "a."

"There are a lot of smart people who wonder about

antimatter," Simons said. "Who have thought about it *for longer than you've been alive*. What does that tell you?"

"I'm not saying they're not smart. I'm saying . . . they just don't know how to work with antimatter."

Simons threw his hands in the air. Yuri turned to Pirkola.

"Here, let me explain."

"How long will it take?" Pirkola asked. "To really explain it and give the mathematical proofs so I'll believe it?" He laid his fork down. "You do have mathematical proof?"

"Of course. Would be . . . really to explain? And you'd want to work it out yourself little bit, to double-check. Four days."

"Four full days," Pirkola said. "That's time we can't lose. Maybe at the end, if we get this done early. I'd love to hear unpublished work from Yuri Strelnikov, boy sensation. But not now."

Simons crumpled his napkin and tossed it onto his tray. Yuri ignored him and focused on Pirkola.

"Our point of divergence is early. I wish it wasn't. But if we work out whole thing, then I show you I'm right, we don't have time to do it again. We'll have wrong approach."

Simons stood. "And if we waste four days on this and don't agree with you, and don't get done in time, what then? We've killed everybody in California to indulge your ego."

Pirkola stood, too, holding his tray. "Look, I really would like to hear your thoughts on this. But we can't handle anything else right now."

Yuri turned to Simons. "If you're not going to listen to me, why am I here? Why not just send me home? You two do equation, and I'll go back to Moscow and watch sky."

Simons flushed. "We need your input," he said. "Is that what you need to hear? You need a compliment every five minutes? We need your input, *based on proven, established theory*."

No, Yuri thought. *I don't need compliments. I don't need to be kidnapped, either, while everyone is looking at the sky.*

They put their trays on a rack outside the kitchen and headed toward the stairwell with its glass wall, but Simons turned back. He pulled his wallet from his back pocket and extracted a photo.

"My daughter," he said, holding the picture out.

Yuri looked but made no effort to take the picture. It showed a pretty brunette in a purple shirt. Looked like a high school senior picture.

"She's older now. Expecting our first grandchild. It's going to be a boy." He tucked the photo back in his wallet. "She's due June ninth."

Impact day.

Simons choked for a moment, looked surprised with himself, then regained control.

"I do a little woodworking—have a shop set up in the garage. I'm making him a wooden rocket ship seat for his bedroom. He won't need it for a year, but it'll probably take me that long to finish it."

He fumbled in his pocket and pulled out a paper, tattered on the fold lines.

"See? Designed it myself. There's a little seat in there, and a window in one side so he can see his mother coming. I'm putting a little bookshelf on the other side. And I got an old harness that's been in space, cut it down to make a seat belt for his bench, so he'll get used to wearing them. It's important that he wear his safety belt."

Simons passed a hand over his eyes and thrust the diagram back in his pocket. Yuri wanted to say something, knew he should, but all he could think of was *ublyudok—bastard. I wanted to hate you.* He just nodded and let Simons walk away.

Yuri worked restlessly that afternoon. He kicked his chair away and stood before his desk on one foot, then the other. He tried squatting against the wall as though he were sitting, working on a clipboard on his knees. The burn in his thighs felt good, but he couldn't hold the pose very long, and it interfered with his concentration. So he sighed, retrieved his chair, and sat again.

Yuri waited that night to see if Pirkola would come by his office for dinner. Was he rude if he went to the cafeteria without him, or foolish to wait, hungry, in his office? He finally decided that if necessary he could plead cultural misunderstanding, and walked down to the cafeteria. The place was busy, filled with the sounds of rattling cutlery, trays sliding down the silver rails, quiet conversations, and, from the kitchen, eruptive *thunk*s and clatters. It smelled of steamed vegetables—broccoli?—but not a bad smell.

By the time Yuri got his food, the tables were full. The cafeteria hadn't been built for the kind of activity the facility was experiencing now. A pair of men ahead of Yuri—he didn't know their specialties—paused, then left the cafeteria with their trays. Probably going to eat upstairs. Yuri needed a break from his office, so he set his tray down at a table for four. Two women sat facing each other, bent in quiet conversation. They looked up as he sat and started to cut his salmon, but he courteously didn't acknowledge them. They had their conversation, and he was separate.

"Um," one of the women said.

"Hi," the other woman said. "You're Yuri Strelnikov, right?"

Yuri glanced up and nodded, then took the cellophane off a bowl of cooked carrots. One really didn't talk with the other people who sat at your table in a cafeteria—with people who weren't of your party. Probably this was an American thing, being overly friendly, the way people made eye contact on the street. It seemed cocky, but probably it wasn't meant that way.

"Okay, then," she said. The women were silent for a moment. "Anyway, it didn't work out. I wound up taking a taxi home." In his peripheral vision, Yuri saw her shrug and glance at him. "I'll give you the details later."

A couple of minutes later the women left, and Yuri finished his dinner in silence. Nobody else sat at the table, even though there were three seats open. Yuri finished his salad and stared balefully at the empty bowl. Americans considered a pile of wet lettuce to be a salad. How had these people won the Cold War?

He left his tray on the rack outside the kitchen and climbed the stairs by the west wall, pausing at the top to look out at the arid landscape. Voices drifted up to him from a couple of men who must have left the cafeteria, too.

"Did you see what Strelnikov did? Sitting with people he didn't know?"

"Yeah, and then he ignored them."

Yuri opened his mouth in protest, then shut it.

"Maybe he thinks everybody wants him around. That he's irresistible."

"I don't think it was that," the second guy said. "I think he just has no social skills. Some of the guys are like that—no clue what's appropriate."

I am not one of those guys. I know those guys, and I am not one of them. Just this week I gave a girl a doughnut!

Yuri retreated to his office.

So there were extra seats in the cafeteria, and people who needed seats. And it was rude for me to sit down, but it wasn't rude that no one invited me to sit. He blew air out sharply. *America should come with a manual. Or is that what the Statue of Liberty is holding?*

When the call for sunset came, Yuri intended to stay in his office, but eventually wandered to the back of the herd of scientists watching in silence as another day slipped away. The need to gather, to look at the orange-streaked sky, was something primitive. This must be what it was like to have a migratory route. Like birds, or turtles. He spoke to no one and kept his eyes down as they ripped off another piece of duct tape. There were thirteen strips left. Yuri watched until the last streaks of color had darkened almost to black, then caught his ride back to the hotel.

The housekeeper had made his bed and put out fresh towels. He opened the middle dresser drawer and lifted the ice bucket. The mouse blinked up at him, sitting by a pile of its own feces.

"I'm sorry, Myshka."

He lowered his hand down beside it and dropped a half-dried scrap of cheese from his lunch sandwich into his open palm. The mouse walked onto his hand, its tiny claws scratching. He gave it a moment to eat, then gently closed his fingers and lowered the mouse into his pocket.

He took the stairs to the hotel's back entrance and slipped out into the night, pushing through the line of scrubby trees and brush between the hotel lot and parking for the restaurant next door. He strode quickly over to the next street, away from the highway, and glanced over his shoulder. He was alone in a strange city.

He started walking.

CHAPTER 8

SOLVING FOR THE UNKNOWN *X*

The night enfolded him, took him in as its own. He stepped through shadow, trying to look purposeful. To attract no attention. No one had said he couldn't leave the hotel, and he knew some of the Americans ate dinner at a restaurant in town. But he was pretty sure that people who watched your computer expected to know where to find you.

He passed a mini mall with a laundromat at the end, saw clothes rotating in dryers, the centrifugal forces keeping them in orbit, fabric moons with no planet. A solar system with no sun. Bored-looking people were reading magazines, and a grizzle-chinned man stood by himself, watching his clothes circling. Yuri wondered if he'd ever become a pathetic old man with nothing to do but watch his clothes dry. Then it occurred to him that he was watching the man watch his clothes spin, and that was surely worse.

He cut through the parking lot of a body shop, closed for the night, and a gray cat concealed behind a garbage can streaked away from him, heading for a stand of some spiky desert plant at the lot edge. He stroked the mouse in his pocket. Cars roared by, lights bouncing, radios blasting sound waves that lengthened in their wakes. In some sector there would be crime. Good to avoid that, but it would be easier if he knew where the bad sections were.

A city, and yet nothing like Moscow, with an aorta of river flowing out of its curled, ancient heart. His home was a huge place now, gone to flab, larger than its ancestral heart could support. The onion domes of the old churches were dwarfed by the stone monstrosities Stalin had built. Moscow was bigger than New York and could be very dangerous, yet he was comfortable in its metro lines, on its diesel-clouded streets.

This hot, dry city felt wrong. The weight of speaking only English for days now, of signs written in the Latin alphabet, was oppressive. It occurred to him that if they didn't stop the asteroid, he would die here. In a city, but alone. The hairs on his neck rose. He looked over his shoulder at the sky, half expecting to see the 1019. He imagined he could hear its soundless scream as it hurtled through the night.

He walked for an hour, looking for the right place. Figured he'd know it when he found it. He finally caught the outline of a band-stand ahead as the residential neighborhood gave way to a park. He cut in toward the building and came to the edge of a deep ravine flanked by a tubular railing. A foot of runoff water gurgled at its bottom, the first open water he'd seen in Pasadena. They probably put the park in because the cut in the land made it unusable for anything else.

He sat by the railing, pulled the mouse from his pocket, and ran a finger down its soft brown back. He touched the end of its whiskers and watched the mouse wrinkle its nose.

"You're American mouse. You should have freedom."

The mouse looked up at him.

"You don't have to worry about June ninth," he promised.

Then he lowered it gently to the ground. The mouse sniffed around at his pocket, then scampered off toward the band shell.

"Good-bye, Myshka."

He raised a hand in farewell.

The air stirred as an owl swooped past, seized the mouse in its talons, and regained altitude, never touching down. Yuri stared.

"*Bozhe moi. Bozhe moi*, I killed Myshka!"

He stood, arms out slightly, as though to retrieve the mouse, to pull it back out of the sky.

The owl swept out of sight. Yuri watched the empty space where it had been for several minutes after it disappeared, and thought of his promise that the mouse didn't need to worry about the asteroid. He snorted softly. True enough.

"I'm horrible person," he said out loud.

He felt empty. He couldn't save a mouse from danger in the sky. Could he save a continent?

He walked to the bridge over the ravine, an arching affair wide enough for strollers to pass and lovers to walk arm in arm, illuminated now with floodlights set in the ground. Posts along the walkway held orange fabric banners advertising an exhibition at a local art museum. He walked to the apex. The evening was still warm, but the railing was cool against his palms. He stared for a moment at the stars reflecting in the dark gorge water, then disappearing as the water rushed on.

Yuri looked up at these misaligned, Western stars. He wondered if the asteroid knew it wasn't in its own corner of the universe, that it was lost. Maybe it was just trying to get home.

He thought about being eternally a foreigner, and about Simons and Pirkola and the approach they were taking to the calculations. They wouldn't listen to him, and they were going to die. So many people were going to die, and it would be his fault.

The mouse had died, and that was his fault, too. He was a mouse killer.

He laughed softly, climbed over the railing, and stood on the concrete lip of the bridge. He stared down at the ravine, tumbled rocks and maybe a half meter of water thirty feet below. Gripping the railing behind him with one hand he leaned out, trying to see his reflection in the water.

He was going to die. If the NEO team stopped the asteroid, if Earth survived for a billion more years, a billion billion, he would die. He'd always plastered his youth over this fact, like a Band-Aid hiding the wound beneath. Living for seventy more years was essentially the same thing as living forever—death was so far in the future that it didn't matter. But every evening, another strip of duct tape pulled away—like the Band-Aid ripping off. Staring at his wavering silhouette in the water below, he couldn't avoid the point. Within a few days, in a catastrophic astronomic collision, or later—but not much later, really—fire or disease, or a common collision on a roadway . . . he would die.

It occurred to him that if he did it now, if he just let go and let the ravine break him, the asteroid would become irrelevant. Fletcher would be nothing, along with his plan to detain him in America. Yuri would slip through his fingers, off the axes of space and time.

Life's constant wasn't the speed of light, or Planck's constant. It was death. He'd learned that from a mouse.

Headlights flared bright beside him, throwing his ghoulish projection across the little park. A motor clunked and roared above the general traffic sounds. He heard the insistent *ping* of a car, door opened with keys still in the ignition. Someone had stopped. Someone had found him.

He twisted, looking over his shoulder, expecting a man in a suit or a soldier. It was a girl, not tall, not thin, running toward him, her car stopped at the base of the bridge. She rushed at him, shouting, her hands waving in front of her, and he noticed there was something wrong with her hair. As her shadow bumped him, he leaned back in surprise.

His grip broke.

Then the wrong-hemisphere stars were upside down and rushing. He reached his arms out, splayed his fingers, grabbing fistfuls of air as the stars slipped through his fingers. He twisted and one hand caught the lip of the bridge below the railing and he swung around, smacking his face against concrete, tasting the iron of blood in his mouth. He scrabbled with his other hand, all thoughts of death gone. He wanted to live. The water rushed below him. It sounded like a city gargling, getting ready to spit him out.

The girl knelt on the bridge, reached through the railing, and grabbed his wrists. It was the girl he'd shared a doughnut with. Her fingers were flecked with paint but warm and strong, and made little troughs where they dug into his flesh, elevating the adjacent area like foothills. He wondered when the last time was he had been touched, skin to skin, by another person. Shaking hands with new colleagues at JPL, of course. And before that?

"You paying attention here? Because I'm trying to save you."

"Right. Sorry."

The girl gave a trial tug on him, but he didn't release his grip on the bars and didn't go anywhere.

"Can you climb up?"

Yuri crabbed his hands up the rails, but they slid back down. "There's nothing to put my foot on."

"Can you swing out a little? Get a little momentum going, and sort of hurl yourself over the railing?"

"No."

"Why not?"

"I'm not monkey."

"Well, that was poor planning."

The girl let go of his wrists and took two tries to climb onto the railing, holding one of the uprights. She was not a natural athlete. She hooked one elbow around the post, stood on one foot and wrapped the other leg around. She was shaking, but she reached up and ripped down the museum banner, tucked it in her waistband and climbed down, making sharp little breaths.

"Ohmygod that was scary."

"I'm hanging off bridge here," Yuri said.

"Well, don't be a grouch about it."

The girl took a deep breath, then climbed up twice more, stripping the poles of their exhibition banners. Then she knotted the ends and knelt before him, tying the jerry-rigged rope around one of his wrists and looping it over the railing.

"Try now. I'll keep your hand from sliding back."

He obeyed, ratcheting his hand up. He threw his loose hand onto the top of the railing, swung a toe up onto the concrete lip, and pulled backward to get momentum to swing over the top. The railing groaned under his weight and bent outward, the top of the railing snapping on one side where it met the next section. Yuri's foot slipped off the bridge. He had both hands on the top of the railing now—progress—but the railing itself was peeled away from the bridge.

The girl scrambled to untie the rope from his wrist.

"Not good idea," Yuri said, but he was afraid to move.

She slipped the knotted banners over the railing and under his nearest arm. She tried to pass it over his back and thread it under his other armpit, but her arms weren't long enough. She pressed

her face into the bars, concentrating, and the result was so comical
that Yuri smiled, even though his biceps were beginning to shake
and his palms were slick with sweat.

Then she got hold of the tail of the fabric and gathered both
ends in her hands.

"Ready?" she asked, pressing a foot onto the bottom railing
for leverage. Without waiting for an answer she yanked upward.

Yuri lost his grip as her foot pushed the bent section of railing
and it snapped off, falling with a clatter onto the rocks below. He
swung loose, twisting slowly over the gorge, suspended in an
orange harness held by a rounded girl.

He screamed.

"We can discuss your attitude later," she said, through teeth
clenched with strain.

The girl leaned back. Yuri swung in and his face bounced off
the concrete. His fingers scrabbled wildly and found purchase
on the bridge surface, and he threw a foot up onto the concrete lip.
He could scramble up now, but the girl kept pulling, smashing him
against the side of the bridge where the railing was missing.

"Don't pull so tight," he shouted, even though she was two
feet away.

She kept her death grip on the fabric, hands shaking with
strain, mouth pulled to the side in concentration. Yuri shifted
his weight, trying to scramble up, and the girl gave another
sharp tug. His body scraped over the concrete lip, banging his
kneecaps. The girl jumped back, letting go of the fabric, but
she wasn't fast enough and he fell into her legs, knocking her

down. He rolled onto his back, groaning, as she scrambled to her feet.

"It's common to fall for someone who's saved your life," she said, "but that was still a little forward."

He looked up at her, not sure if she was joking, then looked back at the hole made by the missing section of railing and squeezed his eyes shut.

"Are you okay? You *jumped*. You were trying to *kill* yourself."

He sat up, and the breeze hit his scraped skin and he shivered.

"I fell."

"You need to go home. Is there somebody at home? Somebody I can call?"

He sat, knees pulled to his chest, arms around his legs, trembling. He shook his head.

"I'm alone." He thought he'd never made a truer statement.

She let that sink in a moment.

"I saw you walking. Did you come all the way from JPL?"

"From my hotel." He looked up at her. "You saw me walking?"

"I thought it was you. I might have followed you a couple of blocks, trying to see if it was or not." She shrugged. "There's a difference between curiosity and stalking, you know." She looked around for a moment, then came to a decision. "Okay, I'm going to take you home. Get in."

She headed back to her car, an old green sedan with one yellow door. Cheapest replacement part, he guessed. He stood, unsteady for a moment. Unsure. He didn't want to walk all the way back to the hotel, and wasn't even sure he could find his way. But having the Americans see him getting out of this girl's car might not be better. Maybe she could drop him off a couple of blocks away, and he could slink in unobserved.

She was already sitting in the driver's seat, her window down, waving him over with an arm out the window. A dozen thin bracelets jangled on her wrist. He tucked his head down and walked over, opening the door behind her. He could see a bag of new paint tubes on the seat, in an art store bag.

"Hey, this isn't a limo service," she said, patting the front seat beside her.

He flushed and walked around the front of the car, the headlights flashing over the white dress shirt sweat-plastered to his chest. He was used to car services and taxis. Used to sitting in the back. He opened the front door and sank into the seat, a combination of relief and worn-out springs.

She ran her finger over the side of his mouth, and came away with a smear of blood. It was a gentle gesture. That was when he realized that girls probably liked injured guys. It would be some kind of hormonal thing. He should file this away—it might have useful applications. She rubbed her hand under her seat, then looked at him from beneath lowered lids.

"Your DNA is all over my car now. There'd be no way to remove it all. So if you try anything, you would *so* get caught."

Oh.

She glanced in the rearview mirror and threw the car into reverse, then stomped on the gas and the engine roared and the body clacked and clattered. He glanced behind them, expecting to see a dozen auto parts tracing their path through the park to the roadway.

She rested her left wrist on the wheel and extended her right hand.

"I'm Dovie Collum."

"Yuri Strelnikov. Is very nice to meet you. Um, again." Her hand was soft and warm.

"Nice to meet you again, too, Yuri Strelnikov. You're Russian?"

He nodded and wished she'd look back at the road.

"What are you doing in Pasadena? Besides pouring coffee and jumping off bridges."

She had bright green glitter around her eyes. It was hard not to stare at it.

"Um, I'm here with NASA's Near Earth Object Program, at JPL."

"Oh, the meteor!"

"Asteroid."

"You're a scientist, huh?" She thought about that for a moment and looked up through the windshield, as though she could see the rock coming. "You're here to save the world."

He didn't say anything, just watched the pink feathers hanging from her mirror sway wildly as she cut the angle off a turn and clunked over the curb.

"How old are you, anyway?" she asked, peering at him.

"Seventeen."

"Huh. And you're a science guy? Really?"

"Um, yes."

He was silent for a moment, tensing as he saw her flip her turn signal on, waiting for the next challenge to the axle, then realized he should show an interest in her.

"And yourself?"

"Sixteen, high school student. Not a science guy." She drummed her fingers on the steering wheel. "It's nine days till summer break. I was going to apply for a job at the video store, but if California's going splat by the time school starts up again, I should probably spend the summer doing something else. So." She looked at him. "What do you think?"

They rocked up and slammed down from the curb. The crystals hanging from her key ring clinked softly.

"Pardon?"

"Should I get a summer job?"

He looked at her for a moment. She was what they were working to save. This girl, with flecks of paint on her knuckles and the troughs around her fingernails, and all the Dovie Collums in California. While he was printing flight schedules and scheming to get home, while he was sitting on a bridge, thinking about jumping. He felt a stab of shame. She had no chance to help shape the work that would guide the rockets. How helpless did she feel? How out of control?

"Yes," he said. "Get summer job."

Dovie smiled widely. It was a great smile, and he stopped feeling the scrapes. She nodded, and her bangs waved to him. She drove on for another ten minutes, careening around corners, testing the limits of modern metallurgy as the car groaned and clicked in unsettling ways. It made him think of submarine movies, with all their menacing creaks.

"Do you have papers to drive?"

"A license? I'm sixteen," she said, and had nosed the car into a residential neighborhood of small postwar houses by the time he realized she hadn't actually said she had a license.

Dovie turned into the driveway of a small purple house with a wheelchair ramp, and the car rocked to a stop.

"Home again, home again, jiggity jig."

She pulled her key ring from the ignition and got out of the car. The door clattered as it shut. Yuri sat alone for a moment, bewildered.

"This isn't my hotel."

She pointed to her ear.

He got out and pushed the door shut, afraid the impact would make the car collapse.

"This isn't my hotel."

It sounded stupid. Of course it wasn't. How would this girl know where he was staying? Maybe he *was* too accustomed to limo services.

"Yeah, but it is my house."

She waved her hand and, without waiting to see if he would follow, walked up the ramp. Yuri hesitated for a moment, swiveling to look at the row of small dwellings, identical in size and orientation to lot, and at this one, the only purple house on the street. The only purple house he'd ever seen. Attached to the siding was a metal rivet for a flagpole, which held a rainbow-hued peace-symbol flag. Only one of those on the block, too.

Dovie opened the front door and motioned to him. He hesitated a moment, absolutely sure that he was dangling as loose as he had been at the bridge, and then he followed Dovie Collum up the ramp and into her house.

CHAPTER 9

NOT A HUMANIST

"I'm home, and I brought a science guy," Dovie called.

Yuri stopped just inside the door, awkward and bleeding from the face. Not the way to make an impression. A young man, maybe eighteen, sat in a wheelchair to the left, watching TV. He glanced up briefly and turned back to his show. A woman stood in the kitchen just beyond the living room, dropping batter into muffin cups. She was lightly dusted with flour.

"Good lord, you're bleeding!" the woman called. "Dovie, sit him down before he dies."

Dovie pulled a chair out from the kitchen table, situated between the kitchen and living room. She raised an eyebrow at him and her glittered shadow caught the light. He slipped out of his shoes, though she'd left hers on, and walked across the living room, leaving depressions in the green carpet. The woman disappeared down a hall and came back with a first aid kit and a wet washcloth.

"These the only boo-boos?"

He looked at her, uncomprehending.

"Yuri's Russian," Dovie said, then explained, "she wants to know where you're hurt."

"Oh. I have multiple superficial abrasions and small laceration to forehead and left lateral mouth, with localized swelling. So, compromised skin integrity and risk for infection, but no skeletal issues."

"I see," Mrs. Collum said, smiling. She dabbed at his forehead with the damp washcloth, then taped a generous amount of gauze over his face. She stood back, looking at her work with approval.

Dovie sat down opposite him.

"This is my mother, Delinda Collum, and my brother, Lennon."

"Lenin? Like revolutionary?"

"No, Lennon with an *o*, like John Lennon."

"I'm very pleased to meet you," he said, swiveling back and forth to look at them both.

"I used to go by Walter," Lennon said. "To rebel." He raised a hand in greeting but kept watching his show.

Mrs. Collum filled the rest of the muffin cups. Dovie pulled two cans of organic unsweetened orange soda with natural flavors out of the refrigerator and plunked one down in front of Yuri. She opened hers and sniffed the fizz with a rapturous look, then continued the introductions.

"This is Yuri Strelnikov. He's one of the meteor scientists down at the Jet Propulsion Lab."

"Why was he bloody?" Mrs. Collum said.

"He . . ."

"He's too young to be one of those guys," Lennon said. "He's feeding you a line, Dovie." Lennon hooked his index finger in the side of his mouth, then pulled it out and narrowed his eyes. "You hitting on my sister?"

Yuri flushed, unsure of the idiom. He opened his soda can to stall for time.

"Say something smart," Dovie whispered.

"I wouldn't hit your sister," Yuri said to Lennon.

"That didn't sound smart," Lennon said, "but the accent did sound Russian."

Mrs. Collum jerked the oven door. It resisted for a moment, then clattered down. She put the muffin pan in. From a corner of the living room a voice shouted, "Give peace a chance! Give peace a chance!"

"We cover his cage in the evening, but sometimes he still gets worked up," Mrs. Collum said. "Lennon, show him the bird."

Lennon thrust his middle fingers up over his head. Dovie laughed.

"Lennon! He's a guest," Mrs. Collum said.

Lennon sighed exaggeratedly and wheeled to a cage in the corner. He pulled off a hand-painted cloth depicting Gandhi and Maya Angelou holding hands, and the motion made his straight, shoulder-length hair swing. A blue-and-yellow parakeet cocked its head and screamed, "Give peace a chance!" Lennon flipped the cloth back over the cage.

Yuri stole a quick glance around. Ivy and a Boston fern drooped from macramé hangers knotted through hooks in the ceiling. The walls were covered in green paint until, halfway up, it changed to blue, which continued across the ceiling. The kitchen counter was littered with brown paper bags labeled "Organic oats," "Organic dried berries," and "Brewer's yeast." Framed photos of Nelson Mandela and Jimi Hendrix hung on either side of the kitchen clock, above the cabinets.

"Give peace a chance!" the parakeet screamed from under its cloth.

"We went through a hippie stage," Mrs. Collum said, by way of explanation.

"Oh. Is it over?" Yuri said.

Dovie snorted orange soda out her nose.

"Sorry," she said, laughing, and grabbed a paper towel. She smeared the puddles around on the table.

A man with Dovie's dark eyes wandered in from the hallway, a paperback folded around his thumb.

"What's going on out here?"

"Dovie brought home a Russian boy from NASA," Mrs. Collum said.

"He was bloody," Lennon added helpfully.

Yuri stood, trying to be polite, painfully aware that gauze almost entirely covered his face. Mr. Collum looked him over, then spoke to Dovie.

"You shouldn't let strange boys in your car."

"We'd already met," Dovie said. "He's the one who sent you the cruller that day."

"The one who made you stand in the street? Huh." He was silent for a moment. "This isn't the start of a collection, is it? Like your rings, or those snails?"

"No. I promise this is the only bloody Russian I'll bring home." She turned to Yuri. "The snails were like two years ago."

Mr. Collum stared at Yuri for a moment. "All right, then. Carry on."

He turned back down the hall. Yuri sat.

"He tried to kill himself," Dovie told her mother. "He jumped off the Hernandez Park bridge and I pulled him back up."

Yuri stared at her. "I didn't try to kill myself. I fell when I turned to see who was there, because you stopped."

"You were on the outside of the railing, looking at the gorge. Then you let go and went down. That counts as jumping."

"She's right," Mrs. Collum said, giving him a sober look. "That's a suicide attempt." She squeezed his shoulders.

"Why'd you do it?" Lennon asked, suddenly interested. He wheeled his chair around with one hand and muted the television.

"I didn't. I fell." Yuri felt his face burn under the gauze.

"So why were you outside the railing?"

Yuri stared at his soda can. Why had he climbed over the railing? He wasn't really going to jump. Was he?

He glanced up. All three of them were looking at him. This would never have happened at home. If something awkward came up, something *emotional*, his mother would have pretended it didn't exist. She wouldn't have asked him about it. She would never, never have mentioned it.

"I . . . was just thinking. About asteroid. Is stressful, you know." He clicked his thumbnail on the soda can. "And my mouse died."

They let that hang for a moment.

"I'm so sorry about your pet," Dovie said, squeezing his forearm.

"So you really are with NASA? Seriously?" Lennon asked.

"I'm with Moscow State University. Russian government lent me to America. I'm physicist."

"Wow. So your head's important, and you got in a car with Dovie?" Lennon said. "You are suicidal."

"She doesn't drive car so much as . . . herd it, I think." Yuri smiled to take any sting out of his words. Lennon and Mrs. Collum laughed, but Dovie looked serious, and for a moment he thought he had offended her.

"You're some kind of freaky genius, then, right? So you shouldn't have been on the outside of that bridge," Dovie said, leaning forward. "Aren't you supposed to be saving us?"

"Not just me."

They were silent for a moment. He shifted under the gauze. Dovie leaned in closer, the light shooting green sparks off her eye shadow.

"How do you go from being like the world's smartest guy, from being *that smart*, to making a decision that bad?"

"Lightning-fast reaction times?"

Nobody laughed. The oven timer dinged and Mrs. Collum ignored it, leaning against the counter, observing him.

He looked from face to face, from Dovie, to Mrs. Collum's nearly identical older version, to Lennon, who had a weariness hiding in the corners of his eyes. Yuri picked at the edge of the table, where the top joined a metal rim. And for the second time that night, he climbed over a restraint without knowing why. He looked in Dovie's dark eyes and told her the truth.

"I heard NEO director say they're not going to let me go home to Moscow. I saw American military information, because of work we're doing. I wasn't supposed to. But after asteroid, then I have to stay here. In America."

Lennon gave a low whistle.

"I don't know anyone in this hemisphere." Yuri shrugged.

"You do now," Mrs. Collum said, giving him a quick shoulder hug. She picked up some potholders off the counter, pulled the muffins out of the oven, and set them on the stovetop to cool.

"Not to be selfish," Lennon said, "but you are going to deal with the asteroid, right?"

"Yeah. We have enough time. Should be okay." He thought about the disagreement with Simons and Pirkola on their approach to destroying the asteroid. It was annoying. Stressful. But he'd convince them. They'd come up with their different answers, and then he'd show them his approach, explain, and persuade.

"So maybe they ought to keep you," Lennon said. "Maybe you're a security threat."

Yuri stared at him.

"Um, no. Is because I saw weapons list one time. It isn't relevant to my research, I don't remember any of it, and I wouldn't tell my government if I did. Russian government is not so free right now. I don't like it so much. Besides, this stuff changes—will be outdated in few months. And I'd guess Moscow already knows most of it, anyway."

"Well, that's a relief," Dovie said.

No one spoke for a moment. Yuri drank his organic unsweetened soda until Lennon motioned him over toward the television. He popped a disc in a console and handed a video game controller to Yuri. A picture came up on the TV—outer space.

"You ever play?"

"Um, no."

"You should be a natural. Sit."

Yuri sat on the sofa and Lennon rolled his chair alongside and took the other controller.

"You're in the blue starship, see? I'm in the red one. We're hurtling through space, and we have to avoid hitting stars and space junk. Alien warships will pop up unexpectedly . . ."

"There aren't alien warships."

"You don't know that. Not for the whole universe."

Mrs. Collum brought a plate of muffins over and set them on the coffee table. Dovie perched on the sofa beside Yuri, and when she sat the cushions moved and Yuri felt himself tilt toward her. For a moment it felt as though he were falling again. She drew her legs up beside her, and he felt faintly dizzy. She was wearing shorts, and her legs were tan and smooth and distracting.

"This isn't whole universe," Yuri said to Lennon. "That's Saturn. See? We're starting in own solar system."

"Well, yeah."

"There aren't aliens in our solar system."

"You don't know that for a fact."

"Actually, I do."

Lennon shrugged.

"Well, they usually pop up farther out in space, but you'd better be ready."

Lennon started the game and went first, to show Yuri how it was done. Yuri tried not to think about Dovie's legs. They moved slightly as she breathed, and that tiny movement was infinitely more fascinating than what Lennon was doing on the screen.

It made Yuri think of a three-body problem. If you knew the position, mass, and velocity of two bodies, figuring their motion was simple. Add a third, and it became incredibly complex. He was fine with Lennon, but when Dovie sat next to him and curled her legs up on the sofa beside him, everything was suddenly complicated. He was sitting up, but he felt like he was falling sideways. Dovie exerted a giant gravitational force. She was the closest thing to Jupiter of anyone he'd ever met, but you probably couldn't say that to a girl.

Lennon stopped after five minutes, when he scraped a piece of space junk and had to go to a space station for repairs.

"Okay," Lennon said. "Let's see what you've got."

Yuri squinted slightly and gave the controls a trial spin, seeing how his ship would move. They were more responsive than he'd expected. He made it almost out of the solar system when he was sucked in by Pluto's gravity and crashed. Lennon stared at him.

"We're all doomed."

"This has nothing to do with real asteroid," Yuri said hotly. "And Pluto doesn't have that much gravity. Is very small thing. In real life, I'd have gotten past it."

"We're all doomed," Lennon said again.

They played for another half hour. Dovie watched Yuri as he played—not the screen, but him—and the right side of his face felt hot. How could he dodge aliens with those legs curving so close to his hip? Lennon was well off into space, and had acquired extra fuel packs and a tentacled girlfriend, when Yuri ended the game by dying for the fourth time.

"I was out of solar system," he said.

"Dude, you were still in the Milky Way. This actually makes me a little nervous."

Yuri stood and put the controller on the coffee table.

"We don't use these. We use math."

"Still."

Dovie took Yuri's hand and pulled him through the kitchen onto a tiny screened-in porch. She had an easel set up on a canvas drop cloth, and there was a little table with a chipped Formica top. A couple of shelves mounted against the house held see-through bins containing tubes of paint, brushes, and paint knives.

"This is where you work?"

"Yeah." She pointed to the bare bulb overhead. "The light's great during the day. Not so much now."

She pulled a sheet of paper off a pad and clipped it to the easel, then tilted her head at Yuri and squinted slightly. She chose a brush and reached over her head to bring down a bin of paint tubes.

"You're going to paint me?" Yuri said. He was flattered. He knew he wasn't exactly handsome, but maybe he had an interesting face. He liked symmetry and precision, but his features had failed to cooperate. Perhaps Dovie appreciated the slight irregularities.

"No," she said. "You're going to paint." She held out the brush.

Confused, he looked from her to the brush to the empty sheet on the easel.

"I don't paint."

"You need to," she said, and her tone was gentle. "No offense, but you're kind of a weird guy."

"I'm weird?"

"You're wearing a suit. That's definitely not normal."

"You . . ." He rolled his hand toward her. "Your hair, the specular reflection around your eyes . . . *I'm* weird?"

"You're both weird," Lennon called in from the living room. "No need to fight over it."

"We're losing the point here," Dovie said, ignoring her brother. "You could have died tonight. I can't let you just leave without dealing with that. You need to paint what's bothering you."

"I don't paint."

"Yeah, well, you obviously don't talk about your feelings, either, so this is what you're stuck with." She put the long, tapered handle of the brush in his hand and closed his fingers around it. The wood was smooth and cool. "You need to paint how you feel." She pulled tubes from the bin and lined them up on the table.

"I try not to have feelings."

"See, that's not actually better."

"I don't even know how I feel," he said, exasperated. "It's not something I sit around and think about." He shifted his weight and put the brush on the table.

"Then paint what you're afraid of," Dovie said, and pushed the brush back into his hand.

He stared at her. This was not normal. Was this an American thing, or a Dovie thing, to acknowledge fear?

"Why don't you have to?" he said, and it sounded belligerent.

She smiled, pulled another sheet of paper off her pad, and spread it on the table. She chose a shorter brush than his, pulled out the chair and sat, then unscrewed the lid from a tube of brown paint.

"Brown?" Yuri said. "You don't seem like someone who would paint with brown."

"I'm painting what I'm afraid of," Dovie said.

"I'm not afraid of anything," Yuri said, and it sounded sharp.

"That's okay," Dovie said as she started to make a series of rectangles across the page with crisp, sure strokes. "Just paint."

Yuri hesitated a moment, then shrugged. Why not? The whole week couldn't get any weirder. He took the light blue-gray and added a touch of cerulean, mixed it, and began to spread it on the top of the paper. By the time he'd covered the whole sheet with pale blue he'd forgotten about Dovie. He added little squares in rows at the very bottom of the paper, and a blob of cadmium yellow orange in the upper-right corner. Squares, and a circle.

He stood back. It looked ridiculous. He knew enough to know the composition was imbalanced, strikingly asymmetrical. It wasn't a picture of anything, certainly not of his feelings or his fears. He felt movement beside him and Dovie was standing there. He shrugged.

"I didn't paint anything," he said, "but it was kind of fun."

"You painted for an hour," Dovie said, gesturing toward his paper. "And you don't think that's anything?"

He looked at it and felt uneasy. "I guess it's asteroid. See in top corner, way above everything? It's asteroid in blue sky." He almost gasped. "And down there, little squares are houses. I painted asteroid coming toward Earth, and I didn't even realize it."

Dovie cocked her head and looked soberly at the picture.

"No, I don't think you did."

He raised his eyebrows.

"It's such a lonely shade of blue, and there's so much of it. The houses at the bottom are rich, warm shades, and way up at the top is this star, so bright and shiny, but all by itself, and so far away from everyone else."

She turned to look at him.

"I think you painted what you're afraid of. I think you painted yourself."

He didn't breathe for a moment. She put her arm around him and squeezed him from the side, and her breast pushed into his bicep and he couldn't even enjoy it because he was thinking: *Artists are sneaks. They have tricky ways of finding things out.*

"I'll clean the brushes later," Dovie said, dropping them in a glass of mineral spirits. She led him back into the kitchen. Just at the last moment he thought to look back and caught a glimpse of her painting. It was completely filled with empty brown rectangles except for one, which trapped a girl.

Yuri made his good-byes and followed Dovie out to her car.

"I'm sorry is so late. I didn't mean to keep you up."

"I liked spending time with you."

He gave her the name of his hotel, and she drove north to the highway, moving slowly as she searched for the right exit.

"Yuri? This thing with the asteroid is serious, isn't it?"

"Yes. But we'll take care of it."

She searched his face, then nodded. "You're special, aren't you?"

He flushed, but made no effort to answer.

"Are we really made of star stuff? You hear that sometimes."

"Yeah. All of elements that allow for life—like carbon—began as hydrogen in stars."

"I think you have more star stuff left."

"My hydrogen hasn't fused into heavier elements yet?"

"Yeah, that's what I meant."

Dovie found the exit on the second try, then prowled the access road until she saw the chain's name in blue neon. She circled once, figuring out the approach, then stopped behind the hotel in the restaurant parking lot.

He turned to look at her and thought he should say something charming and suave. Instead he said, "Your bangs just proved Isaac Newton wrong."

She smiled, and he saw the white gleam of her teeth in the dark.

"With enough hair gel, I can break all the natural laws."

He laughed, then shifted in his seat. "Can I ask you something?"

"Sure."

"Will you teach me to swear in English?"

"What?"

"Other people at JPL are three times my age and speaking their native language. I sound stupid, talking to them."

"I don't believe that for a minute," Dovie said.

"I think it's because I can't swear."

She looked him over carefully. "No, I'm sorry. I don't think you're ready."

"Pardon?"

"Swearing is one of the humanities, and you're no humanist."

"You're refusing to teach me to swear?" He was indignant.

She put her hand on his arm. "I'm saying you're not ready."

"I have Fields Medal!"

"That kinda proves my point."

Yuri crossed his arms. "Well, all language is like that. Are you saying I shouldn't be allowed to talk?"

"Of course not. You're welcome to grunt and point."

He snorted. "Language is stupid anyway. I mean, what makes word bad? In math, number is right or wrong, but never good or bad."

"Language is more complicated, because it deals with people," Dovie said. "Besides, there are other ways to communicate."

And then she leaned in and kissed him. It wasn't a long kiss, just enough to know that her lips tasted of orange from her drink and they had a bounce, a give that was wildly appealing. And then he smiled, embarrassed, and got out of the car.

He lifted a hand in farewell and walked back to the hotel, bouncing a little as he walked. He was in bed, arms folded under his head, when he realized that he was the target of a bureaucratic kidnapping, that tons of rock were hurtling in from space, and that all he could think about was the taste of Dovie. And right about then, with a continent in the balance, he didn't need the distraction.

CHAPTER 10

NO HELMET

JPL the next day was refrigerated and pale blue and sterile. Yuri's face looked better, and he'd removed the gauze before catching his ride in. The driver had glanced at him but hadn't said anything. Twice Yuri found himself tapping a half-chewed eraser on his desk and thinking about light reflection off glitter eye shadow. He suspected his lips were giving off a distinct heat signature—I've been kissed! There had to be a sensor somewhere in the building that could detect that. He refocused, ignoring the ache in his arms, and did his work.

He checked his Moscow State e-mail account. He didn't have a personal account, and tried not to think what that said about him. He had 117 messages, most of which were academia's answer to spam—custodial schedule of the week, hourly workers' time sheets due by Friday—that kind of thing. Two were from students looking for letters of recommendation. Seven were from colleagues in the department, but none from Kryukov. That was a little strange.

He opened the first, from an associate prof with whom he'd always been friendly, a guy in his thirties who studied B-meson decays.

Yuri, not sure if I should mention this while you're trying to save Los Angeles, but weird things are going on here, and I think you have a right to know. Somebody went in your office this morning—Fyodor Laskov. No, I'm not kidding. He claimed you'd done some work together, and he needed to look at his notes. *His* notes. The chair refused to give him the key—but then his father called and how do you say no to the head of the Russian Academy of Sciences? Sedatov went down and watched him—guilty about giving him the key, I think. Laskov spent an hour in your office, trying to boot up your computer. (Nice job on the password by the way, or maybe it's just that he's an idiot. God knows he's never done any decent research of his own.) So he took off with some notes of yours, and a couple of flash drives. I hope to hell you just have porn on those drives, because honestly, I think he's trying to steal your research while you're gone.

This could be serious. You don't have anything in print yet—if there's a dispute over whose research this is, and with his father's backing—they might split the Nobel.

Worse than that, what if they hyphenate your research,
and your name is linked with that asshole's? The
Strelnikov-Laskov Theory of Antimatter?

Get back here fast.

P.S. I think my fingers are going to fall off from typing
that hyphen.

P.P.S. Kryukov wasn't in when Laskov came by. I think
he planned it that way—everybody knows Kryukov's your
protector. But when the old man found out, he pitched a
holy fit.

Yuri stared at the screen for a full minute, visualizing a life
dragging Fyodor Laskov around with a hyphen. There would be
public appearances where they would both speak—Yuri would
have to write the lecture and watch Laskov give it, then step to the
podium for questions. It would make Laskov look like the domi-
nant partner. But it couldn't be done the other way, because Laskov
wouldn't be able to answer the questions. It made Yuri's skin crawl.

And it would never end. Because people didn't make huge
scientific breakthroughs every year. If you made one, it was once,
usually when you were young. Then you spent your career
refining your theories, hammering out the edges. Which meant
that for the rest of his life, Fyodor Laskov's big, ugly face would be
hovering near him.

When he was six, Yuri had memorized the list of Nobel physics
winners. He'd rattled them off for his mother: Röntgen in 1901,
Lorentz-Zeeman in 1902. Amused, his mother explained that

Lorentz and Zeeman were separate researchers. There would be people who saw "Strelnikov-Laskov" and *thought they were the same person.*

Yuri stood up and kicked his garbage can across the room. It crumpled against the wall and rocked back and forth on its undented side until it slowly rolled to a stop. He walked over and gave it another savage kick, and another. His foot hurt, and a sharp tingle sliced up to his knee. And again. And again. The wastebasket was mangled.

The door opened with a soft click. "You okay?" Yuri looked over his shoulder. He didn't know who it was—some American whose work wasn't in jeopardy.

"I might need new garbage can." He gave it another kick, but it was so misshapen that it no longer gave a satisfying crunch.

The man stepped into his office and picked up the phone. Yuri kicked again and sent the crumpled metal rolling. It hit the edge of the bookcase and rattled to a stop, propped against the wall.

"Yeah, somebody get Dr. Strelnikov a new wastebasket, please." The man paused and looked at Yuri, panting slightly and eyeing the remains of his garbage can. "Maybe a couple."

When Simons and Pirkola brought their dinners to his office that evening, Yuri was polite and vague, and listened to their progress without saying much.

"Other groups are doing okay? Solving their problems?" he asked during a lull in the conversation.

"Yeah," Simons said. "Seem to be. Some sections are harder to work out than others. But everybody's going forward."

Yuri nodded absently.

"We'll get done," Pirkola said. "No problem. It's just whether or not it works."

"You don't think it will?" Yuri asked, his mind snapping back to the office. To this office.

"I do. I just wish there was a backup plan."

When the work day was over, and another sunset had sunk beyond the glass wall and into the past, Yuri caught his ride back to the hotel. In his room he cleaned up after the mouse, and scrubbed the ice bucket.

"I'm sorry," he whispered to the empty container.

He sat on his bed in the dark for half an hour, hating Fyodor Laskov. Then he sighed and ran his fingers through his hair. Because for all that he could visualize Laskov's thick lips and stupid ugly mug, and the disappointed way his illustrious father looked at his stupid ugly mug, Yuri kept remembering sparkly green eye shadow. It was interfering with his hatefest.

He found a phone book in a nightstand drawer and flipped through it while he brushed his teeth. There were enough Collums that he didn't think he could cold call, and he couldn't remember Dovie's phone number or her father's first name. Didn't know what he'd say if he found her anyway.

He stood at the window, absently fingering the plastic curtain pull, rolling it between his thumb and forefinger. His room looked out over the back of the hotel. If he craned his neck, he could see most of the restaurant parking lot. And there, partially screened by the trees, was a green car with one yellow door.

He jammed his toes into his shoes and let the heels ease in as he walked, shoving his plastic key card in his pants and finger-combing his hair as he stepped out of his room. He trotted toward the stairwell, embarrassed at how happy he was to have someone swing by for him.

There had been a time in high school when three older guys from his advanced calc class came by. They were heading to a café and wondered if he'd like to study with them. He'd been thrilled. One guy offered him a drink of his dark brown beer, even though Yuri was eleven. Yuri took a swig, thought he might vomit, and held it in his mouth until it became impossible not to swallow. A waitress set a platter mounded with boiled shrimp on the table, and the older boys snapped the heads off and ate the bodies, creating little pyramids of pink heads in front of them. Yuri snapped the legs off, too, and hid them under the edge of the tray. He didn't realize until he went home after the third study session that he'd done all their homework for them. He hadn't been angry with his classmates for using him; he just felt stinging shame at not having seen it.

After that, he vowed to be aloof and make people earn his friendship. That hadn't worked, either. It was like he'd raised the price on something nobody wanted.

Now he was almost to the stairwell when an American stepped out of a room, heading the other direction. The guy nodded to him and kept going. Yuri nodded back, hesitated, then went to the window at the end of the hall, stuck his hands in his pockets and rocked back on his heels. Just admiring the view. When he glanced over his shoulder, the man was gone. Yuri ducked into the stairwell, ran down the steps and out through the hotel's back lot.

He made it past the line of scrubby trees to the adjacent restaurant, and ran bent over to the car. Its windows were down, and a male voice carried out to him.

"You know, that doesn't make you less conspicuous. It just makes you look like an escaped mental patient with orthopedic problems."

Lennon.

Yuri looked through the front passenger window, saw Dovie in the driver's seat, Lennon in the back. He swung into the front.

"I'm glad you came," Yuri said. "I wasn't sure how to get your phone number."

"You ask for it," Dovie said, smiling. Her hair was braided and wrapped around her head, the tips sticking out the top, pointing away from each other, like coiled snakes looking in opposite directions. He almost said, "You have snakes on your head," but stopped himself in time. He was a smooth guy.

"So do you want it?" Dovie asked.

"Huh?"

Lennon snorted. Dovie raised an eyebrow at Yuri. Maybe he wasn't a smooth guy.

"Oh. Miss Collum, may I please have your phone number?"

Dovie handed him a square piece of note paper with her contact information printed in silver ink.

"May I have yours?"

He flushed.

"I don't know it. But I'm in room 427."

"Good enough."

Dovie pulled out of the parking lot in front of a pickup, which hit its brakes and horn simultaneously. She veered into the outside lane, fishtailed, and straightened up.

"Hail Mary, full of grace, the Lord is with thee. Blessed art thou . . ." Lennon mumbled in the backseat.

"Shut up, Lennon. We're not Catholic."

"I am when you're driving. Also Baptist, Jewish, and Hindu. Anybody who'll listen." He turned to Yuri. "I think Hindu will do me the most good. They have thousands of gods."

"Good thinking," Yuri said. "Mathematical approach to religion. I like it."

"So we have a plan," Dovie said. "The general outline. We still have to fill in the details."

"Plan about what?"

"While you're saving us from the meteor . . ."

"Asteroid."

". . . We're going to save you. You know, get you home."

"Okay. Thank you." He hooked his elbow on the back of the seat and looked back and forth between them. "How are you going to do that?"

"Those are the details," Lennon said.

"Oh."

"We're going to start by taking you to the mall. You need

some new clothes," Dovie said, taking a corner with the heel of her hand on the steering wheel. "You have any money?"

"Yeah, but what's wrong with my clothes?"

"You're wearing a white dress shirt," Lennon said. "And gray dress pants. And black dress shoes."

"Yes."

"How old are you?"

"I'm seventeen."

"Going on eighty. You need to blend in if we're going to sneak you out of here."

"That makes certain amount of sense. So we're going with sneaking approach?"

Dovie pulled onto an access road to a mall and took the first right into the lot. The car rocked to a stop and Dovie got out, opened the trunk, and wrestled Lennon's wheelchair out before Yuri realized what she was doing. She set it up, hooked her arms under her brother's armpits, and heaved him up and into the chair, then clicked the wheel locks off.

"Wouldn't van be easier?" Yuri asked.

"Duh," Lennon said. "You know what those things cost?"

"No. No idea."

"I work part-time at the library. So it's a little beyond my means."

As they went into the mall, Lennon's tires crunched on white stones that had spilled from the landscaping around spiky desert plants. The doors hissed shut behind them, and they were blasted with air-conditioning.

The interior was nicely done, with potted plants and skylights and distinct storefronts that gave the impression of a downtown street in some Mediterranean city. People strolled by with drink cups in their hands or wandered in and out of stores. No one seemed to be in a hurry. They passed a couple of middle-aged women leaning against a wall, looking at something on a cell phone.

"You see that?" Yuri said. "If we ever have to figure out who is American spy, it will be very easy."

"Um, what?" Lennon said.

"Look," Yuri said, gesturing expansively. "Everybody standing near wall is *touching* wall. They lean, or put hand on it. It's like you people have magnetic spines. You get within half meter of some wall and—*sloooop*—you touch it." Yuri stood on one foot and then tilted toward the front of a candle store, as though caught in its pull. "You tell Russian to stand by wall, hour later he'll still be standing by wall. Not touching it." He shook his head. "Your spies have no chance."

"Okay," Lennon said. "Somebody's in a mood today."

"And another thing. Did you see, when we came in? We had to wait moment while people exiting used our door because it was already open. Because someone had just gone in. So they made us wait instead of just using their own door."

Dovie shrugged. "No big deal."

"But do you see how lazy is that? I'm not saving California so people can go out wrong door."

"Um, we have some ideas," Dovie said, taking Yuri's hand and pulling him on. "We could try to get you over the Mexican border. It's very porous, and most people don't get shot crossing."

"Shot?"

"You could dress like a Mexican drug lord," Lennon said.

"Why drug lord? Why not just regular Mexican guy? Worker, or student? Mexican physicist?"

"What's the fun in that?" Lennon asked.

"I don't like shooting part," Yuri said. "And I'm blond."

"That wasn't our best idea," Dovie said. "But we thought we'd start with that one, to make the next one look better. What if you dress in drag?"

"Drag?"

"As a girl," Lennon said.

Yuri flushed and shook his head.

"They'd be looking for a guy," Dovie said. "You could walk right past them."

"*No.* Anyway, how would I get on airplane? My passport says I'm male. It's rather specific on that point."

"What about impersonating a pilot?" Lennon said. "We could maybe lock the real pilot up, give you his clothes, and you could get on the plane that way."

Yuri stared at them.

"I don't know how to fly."

"There'd be a co-pilot," Dovie said.

"Thank God you people aren't stopping this asteroid."

"Hey, we're doing the best we can," Lennon said.

"That's chilling thought."

"In here," Dovie said, indicating a clothing store displaying youthful male mannequins. She walked around the store grabbing hangers off the chrome racks, then shoved them at Yuri's chest.

He went in the dressing room, stripped, eyed the clothes, and then sat down on the little seat against the wall. His legs seemed unnaturally white, like the ribs of a long-dead whale beached on an alien shore. He was tired of speaking English all the time. He missed his apartment and his favorite blue cup. He missed stopping at a bakery on the way home from the physics building on Lebedev Street to buy pryaniki, brown spice cookies he could smell through the bag and that left grease stains in its bottom. And he needed to get home. He didn't want to pull American clothes over his Russian underpants.

"How you doing in there?" Dovie called.

He squeezed his eyes shut, struggled into a shirt, then hopped on one foot while pulling on the pants.

"Dovie!" he hissed.

"I'm just outside," she said. "How do they fit?"

"You got wrong size."

"No, I looked, too," Lennon said. "She got them for scrawny-assed."

"My pants are falling off."

"That's how they wear them," Dovie said. "Let's see you."

"No!"

"Come on out," Lennon said. "I want to see you in baggy pants."

"I'd rather die."

"That doesn't mean much, given that you're suicidal."

Yuri stepped out of the offending pants and refolded them. No way he was buying them, and that felt somehow like a victory for him, and for Russia. He left the clothes in the fitting room and emerged humming the Russian national anthem under his breath.

They exited the store and walked to the center of the mall. Some shoppers ambled by, mostly young people, but it wasn't crowded. They passed a cookie store and Yuri stopped and looked over the glass case.

"Do you have pryaniki?" he asked.

"Wha'?" the guy behind the counter said.

"Pryaniki. Small spice cookies."

"We got oatmeal raisin."

Yuri pressed his lips together in frustration. He slapped his hands on the counter, fingers curled under, and said, "My cookies can kick ass of your cookies any day of week."

"Ooh-kay," the counter guy said, rubbing his palms on his apron and glancing past Yuri.

"You might try chocolate chip," Dovie said softly. "Here." She handed a bill over the counter and pointed to a huge chocolate chip cookie with her index finger, a red ring catching the light. "My treat."

The guy wrapped the cookie in waxed paper and handed it to her, then took a step back, away from Yuri.

Dovie ripped a piece off and popped it into Yuri's mouth as they strolled through the mall. It was good, and when Dovie held the cookie out toward him, he pulled another piece off and ate it slowly. They walked in silence for a few minutes, pausing occasionally to look in a shop window.

"We have another idea," Dovie finally said. "It's less entertaining than some of the others, but it might work better for a guy who refuses to change his look."

"My underwears showed!"

"Yeah," Lennon said. "So what about going to the Russian embassy? Or just calling them? You could explain, and they'd come get you."

"You suggested drag before this?"

"We're creative people," Lennon said.

Yuri moved a chocolate chip around on his tongue.

"I thought about this. But they might come and get me now." They looked at him, Dovie's eye shadow scattering the harsh mall lights. "And we're not done with work yet, on asteroid."

"Couldn't they get you as soon as you're done? You tell them after you've figured your stuff out, and they send some spooky black van after you?" Dovie said.

He bit his lip, thinking of his disagreement with his team members. No way they'd use his result if he wasn't there, but he didn't want to explain that to Dovie and Lennon. Knowing about disagreements at JPL could cost them a lot of sleep. Then again, the asteroid would slam into America, not Russia. NASA could deal with it, and he could go home and protect his work, and his reputation. He paused for a long moment.

"I have to stay. Until it's all over with asteroid."

"Your choice," Lennon said.

"Yeah."

They were silent for a moment.

"What about getting into Mexico—" Lennon said.

"No."

"—and keep going? Argentina takes anybody in. There have to be some old Nazis who have died by now. Maybe you could take over one of their hideouts."

"Basic problem," Yuri said, "is twofold. First, none of us have any experience with this. Second, I need point of exit from this country. Some way to get out. And I don't have my passport."

"You *forgot* your *passport*?" Dovie whacked his shoulder with the back of her fingers.

"I didn't *forget*. They took it when I got on plane. To hold for me."

"Ah," Lennon said.

"Yeah. Ah."

They walked into the Target store at the end of one spur of the mall, passed through aisles stocked with bright-colored plastic sand pails, swim noodles, and sunblock, and filed out through an empty checkout lane. Yuri held the door for Dovie and Lennon. It was still warm outside.

"Canada would be best," Dovie said, leading them into the parking lot. "It has a long border, too."

"I like Canada. I'm comfortable in forest zone."

That made Dovie smile.

She pulled a shopping cart out of the cart return and climbed in, using the lower railing of the corral as a step. She pointed to the side of the parking lot, and Yuri started pushing her. When they reached the edge of the lot, Dovie extended her hand and Yuri took it, trying to help her out. But Dovie wasn't a thin girl, and she was starting from two feet in the air. Yuri finally put one arm around her waist and hooked the other behind her knees and lifted her out. He staggered slightly as he put her down, feeling the pull in his sore back and shoulders. He really needed to work out more if he was going to hang off bridges and rescue damsels from shopping carts.

"Now you get in," she said.

He obeyed without a word and didn't think about it until he was in the cart, knees drawn up to his chest, black dress shoes propped against the red plastic. He was not a spontaneous guy. Not a baggy pants guy. Yet he'd just climbed into a shopping cart because this American girl had told him to.

And she was pushing him toward the steeply inclined access road that curved down behind the store.

Yuri grabbed the red plastic rim, and Dovie put her hands on his shoulders and pushed him back down. She had a ring on every finger, and he could feel them all through his shirt, bright bits of metal and sparkle and girl. His shoulders tingled, and the sensation spread down his arms, his legs, everywhere. The rings were excellent conductors of electricity.

"Wait. What . . ."

"It'll be fun," Dovie said.

"I need helmet!"

"You need balls," Lennon said. "I roll around all the time, and you don't hear me screaming about it."

"You gotta learn to live life, not just save it," Dovie said, and gave him a push.

Yuri tucked his head down as the cart wheels rattled violently, the wind flapping his collar and cooling his ears. He reached out instinctively, looking for steering, for levers that weren't there. He was completely out of control, and as he bounced down the access road toward the inevitable crash, it occurred to him that had been true even before he climbed in the cart.

CHAPTER 11

HAPPY HIPPIE HOLIDAY

"Come on," Dovie said, extending a hand down.

The cart had clipped the curb and lay on its side on the grass. Yuri lay beside it, spread-eagle.

"Can't. Dead."

Lennon blew air out in disgust.

"We have cake back at the house," Dovie said, "and Mom said to invite you."

"Cake?"

Yuri sat up, inspecting himself for hemorrhages and lacerations of vital organs. He found a bruise on his left elbow.

"Mm-hmm. It's a holiday."

"May twenty-seventh is holiday in America?"

"It is in our house."

He stood and began to trudge up the hill.

"Something to do with World War Two?"

Dovie and Lennon exchanged a glance.

"We don't celebrate anniversaries of martial destruction or attacks on civilian populations," Lennon said, "whether or not they were technically successful. Anyone causing human death has automatically lost."

"Tell that to defenders at Stalingrad," Yuri muttered, but stepped back to grab the handles of Lennon's chair and pushed him up the hill.

Dovie drove them back to the Collums' little purple house on its lot in the shabby postwar neighborhood. The paisley drapes were open, and light spilled onto the lawn.

"Dad frees Woody Guthrie for holidays," Dovie said. "Be careful where you step."

"The parakeet," Lennon said.

"Oh."

Mr. and Mrs. Collum hugged them all at the door. Yuri held his breath while Mr. Collum embraced him. He wasn't sure why, but he didn't think he'd ever been hugged by a man before, and it seemed like a good idea. Mr. Collum flipped a CD player on, and a man's gravelly voice filled the room with something approximating music. They gathered around the table, where a round cake stood on a glass cake stand. It had chocolate frosting, and a circle with spokes piped on top with white icing. It was a wheel, and done with some artistry. Dovie reached out and took Yuri's hand, and he blushed. Then Mrs. Collum took his other hand and he looked up and realized they were holding hands in a circle. Was this a hippie initiation rite? He hoped no bandana would be involved.

"We are thankful to be together and healthy in a circle of love," Mr. Collum intoned, "on this anniversary of the release of Bob Dylan's album *The Freewheelin' Bob Dylan.*" Yuri stared at him. "First released May 27, 1963, its importance to Dylan's career and to the protest movement was incalculable."

They dropped hands.

"That's the album with 'Blowin' in the Wind,' 'Masters of War,' and 'A Hard Rain's A-Gonna Fall,'" Mrs. Collum said helpfully. "Happy first Freewheelin' Day, Yuri."

"You celebrate this?"

"We don't follow the Judeo-Christian calendar," Mr. Collum said. "Too oppressive. Or official state holidays, designed to instill conformity in the population and inhibit independent thought."

"We celebrate hippie holidays," Dovie said.

"The Greenwich riots . . ." Mr. Collum said.

"Riots?"

". . . the anniversary of the March on Washington. Even the Bonus Army's march on Washington."

"The Bonus Army? But armies . . ."

"Pretty much anybody who marches on Washington," Lennon said.

"Do you follow the Judeo-Christian calendar?" Mrs. Collum asked politely, handing him a slice of cake.

"Don't worry," Lennon said. "She bought it at the bakery, and Dovie decorated it. We can have refined sugar on holidays."

"It's a wheel," Dovie said. "You know, for 'Freewheelin'.'"

"Oh. Um, well, university is closed certain days, so I guess I follow state holidays."

"Can't help that," Mr. Collum said regretfully.

Bob Dylan's voice ground higher on the CD player.

"What would your parents think about this?" Mrs. Collum asked.

"I honestly don't know. Well, my father died when I was very young. But my mother? I've no idea."

"What's she like?" Dovie asked.

"Um . . . she's cardiologist. She's always on call, or at hospital, and I went away to school. I don't really know her very well." No one said anything but Dylan, crooning about the rain that was a-gonna fall. "She's very clean."

Mrs. Collum cut more cake and dumped it on his first slice.

"Oh. That's nice," she said.

"Yes," he said. "Nice. She's nice."

They ate in silence for a moment.

"Um, is there dancing on Freewheelin' Day?" he asked, to change the subject.

"Dancing? The boy wants to dance, Delinda," Mr. Collum said.

"No! No, really. Just asking."

"Dovie could dance Saturday if she wanted to, but she won't," Mr. Collum said.

"*Dad.*"

"Why don't you see if Yuri will take you?"

"*Dad!*"

"Saturday is the prom," Lennon said. "It's the most important dance of the school year."

"*You* never went," Dovie said, then flushed. "Sorry."

"I got dumped that week, asshole."

"I said sorry. And you could have gone."

"It's juniors and seniors. She's a junior," Mrs. Collum said. "It's formal clothes and fancy hairstyles and dancing all evening."

Yuri nodded, thinking about the small house, Dovie's clatter-trap of a car. Wondering if the problem was lack of a date, or lack of money for a dress.

"Do you want me to take you? I think I can get away . . ."

"No, you don't have to do that," Dovie said, blushing.

Yuri glanced past her to Lennon, who was nodding vigorously. So were his parents.

"You'll have to pick me up. Is that okay?"

"Sure. Eight o'clock in the parking lot," Lennon said.

Dovie nodded, still blushing.

No one said anything for a moment.

"Um . . . is there possibly computer I could borrow for moment? To look something up?"

"Yes!" Dovie said, relieved. "Back here!"

She grabbed his hand and led him down the hall, to a little desk wedged next to a stacked washer and dryer. One edge of the monitor touched the washer, and the other touched the wall.

"I'm so sorry about that," she said. "You don't have to take me."

"Will be fun, and I'll learn some things about America. And

about you." She turned pink. "But I'll probably embarrass you, because of my accent. Also, I can't dance."

"You can't dance?"

"No. I've never been to dance."

"Never?"

"I started college when I had twelve years. So, no."

She smiled. Yuri wanted to tell her that when the light danced in her dark eyes it was both particle and ray. Would she think that was poetic? He decided not to take the chance.

He booted up the computer and brought up a map of the United States, staring intently at its outlines, all thoughts of poetry gone.

"See, in middle? Piece of Canada sticks down here. Is farther south than United States around it."

"Yeah. That's the most heavily populated part of Canada."

He clicked to zoom in, adjusted the screen, and zoomed again.

"Detroit in Michigan shares bridge with Canada. I could ask, after asteroid is over, to live there. Then I just cross bridge."

"Detroit in Michigan is a horrible place to live," Dovie said. "They'd never believe you want to be there. They'd smell something fishy."

"Fish? Pardon?"

"It wouldn't work." She curled her tongue up toward her nose, and he saw a slit in her tongue where she must sometimes wear a stud. He stared at it. "Unless there was some reason to go there. Hey, see if there are any conferences or anything." Then she leaned past him and typed in the search box herself, her rings hovering over the keyboard.

"You found one." He leaned forward, took the mouse from her hand, felt his finger brush against hers. "But it's in two weeks," he said, disappointed. "I need to get back sooner."

"What about in Ann Arbor? The University of Michigan is there. Would it be close enough for you to get across the bridge?"

He leaned in to the map and traced a finger west of Detroit to Ann Arbor, away from the bridge.

"No. Not if they're keeping watch at all. Would be couple hour taxi ride first. I'd have to be very near bridge before they realize, to have chance to get across."

She sighed. "What would you do if you got into Canada? Since you don't have your passport?"

"Call Russian embassy, probably. They could get me home."

Dovie was silent for a moment.

"Do you know things that would hurt this country? Get us bombed?"

"No! No. Is just . . . like how many missiles of this type, or how far can this airplane really fly. Like that. And *I don't remember any of it.* I only looked at it for maybe one minute. It'll all be outdated in five years anyway, but by then I'll have lost everything. My apartment, my job." *My research.*

"You have an apartment?"

He nodded.

"But I go to restaurants. I'm terrible cook."

"Maybe my mom could give you some pointers."

They laughed and then were quiet for a moment.

"Will this be what you tell your grandkids about someday?" Dovie said. "Going to America and destroying an asteroid?"

"No," Yuri said. "I'll tell them about winning Nobel."

Dovie snorted, then saw that he was serious and stared. "Could you win one? Seriously?"

He nodded. "I have excellent chance."

"Is that what you want?" she asked.

It was his turn to stare. "Nobel in physics is greatest honor in world! I've worked toward it my whole life."

"To get the Nobel, or to do the work?"

He frowned. "What do you mean?"

"I mean if you could only do one—if it came down to it— would you rather have made a great contribution without recognition, or get a great honor for work that didn't help anybody that much?"

He hesitated.

"Ah," she said.

She didn't understand, but that was okay. The Nobel was the ultimate Band-Aid—winning it would fix anything.

Yuri stood, and Dovie led him back to the front rooms. They passed the little porch she used as a studio, and he saw that she'd framed his painting. He flushed with pleasure. In the kitchen, Mrs. Collum was putting the remains of the cake in the refrigerator. Mr. Collum was lying on the sofa reading, and Lennon was playing the space game. He held a control out toward Yuri and jacked an eyebrow, but Yuri shook his head. Bob Dylan sang as though he were filing keys with his voice box.

Yuri shifted his weight.

"Um, in America," he said, looking at no one in particular, "does guy pay for girl's dress for dance?" He pulled out his wallet.

"No," Dovie said. "Of course not."

"Yes," Lennon said, "unless he's a huge jackass. And he gets her flowers."

"You should get her flowers," Mrs. Collum said. "But, Dovie, you could wear that yellow print. It's not formal, but it would pass."

Dovie's fingers curled at her thighs.

"Or you could borrow one from that girl in your art class," Mr. Collum said.

Dovie stiffened.

"Carlie Sinclair?" Lennon said. "Are you . . . Carlie Sinclair? That whole family is jerks."

"They're jerks with a lot of clothes," Mr. Collum said.

Yuri rolled four one-hundred dollar bills inside a fifty. He figured it looked like two fifties, maybe three, the way he held it.

"My government gave me money when I left. I'm not sure what am I supposed to do with it, because NASA provides food and housing. I really don't need it for anything," he said, shrugging.

He tucked the money half under the empty cake stand.

"I don't know what dress costs in America . . ."

"You know how much a dress costs in Russia?" Lennon said. "Kinky."

"Um . . ."

"Lennon, if Yuri is a cross-dresser, we don't like him any less," Mrs. Collum said, removing the bills and pushing them back in Yuri's hand. "We celebrate his unique individuality."

"You should see the pants he was wearing earlier," Lennon said. "Baggy things that showed his underwears."

"I'll get you out of here," Dovie said, hooking Yuri's arm and leading him to the door.

"Thank you."

Yuri waved good night to the Collums. Lennon grinned and jerked his head.

Passing the mail table by the door, Yuri tucked the bills under a letter opener. Dovie would find them later.

As they walked to the green-and-yellow car, Dovie slipped her fingers down his forearm and into his hand.

"Oh my gosh, I'm so sorry about my family—everything about them."

"I like them," Yuri said. "I like them very much."

"I couldn't take your money, though. It's not right."

"Why not? I don't need it, and anyway I have more. Besides, it's my way of being freewheelin'. You have to let me celebrate this important holiday."

She laughed.

"What did you think of Bob Dylan?"

"He sounds like goat caught in hailstorm."

She laughed again, but not for very long, because when they reached the car, he bent down and kissed her. The second time in his life he'd kissed a girl—twice in two days. It was as though the sky was falling.

CHAPTER 12

HAMSTER SAVIOR

Dovie let him out in front of the restaurant, so that the building blocked the sight line from the hotel. She waved and clattered off, and Yuri walked back to the hotel, head down, no thought to anyone watching from the shadows. He was thinking about how women's bodies have a lower percentage of water, and wondering if that's what makes their lips soft and resistant at the same time. He decided it probably had to do with connective tissue.

He showered, then went to sleep, and in the morning dreamed of Dovie in a yellow print dress, holding a bouquet of flowers, smiling at him. Then tiny asteroids began to hurtle out of the flowers, like weaponized bees, shooting all over a dance floor and hitting dancers like hail while Bob Dylan sang "A Hard Rain's A-Gonna Fall." The dancers turned into mice, fell and lay still, paws curled. And Dovie looked at him, a trickle of blood running down the side of her face, and she said, "You didn't save us."

He woke up screaming.

At JPL the next morning Fletcher looked at him when he walked in, but didn't say anything. Yuri went to his office and reviewed the work he'd done the day before. It was good. He knew it was good. The calculations were complex, and he was double-checking himself as he went along. Another day and he'd have his answer. Then he'd explain it to Simons and Pirkola.

It occurred to him that one of the other astrophysicists might be of some help, might have some influence over his team members. He walked down to the cafeteria, trying to think who he might talk to, wishing he'd paid attention to social interactions between the NEO Program employees. Who ate with whom, who chatted with whom. Where people stood at sunset, watching another day dissolve into the contrail of time, streaming behind them as they hurtled into the future. But that wasn't the kind of thing he knew.

He passed one of the American security guys in the hall, nodded vacantly as he went by, and entered the cafeteria on the floor below. It was nearly deserted. He took an orange juice and swiped his name tag, then walked over to a couple of planetary dynamicists talking at a table. One of them pushed out a chair as he approached.

"Yuri Strelnikov! Russia's boy genius. What brings you down here?"

"Orange juice," Yuri said with a smile, lifting the bottle so they could see.

The guard he had seen upstairs walked past the entrance to the cafeteria, not breaking stride, but sweeping it with his eyes as he went by.

The men introduced themselves, although Yuri already knew both by reputation. He perched on the edge of the chair. The man had pushed it out for him, but Yuri was no longer sure of the rules for when one could sit.

"I was wondering, um, are you familiar at all with antimatter?"

The men glanced at each other.

"Sure," one of the men said. "Just the basics. The math to contain it is incredibly complex."

"I did some theoretical work in Moscow earlier this year . . ."

"Theoretical?"

"Well, yes, is unpublished . . ."

"This year?" the other man said. "It's the end of May."

"My work has bearing on what we're doing. I can't get Zach Simons to listen about it," he said, and instantly regretted dumping that out.

The men exchanged a look.

"Simons knows what he's doing."

"Sure, but . . ."

"You don't agree with his approach, you need to take it up with him."

"Right," Yuri said, nodding to them and trying to smile.

He left, threading through empty tables, making his way past the glass wall and up the stairs. As he turned, he caught the reflection of the same security guard walking down the hall from the cafeteria.

Three times. Not a coincidence. He was being watched.

Yuri stayed in his office the rest of the day, working and making real progress. He only went downstairs for a late lunch and dinner, and managed to avoid crowds, conversations, and eye contact. Triple score. At the hotel that night he flipped on the television and found an NHL play-off game in the second period. He hung up his suit and stretched out on the bed to watch. When the room phone rang he jumped, and wrapped the bedspread around his waist to answer it.

"Did your day go okay?" Dovie asked. "Because mine didn't, and if I start complaining and it turns out you had a bad day, too, I'll look like a jerk."

He smiled. "I had little bit of frustration, but nothing big, and I got very much done." He sat on the bed. "I want to hear about your day."

"Excellent." She took a breath. "So I already told you my math teacher's an a-hole, right?" She paused. "I'll get to that. But there's this girl who's a jerk . . ."

"There are very many jerks in your school."

"High school is a jerk zoo, Yuri. You should come down sometime and see the wildlife."

He walked to the balcony window, holding the bedspread up with one hand, and looked out over the city. His room faced away from Dovie's house, but it still made him feel closer.

"So her name is Kelli, and she's annoying, and hot, and she wears these low-cut shirts every day. The dress code says your bra straps can't show—well, her shirts cover the straps, but they sure don't cover anything else."

Yuri hung his head for a moment. He was facing an incoming asteroid, and a conversation with Dovie about another girl's breasts. One situation was incredibly dangerous, and it wasn't the BR1019. "I don't understand what is problem to you if this girl has too much, uh, showing." His accent turned the final *g* into a *k*.

"I don't care what she's showink, Yuri. But she's in my art class, and she makes lopsided crap and gets *A*s because the teacher's staring down her shirt the whole time."

"You have horrible teachers."

"Not all of them. The Spanish teacher is fabulous."

"Okay. But are *you* getting good grade in art?"

"Yeah. I'm getting As because I'm *talented*." He could hear her move around, and wondered suddenly if she was in her bedroom. Maybe she was in her underwear, too. It was almost like they were having sex. "Yuri? You there?"

"Hmm? Oh, yes."

"Anyway, tomorrow I have to get up and go back into the zoo. I wish I could take a whip with me, like a lion tamer."

He was in his underwear, talking with Dovie about breasts and whips. He fell backward on the bed. She was silent, and when she spoke, it was almost a whisper. "And I don't think I can stand to go to math tomorrow."

"Algebra is still swearing at you? I could maybe help, you know."

"No, you can't."

"I can. I guarantee . . ."

"You don't understand. Once a month Mr. Reynolds does this thing where we each have to solve a problem at the marker board."

"Okay."

"He keeps a snake in a tank by his desk, and a tank of dwarf hamsters in the back of the room. They breed like crazy. And if you get your problem wrong, you have to choose a baby hamster and bring it up and feed it to the snake." He didn't say anything. "Yuri?"

"Because you got problem wrong?"

"Yeah." She started to cry softly. "We never get to the back row before all the babies are in the snake tank. But we sit alphabetically."

"And your name starts with C."

"Yeah." She sniffed.

"Principal allows this?"

"Oh, yeah. You haven't met the principal."

"This is not way to motivate students."

She made soft, little gasps.

"Dovie? I'm coming with you tomorrow."

"Um, meteor? Hello?" Dovie said.

"No, I got very much done today. It will be okay."

"You seriously want to come to school with me?"

"I can hold up fingers when teacher's not looking, so everybody gets problems right."

"He'll just make them harder."

Yuri snorted.

"Oh, yeah." She was silent for a moment. "He'll feed them to the snake later."

"But you won't have to see it."

"Yeah. That would be nice."

"Besides, I want to see this American jerk zoo."

"Huh." She was silent for a moment. "I'll be by at seven thirty. Wear the most casual clothing you've got."

Yuri hung up, smiling. He had a mission. He was a hamster savior. Then he turned to the hanging bar by the bathroom. Which suit was more casual, the gray or the black?

CHAPTER 13

THE JERK ZOO

Yuri left the hotel before six in the morning, when there was only one guard in the lobby, absorbed in watching the night clerk carry cups of waffle batter to the breakfast nook. He ate in the restaurant across the parking lot and was standing outside when Dovie's car rattled to a stop at 7:34.

"Hop in." He did. "I brought some clothes." She pointed to a bundle in the backseat. "I didn't think you had anything casual."

"I'm wearing blue shirt and no tie," he protested.

She smiled at him. "You're a wild man."

He hesitated, then picked through the clothing. "Where did you get this?"

"The lady across the street has a son your size in college. I told her it was for charity."

"Um, none of these shirts have collars."

"Welcome to the jungle."

He struggled out of his dress shirt, folded it nearly in thirds, and laid it on the backseat. It was the second time in a day he had been sort of naked with Dovie. Then he slipped into a red T-shirt with a band name emblazoned on the front, and crawled into the back to try on a pair of jeans. He made Dovie tilt her rearview mirror up. He found a pair that fit well enough once he added his belt. He didn't change out of his black dress shoes. By the time he was dressed, Dovie was pulling into the parking lot of a redbrick high school.

"Do I need to go to administration office first, before classroom?" Yuri asked.

Dovie looked horrified. "Okay, Yuri, do *not* go to the office for any reason. If a teacher sends you there, just leave the building. It's not like they can do anything to you."

They started up the sidewalk to the front of the building.

"Do they keep most vicious zoo animals in office?"

"Actually, yes—they're there quite a bit. But it's the principal we're avoiding."

"Ah."

They climbed the front steps and were jostled as they entered the building. The walls were painted beige with a hand-applied grime finish. The floor was green and cream linoleum squares, and a bank of putty-colored lockers ran down both sides of the halls. But it was the noise that struck Yuri—lockers slamming, books dropping, people calling to each other and shouting, footsteps and muttered curses and apologies and a guy walking by them singing, *singing*, in public. Dovie caught his look.

"That's James. We like him."

"Okay." Dovie lived in this surging, pushing, locker-slamming world, where guys in collarless shirts walked by singing, and it was all normal to her. For a moment Yuri imagined singing in a duet with James in the hall of the monolithic Moscow State physics building—one black guy, one white guy, and a dozen stunned physicists. He smiled at the picture.

Dovie led him to her locker.

"Three hundred seventeen. They gave you prime number," he said.

"Yeah, I paid extra for that." He looked at her, not sure if she was kidding. She pulled a notebook and pencil pouch from her backpack, then stuffed the rest in her locker and slammed the door shut. "First hour is English, and if we run we might make it on time."

Dovie started a shuffle-jog down the hallway. Yuri broke into a trot to keep up with her. It was undignified and he was going to say something about it, but the bell rang, loud and jarring, and then Dovie disappeared into an open doorway. Yuri took a breath and followed her in.

Thirty students sprawled in chairs with attached desks. The teacher was a Chinese woman in a floral print dress.

"You're early, Dovie," she said, and everyone laughed.

"Punctuality was imposed on an unwilling populace during the Industrial Revolution, as part of the move from cottage industry to factory production. It runs counter to our biological needs, and is evidence of the extent to which our industrial over-lords control our lives. I'm late because I'm raging against the machine, Mrs. Lee."

"Rage on, Dovie," Mrs. Lee said, smiling. Yuri blinked. This was not a normal student-teacher interaction.

"Um, this is Yuri Strelnikov. He's visiting today."

"Welcome, Yuri." Mrs. Lee waved toward the seats. "We're glad to have you join the fight against our industrial overlords."

Yuri had absolutely no idea what to say to that.

Dovie sat down and opened her notebook, and Yuri sat in the only open seat, directly behind her. He took the sheet of paper and pen she handed back to him.

"Today," Mrs. Lee said, clasping her hands, "we continue our poetry unit."

Yuri kicked Dovie's foot.

"You'll all be writing a haiku, and I'll ask some of you to read them out loud." Mrs. Lee moved to the marker board. "A haiku is a poem, often about beauty or the natural world, which has three lines of five, seven, and five syllables." Yuri kicked Dovie's foot again. She didn't turn around. "I want you to write about something found in nature that moves you."

Mrs. Lee moved to the board and picked up a green marker. "I'll write an example, so you can refer to it if you forget the structure."

She uncapped the marker and in neat letters printed:

A dewdrop glistens
below a drooping petal
then silently falls.

She turned to the class. "I'm going to do some grading up here.

If you have any trouble, come right up and I'll try to help." She smiled warmly and sat at her desk.

Yuri kicked Dovie's foot twice. She didn't turn around. He leaned forward. "Dovie," he hissed. "You didn't tell me there was poetry involved."

"You'll be fine, Dewdrop."

Yuri sat back in his chair. He couldn't leave now. He had dwarf hamsters to save. Besides, he really wanted to make it to art class to see the objectionable breasts. He stared at the paper. Something natural? That moved him? He didn't spend a lot of time outside. Haikus were a torture more appropriate for botanists. At least the form was spare, like an equation.

And then he got it—his very first poem idea—and smiled to himself. He'd just have to make the syllable count work. Yuri leaned over the desk and wrote his poem. Then he pulled out his phone and sent a text to Fletcher.

Coming in little late this morning—overslept.

There were dozens of people working at JPL. He could take a couple of hours off. It would be fine.

A few minutes later Mrs. Lee stood and rolled her neck. "How are your haikus coming?" The class shuffled restlessly. Mrs. Lee called on several students, including a guy in the back row who started a poem about his girlfriend's butt. The teacher cut him off before he could finish. Yuri thought haiku might have more potential than he'd realized.

"Dovie?"

"Oh. Um. 'Yellow, red, and blue:/Beauty's holy trinity,/from which all is made.'"

"Color is what moves you," Mrs. Lee said. "Of course." Her gaze shifted backward. "Was it Yuri? Would you share your poem with us?"

Yuri took a breath. He rose before he remembered that no one else had stood to recite, but he couldn't just sit down again. He cleared his throat. "'Total net force is/mass times acceleration./ These forces move me.'" He sat down.

Mrs. Lee laughed. "How droll! I asked for things that move you, and you gave me laws of motion!" She clapped. Dovie turned in her seat and scowled at him.

When the bell rang and they filed out, Dovie said, "I can't believe you got away with that."

"You're just jealous because I have conquered world of literature, as well as science."

"It was like a formula or something."

"Yes. And I was droll."

Dovie rolled her eyes.

"I looked it up. It's good thing."

"Okay, Science Boy. Let's get you to band."

That took a moment to sink in.

"Band? Dovie, I don't play instrument."

She gave him a shark smile. "This is your chance to conquer the world of music."

The band room was a cavern with sound-absorbing panels high

on the walls and instrument cases at the bottom. Dovie threaded through chairs and music stands to the far wall, where she opened a black case and pulled out a clarinet. She grabbed the book from under her case and led Yuri to the front, dodging a guy blasting his cornet at anyone who passed by.

"Mr. Shekla? I have a friend with me today. Is there something he could play?"

"No," Yuri said. "I can just listen." *I'm only here to save the hamsters.*

"That's no fun," Mr. Shekla said. "You don't play an instrument?" Yuri shook his head. The band teacher looked at him over reading glasses, straight across the top edge. He stroked his gray soul patch. "Can you count?"

Dovie snorted.

"Yes," Yuri said. "I can count."

"Grand! One of our percussionists is out today. You can play the triangle."

"At least geometry is involved," Yuri whispered to Dovie. "Maybe I'll be okay."

Dovie raised her eyebrows and, clarinet in hand, led him to the back of the room, populated by a row of snares, a bass drum, and two slackers sticking drumsticks up each other's noses.

"So this is Yuri," Dovie said to the drummers. "He's going to play the triangle. Can you set out the music for him?"

The drummers exchanged a look. One motioned to an open band book on the stand. "He can look on with me."

"No, is okay," Yuri said. "I don't read music."

"Dude, you just hit the triangle whenever you see a little X." The guy pointed a finger. "One, two, three, *ding!*"

"Dovie," Yuri hissed. "This is bad idea. I'm going to embarrass myself playing triangle."

"It's kind of embarrassing to be the triangle player in the first place," Dovie whispered back. She took the instrument from the drummer and handed it to Yuri, along with a little metal stick. "Hit it from the outside. Good luck."

The band teacher stepped onto a wooden box, raised a thin baton, and gave the down stroke. The brass started; then the clarinets came in and Yuri watched Dovie. One drummer beat the bass drum with a muffled mallet, while the guy beside him hit a wood block. A minute into the piece the guy stuck an index finger onto the score and moved it right, one, two, three. He nodded to Yuri. Yuri hit the triangle and Mr. Shekla beamed at him.

Score. He'd conquered music, too.

When the wood block player turned the page, there were little Xs all over the place, but Yuri had the hang of it now. He counted to four for each measure and struck the little silver triangle whenever he saw an X. There was only one more page to turn in the music when the bass drummer nudged the guy next to Yuri and jerked his head toward the cymbals on their stand. The near guy hesitated, then leaned in to Yuri and whispered, "Crap. We forgot to get you the cymbals."

"I'm playing triangle," Yuri said.

"You're supposed to switch to cymbals at the end," the wood

block player said. "You don't play anymore until the last measure, but then you're supposed to be on cymbals."

Mr. Shekla gave them a sharp look. Yuri wasn't sure if it was because of the whispering or because he hadn't switched instruments yet. He didn't want to embarrass Dovie, or himself, so he laid the triangle down, keeping a finger on it to prevent reverberations, and carefully lifted the cymbals from their stand. He'd seen them played at the symphony—a big crash at the end, each piece held outward to maximize the sound waves. He held them at his thighs, squeezing the handles, waiting.

The piece softened as the brass and percussion dropped out, then the clarinets and bassoon fell quiet. The music sounded like raindrops, slow and soft. Yuri wondered why the composer had chosen to put a crash at the end of the piece. Maybe it was supposed to be a renewal of the storm, or a crack of thunder. Who knew what some crazy musician was thinking?

The drummer turned the last page and only the flutes played, whispering, then faint. The drummer stuck his finger on the last measure and Yuri counted in his head, one, two. He brought the cymbals up. Three. And he smashed them together for all he was worth, moving them outward to let the vibrations bounce off the walls.

The whole row of trombonists in front of him lurched, smacking each other with their slides and knocking over a music stand. One of them yelled, "Jesus H. Christ!" The entire band turned to stare at him, and Mr. Shekla stood with his baton pointing directly at Yuri, a startled expression on his face. The room quieted, magnifying the last echoes of the cymbals and the clatter as a second teetering music stand fell over. Then everyone began to laugh.

"You see how difficult composition is?" Mr. Shekla said. "You change one note, and it gives the piece a rather different feel. I think we'll stop there."

Yuri turned to the drummers. "You tricked me."

They snorted and draped their arms over each other. "You should see your face, dude," the bass drummer said. "You're bright red." He slapped his friend's back.

"Come on," Dovie said, taking his arm. "Let's get going."

"I don't think I conquered music," Yuri said, waiting while she stowed her clarinet, then walking with her out of the band room.

"Depends on whether volume counts," she said. "Oh, don't give me that look. You have to admit it was kind of funny."

He exhaled in disgust. "High school is boredom punctuated by humiliation."

"You got that right, Science Boy."

He followed her down the hall to a set of wide double doors.

"Next class can't be as embarrassing as that," he said. "What is next anyway?"

Dovie pushed the doors open. "Gym."

CHAPTER 14

SNAKES OF ALL SORTS

The gym had thin wooden floorboards lacquered gold, with basketball hoops at each end and a trapezoidal scoreboard looming over the middle of the court. There was a raised stage at the far end of the floor.

"You'll need to tell Mr. Pisotto you're here," Dovie said. "Don't piss him off. He broke a clipboard over a kid's head last year."

"No. Really?"

She nodded.

"He wasn't terminated?"

"The school board suspended him for a week—with pay."

"That's called vacation."

Dovie tapped her forehead. "Boys' locker room is in there."

She walked to the girls' locker room and left him standing alone in the gym. Yuri fought the urge to follow her. Why did he feel more out of place here, with people his own age, than at

NASA? He pulled out his cell phone and found a text from Fletcher.

Wake up yet?

It had come in ten minutes before.

Yes. I'm going to work some at hotel before I
come in.

He pressed "send" and walked through the swinging door to the boys' locker room.

He could hear it, and smell it, before he went through the door, and it was an entirely foreign place, like the ocean floor. Guys were changing into gym shorts between stands of lockers. The teacher was leaning against a wall. He was holding a clipboard. Yuri walked up to him.

"Um, I'm visiting school today. I'll just go sit outside and watch."

"You have a pass to get you out of gym?"

"A pass?" Yuri thought for a moment about asking Karl Fletcher for a note to get out of gym class. "No, I don't." He brightened. "I also don't have exercise clothing. Maybe tomorrow." Tomorrow he would be back at JPL. In fact, he really should go in soon. He'd gotten a lot done the previous day and could afford to take a few hours off, but it would still be acutely embarrassing if anyone at JPL discovered what he'd done. Where he'd gone. If algebra wasn't the next class, he would have to save those hamsters some other way.

"You can wear what you have on for today. You got gym shoes?"

"No."

"Then just wear your socks."

Yuri hesitated. Mr. Pisotto crossed his arms. He was wearing sweatpants and a polo shirt that stretched tight across his chest, making sure everyone saw that he had muscles. The clipboard protruded from his armpit. Yuri sat on the nearest bench, untied the strings of his dress shoes, and placed them under the bench. He spent a lot of time lining up the toes.

"All right, ladies, get on out there," Mr. Pisotto shouted, leading the way into the gym.

By the time Yuri padded out in his black dress socks, Mr. Pisotto had sent dozens of low, wheeled platforms careening across the gold floor.

"Everybody grab a scooter!" he bellowed, then blew the whistle around his neck for emphasis. Yuri looked for Dovie and found her standing across the gym with the girls. She gave a finger wave beside her thigh.

Mr. Pisotto began a circuit of the floor, dropping orange traffic cones in an oval. "You know how to do this," he shouted. "Lay on your back, hands up, use your feet only. Ready?"

Yuri hastily sat on the edge of a scooter and looked over at Dovie. She was tying up the long hair of the girl beside her with some kind of hair elastic. He was on his own. Mr. Pisotto blew the whistle and Yuri was suddenly the only stationary object in an asteroid belt. He lay on his back, crossed his arms over his chest, and pushed off.

He might be able to catch up with Dovie and they could chat while they crabbed around on the ridiculous little platforms. It was undignified, but it was also a little bit . . . fun. He continued to think that until the girls shot past him. He pushed off on his heels, trying to increase thrust with his thighs, but his dress socks couldn't gain traction on the lacquer-slick floor.

And then Mr. Pisotto was standing over him, holding a rubber ball the color and size of Jupiter's red spot. "Keep it in the air," he bellowed, and dropped it over Yuri's face. Yuri threw his arms up reflexively, causing the ball to fly into the floor and bounce away. "Good job, cupcake," Mr. Pisotto said. Laughter rose over the whirring of wheels rolling across the gym floor. Yuri flushed.

It occurred to him that he was better at calculating bodies in motion than being one. He concentrated on speed and avoiding the ball as it arced overhead, batted deftly by some kids, and desperately by others. Nobody else drove it into the floor. He swerved once to avoid the ball and bumped elbows with a guy who glared at him and muttered, "Watch it, prick."

On the next lap, the guy thumped a wheel over Yuri's foot. Yuri peeled off his sock, running a finger along the red mark the wheel had left.

James, the guy who'd sung in the hallway, berthed his scooter alongside Yuri. "You okay?"

"That—jerk—ran over me. Intentionally."

"Yeah," James said in a low voice. "Watch out for that guy."

Mr. Pisotto walked over. "Any reason you're sitting there on your ass?"

"He ran me over!"

"If you moved a little faster, you might stay out of everybody's way." Mr. Pisotto started to stalk away, then turned. "Your last school must have had a crappy gym program."

Yuri paused for a moment. "Yes, it did."

He put his sock back on and lay down, pushing off as hard as he could. He was almost around another lap when the jerk caught up with him and hooked a foot behind Yuri's knees, dragging him off his scooter. His head did a double bounce, first on the platform as his butt hit the gym floor, and then on the boards as the scooter flew away from him.

"Oops," the jerk said as he sailed by.

Yuri crawled back on his scooter and stared at the ceiling. He could just leave. But he imagined Dovie cradling a dwarf hamster in her hand, carrying it to the snake. He had to save the hamsters to save Dovie. He also needed to get back to JPL, but first he had to deal with this guy. Yuri might not have been an especially good athlete, but he did have a fine grasp of momentum and torque and velocity.

Total net force is mass times acceleration. His mass was up by bacon and a short stack from the restaurant by the hotel. They didn't have kasha. But the acceleration. He exhaled in frustration, stripped his socks off on the fly, and dropped back until his prey was on the opposite side of the oval. He built his speed and then pivoted and shot across the center of the gym, between the orange cones, driving his heels down together, his thighs bunching. He kept his head tilted back so he could see the jerk, made a slight adjustment to his speed, and saw the guy's eyes widen right before Yuri T-boned him and drove him through the swinging door of the girls' locker room.

Yuri's scooter skidded and slammed the wall just past the door, but the collision had transferred most of his momentum. He jumped up and darted into the boys' locker room. Behind him the gym erupted in howls and applause. He slipped on his shoes and looked for a second exit—the fire code would require one. He found the door and beyond it, an empty hallway. Yuri grinned and skulked down the corridor, more pleased with himself than was reasonable.

Dovie found him at her locker after gym. Her eyes widened, the movement sending light sparking off her glitter eye shadow.

"Yuri, you are in so much trouble. Also, you're a folk hero. Nobody knows who you are or where you came from." She retrieved a book and her pencil pouch from her locker and swung the door shut. "You rode into town, slammed Jake Bortell into the girls' locker room, and rode off into the sunset."

"I'm cowboy," he said. "But my horse is stupid scooter."

"Wherever the sagebrush tumbles, your story will be told. Also, you should avoid Mr. Pisotto for the rest of the day."

She led him up a floor. "You think you can stay out of trouble?"

"Is it art? I'll just sit quietly and observe," he said.

She shot him a suspicious look.

"No. Now we have algebra."

Yuri grinned. "Which way?"

"We wait for my friends. None of us walk in alone."

He checked his phone. He had a text from Fletcher.

You'll work better here. Sending a car for you.

It had come in fifteen minutes before—while he was making laps on a scooter. *Mat' tvoyu.* He showed Dovie his phone screen. "Oh, no," she said. "The car will be there by now." He nodded.

James came up, and the girl with long hair from gym class— Mary, whose photo he'd seen on Dovie's phone when she left it at JPL. Dovie introduced them. "Yuri's got a problem," she said. "He has to get back to work." She swallowed. "I'll skip class and give you a ride."

"You can't give him a ride someplace now," Mary said, her eyes widening. "It'll be unexcused, and you'll have to see Mrs. Cronick."

"The principal," James explained. "Ruiner of futures. Destroyer of civilizations. Where she has passed, you find only flooded fields, burning shacks, and lone dogs howling in terror."

"I'll call taxi," Yuri said. He texted Fletcher:

I missed car. Decided to walk in because such nice day. Will be there in 45 minutes.

He hit "send" and wondered how good NASA's bullshit detector was. Their other detectors were pretty good.

I'll go to math and leave when taxi gets here.

James called the taxi for him because Yuri hadn't changed his data plan before he left Moscow.

Yuri, Dovie, James, and Mary walked down the hall to algebra. Time to save some hamsters.

In forty-five minutes, the asteroid would be 119,000 miles closer.

Mr. Reynolds wasn't in the room yet, but his desk was at the front, beside a glass tank. The snake inside was black with irregular brown blotches, and bigger than Yuri had expected. It stared at him with black eyes as he walked past, and darted its forked tongue out. Yuri pulled a spare chair over and sat in the back corner. Dovie, Mary, and James leaned against a bookcase beside him. He glanced around the room, looking for Jake Bortell, his scooting nemesis, but didn't see him.

"Mr. Reynolds always comes in late," Mary explained. "He talks with the teacher next door."

A kid in front of them turned around. "Hey, it's Crash!" Several kids waved.

"Crash?" Yuri said.

"You already have a nickname," Mary said, bouncing a pencil on her algebra text.

"Because of cymbals?" Yuri said.

"Okay, that sounds like a good story," Mary said, "but no. It's because of slamming Jake Bortell in gym class."

"Ah." His list of people to avoid was growing exponentially. "I'm clearly not genius at high school."

"Nobody is," Dovie said. "It's not something you excel at; it's just something you try to survive."

That reminded Yuri. "In gym class, with scooters—they grade you on this?"

The girls pulled comically sad faces and nodded.

"But this is stupid. Scooting is not important skill. It has neither theoretical importance nor practical application."

"*Where* did you get him?" James asked.

"Hold on there," Mary said, twirling a pencil. "My great-grandfather was at Normandy. When the troops hit the beaches, they rode scooters in counterclockwise circles while keeping a ball in the air. If they hadn't been able to do that, Hitler would have won." Dovie snorted. Mary pointed the pencil at Yuri. "The price of liberty is eternal gym class."

Mr. Reynolds walked in. He was a thick, solid man wearing a trace of a sneer. Yuri took an instant dislike to him. Dovie, Mary, and James scattered to their seats. The teacher saw Yuri.

"Hey, who are you?"

Yuri rose. "I'm just visiting."

Mr. Reynolds stared at him for a moment. "They didn't tell me anyone was coming."

Yuri held his breath.

"Yeah, okay." The teacher turned to the rest of the class and rubbed his palms together. "Today is Feed the Snake Day. If you don't know your quadratic equations, you're going to be responsible for killing one of the fuzz faces in the back." The class was absolutely silent.

Yuri looked over and saw the dwarf hamster tank. He couldn't see the animals, but with his peripheral vision he saw Dovie stiffen.

"I hope you studied," Mr. Reynolds said. He moved to the marker board and, working from a sheet of paper, wrote $(1-i)$ $(\sqrt{-9})$. "Okay, Devon Ayres. Come up, simplify, and save a hamster."

A tall guy with a mass of dark curls swung out of the first seat. He started working the problem, and got about halfway through before he seemed to be in trouble. It occurred to Yuri that maybe he could make a bet with the teacher—he would do all the problems, for all the hamsters. But the teacher might not go for it, and then Yuri would be on his radar. Devon gave a glance back at the class and Yuri held up three fingers, then pointed at his eye three times. Devon stared at him for a moment, then wrote $3 + 3i$ on the board. Mr. Reynolds looked disappointed as he dismissed him.

Ayisha Billingsley was doing fine finding the domain and range of the relation given for problem two, so Yuri watched the back of Dovie's head.

A guy went up next, worked a problem, shrugged, and stepped away before Yuri could make contact. They should have let people know before class that he could help. Why hadn't they done that? Mr. Reynolds gave it a long look but finally nodded and called up a girl who trembled as she picked up the marker.

$x^2 + 5x = 14$ appeared on the board. "Solve for x," Mr. Reynolds said. Yuri frowned. There were two answers: x equaled 2 and -7. Did she know that? Did she understand that there was more than one answer?

The girl wrote the equation in order of descending degrees, but when she tried to write the quadratic formula, substitute, and simplify, it went to pieces. She dropped the marker.

"A fuzz face is sweating back there," Mr. Reynolds called. He still had the trace of a sneer, and Yuri wanted to write 2 on one fist, −7 on the other and give Mr. Reynolds the answers himself. The girl kicked the marker when she tried to pick it up, and when she finally grabbed it and stood, her face was blotched red and she had a tear track down her cheek. Dovie was next, and she was already starting to tremble. Yuri held up two fingers, but the girl didn't understand. She turned back to the board with a soft moan.

Mr. Reynolds turned and saw Yuri with his fingers in the air. "Yes? You have a question?"

"Um, just stretching."

Mr. Reynolds narrowed his eyes, then turned to the board. "Give up, Lupe? Ready to feed the snake?"

"She had answers up there," Yuri said. "She wrote two and negative seven. Are those right?" Mr. Reynolds gave him a long look. Lupe took the opportunity to write the answers on the board. Mr. Reynolds stared at her work, then at Yuri. The teacher wasn't, as it turned out, a fool.

"I think," Mr. Reynolds said, "that you just cheated in my class." He twirled the marker. "Why don't you come up here and do a problem for us, if you know so many answers?"

"Sure," Yuri said, trying not to smile. He walked to the front as slowly as he could. Dovie was next, and he needed to kill some time. While Mr. Reynolds wrote a problem on the board, Yuri looked at the cage in the back. A hamster, all fuzz and tiny face, stood on its back legs and put its pink front toes against the glass. Dovie sat, arms across her chest, head down, tapping her foot. He caught her eye and smiled.

Mr. Reynolds grabbed a marker and attacked the board, his hasty scrawl leaving a faint chemical stink hovering in the air. He held the marker out. "There—I never caught your name."

"They call me Crash."

Yuri took the marker, glanced at the problem, $-x^2 - 2x = -4$, then wrote $x = -1 + \sqrt{5} \approx 1.24$, and below it, $x = -1 - \sqrt{5} \approx -3.24$. He capped the pen and laid it on the tray, and smiled at Dovie. In the back, the hamster raised a pink paw in salute.

"Wrong," Mr. Reynolds said.

Yuri wheeled to look at his answers. He scanned them twice. "No, is right."

"You didn't show your work," Mr. Reynolds said. "That's a requirement. Therefore, the answers are wrong."

The class groaned. Yuri stared at him. *You are the snake. Dovie is the hamster, and you are the snake.* Mr. Reynolds sneered and his trapdoor mouth opened. "Please go to the back of the room, *Crash*, and choose two hamsters, since you didn't show your work for either answer. It's time to feed the snake."

Dovie stared at her desktop. Yuri walked back to the hamster cage. He watched them for a moment. They were the size of his pinkie finger and, well, pretty cute. When he got back to Moscow he should get one as a pet. "I can't decide," he said. "Could next student make decision?"

Mr. Reynolds's sneer widened. "Sure. Dovie Collum, go back there and help him choose."

Dovie stood, her face ashen, staring at him. *Come on, Dovie. Trust me.* She walked to the back. He whispered "Lid is stuck" as she reached him. She put a hand on the cover and he laid his palm over her fingers, keeping her from lifting it. "Is stuck."

"Oh," she said. "Yes." He wandered backward, away from the tank. "Mr. Reynolds?" she called. "The lid is stuck. I can't get them out."

The teacher exhaled in disgust and stalked to the back of the room. Yuri trotted forward and hefted the snake tank up. He'd calculated the volume and estimated its weight with the snake at under sixty pounds. Difficult, but not impossible. A guy he didn't know stepped sideways to open the door for him and gave him a tight nod as Yuri crabbed sideways out of the classroom. Yuri nodded back and saw a dozen students rise, blocking the door—buying him time.

The best way to save a hamster was to get rid of the snake.

He struggled down the stairs, imagined falling, the glass tank shattering and the snake coiling around his neck. Expecting to be stopped. As soon as he was down the stairs, he trotted across the green and cream linoleum squares, pushed the school door open with the tank, and was at the edge of the road, breathing heavily with exertion and adrenaline, when the taxi pulled up.

Yuri paid the driver extra to take him back to his hotel so he could change out of the borrowed jeans and red T-shirt, then gave him another twenty to take the snake to the Humane Society.

At JPL, Yuri went straight to his office and booted up his computer. He was working mostly by hand, but nothing looked as derelict as a black screen. He spread out yesterday's work and by the time Karl Fletcher poked his head in the door, he not only looked like he was working, he actually was.

"You sick or something?"

"Hmm?" Yuri looked up, a pencil in his hand, his hair already crumpled from grabbing it with his fist. "Oh, maybe I was fighting something off." Jake Bortell, prankster percussionists, and a python-wielding psychopath. "I'm here now."

Fletcher gave him a long, cool look. "Right." He turned to go, then paused. "Don't do this again. My heartburn is already eating the backs of my eyeballs, without wondering if we lost Russia's boy wonder."

Yuri tried to look innocent, and then Fletcher was gone and he slumped in his chair. He hadn't made it through a single day of high school. He hadn't made it to lunch.

It was eleven days to impact.

CHAPTER 15

WINGS

Yuri went in early the next morning, making up time. He worked steadily through the morning, looking up the first time Karl Fletcher poked his head in without knocking, and ignoring him the second time. He was there, and he was working.

In the afternoon he went down to the cafeteria for an orange juice. Maybe this was why so many adults were overweight. You could take a break for food; you couldn't take one to go for a walk. He shut his office door with a soft click and got back to work.

It was four o'clock when his phone rang. He expected Simons, maybe Pirkola, but it was Dovie.

"You need to come to our house for dinner."

"Oh. Why?"

"Thank you for the invitation, Dovie. I'd be delighted, Dovie."

"Yeah," Yuri said. "But seriously, why?"

Dovie sighed audibly. "Lennon's feeling down. Mom and I

think we should have some people around, so Dad's going to grill. Mary's coming over, and a couple of Lennon's friends, and you should come, too. You ever eaten a hot dog? It's not really dog— it's pig lips and cow anus. You'll love it. I'll get you at the hotel in half an hour."

The cow anus distracted him, and Dovie hung up before he could ask why Lennon was upset. Maybe he knew what was for dinner. Yuri took the car service back to the hotel, removed his tie, and unfastened his top button—a bold sartorial move. He grinned at himself in the mirror—he had been invited somewhere.

When Dovie bounced to a stop in the restaurant lot, her friend Mary was in the front seat, so Yuri climbed into the back.

"What happened to Lennon?" he asked, scrambling to fasten his seat belt as Dovie accelerated onto the road, one tire clipping the curb.

"There's this hot YA librarian," Dovie said. "He asked her out and she said no."

"Oh."

"Yeah. He launched a monthlong charm offensive and asked her at the end of it. Now he's really bummed."

"So you're having party because girl rejected him?"

Mary turned around and stared at him. She could do something with her eyes that was a little frightening.

"*No*," she said. "We're trying to *support* him."

Yuri sat back in his seat and decided to be quiet for a while.

When they got to the Collums' house, Dovie led them around to the backyard. Mr. Collum was standing at a little round grill, wearing short pants. Mrs. Collum set ceramic plates on a picnic table to hold down a tablecloth stirred by the breeze, while Lennon sat between a couple of guys by a red cooler. One of the guys looked at them, tilted his chin up in greeting, and lifted the cooler lid with the side of his foot. Cool guy, cool move. Yuri made a mental note to use it sometime—possibly not while wearing dress shoes.

The cooler had beer and a variety of organic sodas. Yuri grabbed a can labeled "naturally sweetened lemonade," shook off the ice water from the cooler, and popped the tab. Naturally sweetened his ass.

"Mike," Lennon said, pointing at the guy by the cooler. "Paul." He pointed at the other guy. "This is Yuri, the Russian astrophysics genius who hangs out here on occasion."

"Hey," Paul said. Yuri shook hands with both guys.

"Your dad is cooking hot dogs?" Yuri said. "Doesn't seem like something your parents would let you eat."

"They use waste meats in them, and we're opposed to waste."

"Yeah, every time they have a picnic they save the Third World," Mike said.

"We can have whatever someone else doesn't want," Lennon said. "Kind of like my love life."

"Food's ready!" Mr. Collum called.

They sat at the picnic table and ate. Yuri stole glances at Lennon, seated at the end. The pinch around his eyes was tighter. But mostly he watched Mike and Paul. They bantered easily with everyone at the table except him—apparently he was as foreign to them as they were to him. He tried to think of something to say but drew a complete blank. He thought they were trying, too. Paul looked up at him once, opened his mouth, then shifted his eyes to Mary and pointed. "Ketchup." Mary passed him the bottle, and Paul didn't look at him again.

"It was nice of you all to come over and pretend you're not worried about me," Lennon said, balling his napkin and pitching it at the side of Mike's face. "But my life sucks, and it's not gonna stop sucking. So the Friends-of-Lennon Club may have to agree to disband."

"I don't have many friends," Yuri said. "But I'm pretty sure that's not what they do." Everyone looked at him. "Disband," he said. "I thought it means 'separate.' Did I say something wrong?"

"No," Mrs. Collum said, "you said something just right." And she leaned across the table, put a hand on each of his cheeks, and gave his head a squeeze.

"Not too hard, Mom," Dovie said. "Don't squeeze the brains out."

"*Pssshhh*," Paul said, making a brain-squirt sound.

"Even at my pity party my friends get the attention," Lennon said.

Friends. They were friends—Lennon had just said so.

"I'm smart and funny and I know the dialogue from *The Godfather* by heart," Lennon said. Mary and Dovie exchanged a glance. "She didn't want to go out with me because of the chair."

"Well, duh," Paul said. "It's an ugly-ass chair."

"Yeah," Mike said. "I wouldn't date you, either. It ruins your T-shirt's classy effect."

"You know," Yuri said, "what it needs are accessories."

"A cup holder?" Lennon said, exhaling derisively. "You're gonna change my life with a cup holder?"

"I was thinking jet power," Yuri said.

Lennon's eyes popped.

"Why should your chair not be customized? It's only normal thing here," he said, waving a hand toward the back of the purple house, then flushing. He probably shouldn't have said that. But Mr. and Mrs. Collum were beaming.

"Dude," Mike said, extending a fist, "the Friends-of-Lennon Club has a mission." Yuri bumped his fist. He was now a dude.

"I've got some stuff in the truck," Paul said. "Hey, Mrs. C, can we use your craft supplies?"

"Of course!" Delinda Collum said. "You know where everything is. You boys help yourselves."

Paul grinned at him. *You boys.* Yuri had never been one of "you boys" before. Ever.

"Wait," Lennon said suspiciously. "What are you guys going to do?"

"None of your business," Mike said. "You're not a member of the Friends-of-Lennon Club."

"That's because I'm *Lennon*!"

Mike shrugged. Paul motioned to Yuri, and they walked together to a white truck parked in front of the house. Paul pulled a toolbox out and handed it to him, then grabbed some lumber and metal piping and hauled it to the backyard. Yuri walked beside him, bouncing the toolbox up and down. It was heavy, and felt good in his hands.

They dumped the materials in the yard and looked at what they had. Lennon rolled over to inspect it.

"You can't make anything with that pile of crap," he said.

"That's the spirit!" Paul said, chucking him in the shoulder.

"Ow."

Mike motioned Dovie and Mary over, and they huddled, whispering for a moment.

"You know it's *my* chair?" Lennon said.

"You gotta learn to share, man," Mike said.

Dovie went to work with a pencil on a thin piece of wood, then Mike took it into the garage, and the sound of power tools and smell of sawdust settled over the yard.

"Am I getting jet packs?" Lennon asked.

Yuri shook his head. "We don't have right equipment. But we're doing something else."

"It's possible that you may want to dismantle this eventually," Mary said, "but it'll be fun for now."

"Oh, crap," Lennon said, but he was smiling.

"Is this okay?" Dovie said, holding up a small can of paint.

"What is it?"

"Glow in the dark," Dovie said.

"Why would I want . . ."

"It's not a bad idea," Mr. Collum called from the garage. "Could be a useful safety feature."

"Eh," Lennon said. "Just don't write 'Lennon sucks' with it."

"Well, shoot," Dovie said. "Plan's off, everybody!"

"Ha-ha," Lennon said. He leaned over, watching as Dovie painted his spokes. Mary crawled under the chair and Mike helped from the outside, and Paul and Mr. Collum and Yuri worked on the back.

Mrs. Collum motioned them all in for a photo when they were done. "Ta-da!" she said.

"Anybody want to explain what you did to my personal property?" Lennon said. "While I was *sitting* in it?"

"Okay," Mike said. "We had limited equipment, remember."

"And ability," Lennon said.

"Ouch," Mike said, clasping his hands over his heart.

"We did the basics," Dovie said. "Glow-in-the-dark spokes, bat wings . . ."

"And a bat signal!" Mrs. Collum said, clasping her hands together.

Lennon looked at Yuri. "Take me with you to Moscow."

Yuri grinned. "Look at your wings first. Is very ingenious."

Mike pushed a handle, and two wings of black fabric stretched on a piping frame swung forward. Lennon took the handle and pumped it back and forth, making the wings flap.

"I actually kinda like these," he said. "I mean, they've gotta go, but I like them."

"Nice on a hot day," Paul said.

"Show him the bat signal!" Mrs. Collum said.

"Press this button," Mary said. Lennon gave her a deeply

suspicious look, then pushed it. A circle of light appeared faintly in the shadow of the trees, the bat outline dark in the middle.

"It'll be better at night," Dovie said.

"We mounted a flashlight under the chair and angled it forward," Mike said. "You can switch out the cover if you want, and project different images."

"Everything except class," Lennon said.

"Your words, they cut like a knife," Paul said, staggering around with his hands over his belly.

Lennon grinned, wheeled his chair hard around, and cut circles in the grass, his wings flapping like mad. "You guys are idiots," he said, rolling back to them. "Thank you."

"Hey, you want to go to the movies?" Mike said. "They're showing a . . ."

"Vampire film!" Paul said. "Dude, halfway through you could . . ."

"Unfold my wings!" Lennon said. "Ha! I'm in."

"You coming, Yuri?" Mike said.

For a moment Yuri almost said yes to going to a vampire movie with these guys. It could be fun. Who knew? He might even come back with a tattoo. "Oh, no thanks. But have fun."

"You can go if you want," Dovie said, but the guys were already around to the front of the house.

"No," he said. "But I'm glad you invited me today."

She put a hand on his forearm. "Thanks for coming. I worry about Len sometimes. He gets depressed."

"About wheelchair?"

"About the chair, about high school students' reading habits, about how fast cottage cheese expires." She shrugged. "He's kind of aimless sometimes. Sarcastic, but aimless."

She picked up a stack of plates, and he grabbed the ketchup and mustard bottles and followed her into the house.

"He seemed happier when he left."

"Yeah, he'll be okay for now. Growing up is just hard, you know? He wants to leave home, but he needs a better job first."

She set the plates on the counter and Yuri put the bottles beside them. Mary came in with some glasses.

"Hey," Dovie said. "Distract Mom if she comes in, okay? I want to show Yuri something in my bedroom."

"Sure," Mary said, opening the refrigerator to put the condiments away.

Dovie took Yuri's fingertips and led him down the hall, past the computer by the clothes washer, and the brush of her skin was the sexiest thing he had ever known. *Dovie's bedroom. Was there any chance that it was customary to end American picnics with sex? It would be a fine tradition.*

They stepped through the doorway. The walls were hand painted with huge flowers, old-fashioned things from overgrown cottage gardens. The scale made him feel like a bug. A very, very horny bug. In the middle, Dovie's bed was arched with white garden lattice covered with paper flowers.

"It's beautiful," Yuri said.

"I wanted to feel like a fairy," Dovie said. "Lennon says it's a firetrap."

Yuri turned in a circle, then looked up. "You have little stars on ceiling."

"Yeah, I did them with glow-in-the-dark paint. That's what I put on Lennon's spokes."

Yuri squirmed, trying not to point out the obvious. It was a pretty room, completely individual, and Dovie's talent was evident—but he couldn't help himself. "Stars are wrong."

"What?"

"They're not just wrong hemisphere. It's as if you painted them randomly."

"I did. I was just going for pretty." He gaped at her. "Yes," she said. "My fairy-princess bedroom has an appallingly low level of academic rigor." He nodded. It was true.

"Sit." She pointed to the bed. He sat.

Dovie went to the closet and came back with a ceramic piece, glazed in a profusion of brilliant colors. She sat beside him, making the mattress bounce.

"I don't know what it is, but it's beautiful," he said.

"It's a cookie jar I made in art class. See? The lid lifts off."

It was a bed, with flowers and vines interwoven through the brass headboard, and a whole jungle on the bedspread, all done in clay. It was a verdant, writhing explosion of life, in colors stolen from parrots and tropical fish. Dovie lifted the bedspread off to reveal the cavity within, then replaced it with a clink.

Yuri touched a bird's tiny wing, scarlet and perfect. "It's beautiful. It's . . . really good, Dovie. You have serious talent."

"Yeah," she said. "But it didn't make it into the art show."

He stared at her.

"The teacher said it's too colorful, that I need to 'prune my palette'—so some elements are more prominent. So the eye knows where to go."

"But your result is amazing." He peered close to look at the detail—the stamens in a lily twining around the bedpost, a ladybug crawling up a vine. "Surely other students didn't make anything better than this?"

"No," Dovie said acidly. "They didn't. Besides, I titled the piece *Dreamland*. You're supposed to be able to dream wildly, right?"

Yuri didn't answer. He didn't know what to say.

"The girl in my art class that I don't like? Her cookie jar made it into the show, because she's most improved. She made a box. A *box*, Yuri."

"I'm sorry."

Dovie put the cookie jar back in her closet and stood, leaning against its door. "I grew up in a purple house with hippie parents— it's safe, you know? It's fun. And I'm going to have to go out on my own someday pretty soon. And the world is already telling me to be less. To *prune my palette*." Her eyes were wet. "I don't want to do that." She smiled weakly, and a tear spilled down her cheek. "Len doesn't want to stay here, and I guess I don't want to leave."

She pushed away from the closet.

"It doesn't matter anyway if the meteor hits, right?"

He stood. "Asteroid won't hit."

She wiped her hand across her cheek. "Then I guess I'll have to grow up."

They walked out to Dovie's car, picking up Mary and saying good-bye to Mr. and Mrs. Collum on the way. Yuri settled into the lumpy backseat.

"Mary," he said. "I want Dovie to teach me to swear, and she says I'm not ready."

"Hmm." Mary squinted back at him thoughtfully.

"It's not safe to know how to swear but not how to deal with people," Dovie said. "It's like walking around with your mouth loaded and the safety off."

"Yeah," Mary said. "He did really well today, though."

Yuri beamed and shot Dovie a look.

"Yeah," Dovie said. "Keep up the social mingling and we'll teach you some bad words. Human interaction is a precursor. Get it? Pre-curser?" And she accelerated back toward his hotel.

CHAPTER 16

PROBLEMS WITH ROCKS

Dovie dropped him off in the restaurant lot, and he walked to the hotel, hands shoved in his pockets. It was late enough that the air was cooling a little, and he could feel it on his neck. No tie. He reached the building.

He extended his plastic key card, ready to swipe it through the scanner, when a clot of shadow detached from behind a shrub and stepped between him and the door. It was one of the American security men, a big guy with short hair, arms crossed over his chest, staring at Yuri. Yuri took a sharp breath but didn't want to show that he was startled. He leaned toward the scanner, hoping the guy would move, but he stayed planted. Silence stretched, then snapped.

"I'm trying to get into hotel."

"Yeah. Where were you?"

He hesitated. "I took walk."

"Where'd you go?"

"Around." He shrugged.

"Uh-huh. You meet anybody?"

"I don't know lot of people in North America."

"Uh-huh. You have a handler?"

Yuri stared at him, genuinely taken aback. He thought he might be in trouble for fraternizing with locals, or leaving the building on general principle. It hadn't occurred to him that they might think he was actually up to something. He thought about the flight schedules he'd printed and wondered if that had made Fletcher suspicious. Of course, breaking into his office and trying to photograph documents might have added to the impression.

The man stared him down, then swiped his own card and held the door. Yuri walked up the stairs to the fourth floor. Didn't want to be alone in an elevator with the guy. He could hear the man's heavy tread behind him.

He held his key out as he neared his room, wanting to shut the door before the man could say anything else. Not wanting to run to do it. It would only make him look guilty, and undignified. But the security guard put an arm across the door, so that Yuri's face was in his shoulder. The thing was the size of a ham.

"You're not supposed to be out of the building, Dr. Strelnikov."

Yuri turned to look at him, and the guy's face was right above his. Not angry, just matter-of-fact.

"Nobody said," Yuri muttered, and swiped his way into the room. The guy made him duck under his arm. Yuri kicked the door with his foot before he turned around and threw the dead bolt and chained the door.

He wasn't supposed to leave the hotel. But Saturday was the prom.

Yuri kept a laser focus on his work for the next couple of days, but by Saturday afternoon he was fidgety. He stood at his desk, bouncing a pencil on the metal band that had held its eraser in before he chewed it off. He walked to the cafeteria, got an orange juice and drank a little, then reviewed what he had done that morning, looking at how it fit into the totality of the work. He was in good shape—done, really, except for double- and triple-checking. And then he had to persuade Simons and Pirkola. They were still working, but he was the one who wasn't supposed to leave the hotel—and the dance was tonight. No time to reestablish trust with Fletcher and get his blessing to go to the prom. That meant sneaking out, or blowing off Dovie, leaving her standing alone in the parking lot. No flowers, no date. He was pretty sure that would be a big deal to her.

Dinner with Simons and Pirkola was fast, and the conversation terse. Yuri was thinking about how to get out of the hotel if a guard was watching him there, too. Maybe it would be better just to leave from the NEO building. They would know he'd left, but they'd never find him, never think to look at a high school dance. Still, it would be harder to get out to see her another day, if he threw it in their faces like that.

Pirkola cupped his hands over his face. Behind them, his face turned red.

"Goddammit, my stone came back."

"Can it come back? I mean, it'd be another stone, wouldn't it?" Simons said.

"I don't care. I've got a freaking kidney stone, and it freaking hurts."

"Is pain bad?" Yuri asked.

"Yes, pain is bad."

Yuri flushed. Someday he was going to have to learn how to use English articles.

"This pain is a freaking galaxy of red giants," Pirkola said.

"You've got trouble with rocks of all sizes," Simons said, pushing a green bean into his potatoes. He looked up. "Something's going on."

"I'm gonna have to go back to the hospital. Have them zap this thing."

"I don't know what the problem is, but an hour ago a couple of people were running to Fletcher's office. They wanted him immediately, but he wasn't in," Simons said. "He was off campus talking to some Pentagon brass."

"Who was looking for him?" Yuri asked, just to sound interested. He wasn't thinking about Fletcher. He was thinking about the way Dovie's legs rose and fell fractionally when they were tucked beside him on her sofa.

"Some guys from spectral," Simons said.

"God, this hurts," Pirkola said. "I'm gonna get out of here."

"Me, too," Yuri said, yawning. "I'm going to make early night of it, get some sleep. I think I'm still fighting against virus."

Three minutes later he'd gotten Simons and Pirkola out of his office, rubbed his hockey puck for luck, and was slipping down the back hallway when he saw two men pound on Karl Fletcher's door. One of them held a printout pinched between his index finger and thumb. It looked like he'd carry it with tongs if he could. Yuri hesitated. He didn't want the director to see him leave. From down the hall he could hear Fletcher bark permission to enter, and the men disappeared into the office. Yuri waited a moment, then continued down the hall. As he passed the door, he caught a fragment of conversation.

"We made assumptions based on incomplete data," a man's voice said. "And just on the probabilities. Guess it shouldn't be a surprise."

"It's a little bit of a surprise," Fletcher said. "It's a little bit of a goddamn surprise."

"Yeah," the man said.

Yuri hesitated in the hall. A problem with the asteroid? *Mat' tvoyu*—he'd have to stay.

"We couldn't reach you." It was the other man. "They didn't want to transfer us to your cell."

"Yeah. I was talking with the Pentagon," Fletcher said. He sounded distracted.

Yuri could hear papers flip. Fletcher must be looking at the report. Then the click of plastic as he tapped his office phone.

"Yeah, get me the White House."

Ah, something political. The Pentagon, the White House. Not a science problem.

Yuri walked into the lobby, and the front desk called a car for him. He stepped out to the curb to meet it, opened the door himself, and sank into the backseat. He thought of Dovie and smiled at the driver.

"Hotel, please."

The man nodded and accelerated down Oak Grove Drive, away from JPL.

CHAPTER 17

CATCH A FALLING STAR

In his hotel room Yuri shaved, more for the ritual of it than any real need, and put on a fresh white shirt and his gray suit. He practiced his lady-killer smile in the mirror. It hadn't produced much carnage yet, but he had hopes. He added a raised eyebrow and decided it made him look sophisticated. How could she resist?

He didn't know if he needed a tuxedo or not, but this was as good as it was going to get. Besides, he had the eyebrow thing. He threw his suit jacket over his shoulder, Mr. Casual, and took the elevator down to the lobby. A guard stood leaning against a post, arms crossed, alert. Not menacing, but not someone you could get around, either. Yuri picked up a newspaper off a folded stack and headed to the stairwell by the back door.

"Good evening, Dr. Strelnikov."

It was the guard from the other evening, the one who'd

confronted him. The rear door was propped open, and he was standing just outside, in the parking lot.

"Good evening." Yuri lifted the newspaper in explanation and trudged back upstairs. No way to get out of the lobby undetected.

He tossed the newspaper on his bed and went directly to the balcony. If he didn't do this fast, he wasn't going to do it. He stood on the lone chair and shut his eyes for a moment, trying to steady his breathing. Felt his gut twist. Then he imagined Dovie standing by her car in the yellow print dress, looking across the parking lot, waiting. He stepped out onto the railing.

He reached up. The parapet was low, and he got a solid hold on the top. Not so hard. But now what? He pushed off with his legs, pulling up at the same time. He swung free from the building, but didn't make much upward progress. He hung for a moment, imagining some American official explaining his strange death to his colleagues in the physics department at Moscow State. "Yes, climbing up the side of his hotel," the official would say.

Yuri pulled again, swung sideways a little, back and forth like a pendulum, hoping the lobby guard was still inside the building. He managed to land his left foot over the parapet, and crabbed his palms until he was sprawled on the top of the hotel.

Below him, his room telephone rang.

He stared down through the roof. It could only be Dovie—NEO was winding down for the night. Was she calling to cancel? After he'd dangled off the fourth floor of a building for her? His cell phone was in the pocket of the pants he'd worn to work—no way to check. He'd find out later what she wanted—he wasn't climbing down to answer a phone.

The roof appeared flat from the ground. Standing on it, however, he could see that it was divided into sections, each slightly pitched toward a basket-covered drain. He trotted bent over at the waist, tripped once on a condensate drainpipe but kept his balance. He reached the edge.

He grabbed the parapet and eased himself out, four stories in the air, feet searching for the fourth-floor balcony railing. Because the parapet extended out slightly, he had to swing in, toward the hotel, to find the railing. And he couldn't see what he was doing. His heart slammed in his chest. He could feel his pulse ticking in his neck, feel it quiver in his fingertips. His mother would say something about tonic regulation of his vagal pathway. But she wasn't hanging off a roof.

His feet found the railing, and he shifted so that he would fall inward onto the balcony. No way could he try to balance on the balls of his feet, as likely to fall off one way as the other. So he dropped down to the balcony, half rolling into the small area, to find himself at the feet of an elderly woman in a bathrobe, sitting with a cup of coffee and a newspaper. Her legs didn't taper at the ankle—they just became feet stuffed into lavender slippers that brought out the purple splotches on her skin.

"Evening," he said, his accent changing the final consonant to a k. She stared at him.

He grabbed the railing and swung down, letting his hands slide over the posts, his feet kicking out, then finding the next railing. He could hear an American baseball game playing on the television in the third-floor room as he landed, then clambered down to the second-floor balcony. He was waiting for the woman above to scream, wondering if she was calling the front desk, if someone would come out the lobby door right as he landed. After all this. He heard the same baseball game from the second-floor room and wasn't sure he'd hear if she was on the telephone.

He dropped from the second-floor balcony to the ground, staggered for a moment, but kept his footing. No guard. She hadn't called, or he'd been faster. He slipped between cars, eyes down, heading for the street that ran in front of the restaurant. A couple of weary businessmen stared at him but kept going into the hotel. Checking in, probably—no search in their pockets for key cards. They'd just seen a guy in a gray suit clamber down the hotel facade. Not likely they weren't going to mention it to the clerk.

Yuri trotted across the road, turning at the first side street to block himself from sight, then turned again. He needed to clear out for now in case the guards realized he was gone, and get flowers before Dovie showed up. He kept moving, found a bouquet in a stiff plastic sleeve at an overlit grocery store a mile down, paid cash, and got out as fast as he could. He walked back toward the hotel, wanting to catch Dovie before she got to the restaurant lot. Not wanting to think about her two-tone car rattling toward the hotel, maybe parking in sight of a guard, and Yuri being unable to approach it. He mumbled the list of Nobel winners under his breath to calm his nerves.

Dovie was singing when he saw her, bouncing her wrists on the top of the steering wheel, her head bobbing from side to side. He stepped out, waved the flowers to her, and her eyes flew wide. She jerked the wheel and he darted away from the road, heard tires hit the curb and caught the odor of scorched rubber. The wheels churned up grass along the last lot before the corner, missed a fire hydrant, and slammed off the curb onto a side street. The car rocked to a stop. Dovie leaned over and opened the passenger door, but her arms weren't long enough to push it wide.

"You startled me!"

"I thought you were going to hit me," Yuri said, swinging into the front seat.

"Well, I didn't expect you along here."

He looked at her. Dovie had undone herself for the evening. Instead of bright glitter around her eyes, she had soft brown shadows, and her hair was twisted up in a neat braid that nestled over the curve of her head. Her dress was soft pink silk that puddled around the accelerator.

"You look beautiful." He suddenly remembered the eyebrow move and cocked it while he smiled. Better late than never.

"You sound surprised."

She gave him a sideways grin as she pulled away and headed for the high school, and he saw the silver glint of a tongue stud. Maybe she wore it for formal occasions. Yuri stretched his legs, pushing his back into the seat. He glanced himself over, and figured he looked pretty good considering what he'd just done. He grinned.

"These are for you." He held up the bouquet by its stems, the stiff cellophane crinkling in his hand.

Dovie laughed.

"They're lovely. Thank you."

"Um. Are they wrong colors?"

"Really, they're pretty. It's just the guy usually brings a corsage, not a full bouquet."

"Oh. What does corsage mean?"

"Like to pin on your dress, or for your wrist."

"Ah." He flushed. "I'm sorry. I failed my first American high school task."

"Unless you count band," Dovie said. "Or gym. Or . . ."

"Do not say algebra," Yuri said. "I got those problems right."

She laughed. He stared at the flowers. Why hadn't he thought about this? What was she supposed to do with a bouquet all night—just walk around and hold it? Her friends would laugh. *She* had laughed.

"I have idea." He snapped a sprig of pink baby's breath off. "Turn your head." He waggled his finger toward her window. She turned, exposing the braid that coiled up the back of her head. Yuri tucked the sprig where one plait rolled under another.

"That okay?"

She nodded. He snapped off a pink alstroemeria and slipped it in the next junction, where the underneath plait emerged.

"Use some yellow ones, too," Dovie said, driving with her right eye on the road, and her face to the side window.

"Can you drive okay while I do this?"

"No, but I can't drive okay while you're not doing it, either."

He laughed. He had her braid exploding in bloom by the time they bounced into the high school parking lot and stopped, facing the building.

They got out of the car, and Dovie poked an alstroemeria bloom into his top buttonhole. She looked up at the darkening sky. "Did you wish on the first star as a little boy in Russia?"

"No. First star is actually Venus. I would be wishing on planet."

She laughed and turned toward the school, and her expression grew serious. "Did you really look at the building the other day?" Dovie said. "Did you see all the rectangles? The building itself, each brick, the doors, the windows, the panes in the windows. It's like the architect only knew one shape."

"Oh, yeah," Yuri said. "I see what you mean."

Light spilled from the windows and an open double door, and couples ran lightly up the outside stairs, holding hands. Dovie hooked one hand around his elbow and elevated her skirt with the other as she led him up the exterior flight of steps and into the corridor.

"Some squares, finally," Dovie said, pointing to the green and cream linoleum tiles. "You'd think the guy's progressing, but there's all those stairs up, and then the stairs back down." She gestured to the well-coifed heads descending before them in regular jolts. "It's impossible in a wheelchair."

"Oh. Lennon. Did he study here?" Of course he did.

"Yeah. There's wheelchair access behind the building. So you can get in, but you can't feel good doing it."

The steps down funneled them into a rustling parade of colored dresses. Excited chatter bounced off the stairwell walls, creating overlapping echoes. It was hard to hear.

"Can I ask? Why Lennon, um . . ."

"The wheelchair? He fell out of a tree, at that white house three down from us." She looked at him, but he shook his head. Who notices a white house on a block with a purple one? "He was eight. He tells people it was a drunk driver. He gets more sympathy that way."

They stood, trapped, at the foot of the stairs, caught in warm, humid air recently exhaled by a hundred would-be dancers, whose finery twitched with their nervous energy. Several girls hit their dates with elbows as they tugged on strapless dresses. Then they were through the doors and into the gym, heels clicking on polished gold boards. A woman herded them toward a freestanding archway covered with crepe paper and dangling foil stars, and a man snapped their picture, then took their names. The woman motioned them forward and turned to the next couple.

"Do you want to get some punch?" Dovie asked.

Yuri stared at the gym. Blue and white crepe paper twisted from the corners to the center of the ceiling, where a silver star with a sagging black-foil tail hung suspended. A banner along the far wall read, "Catch a Falling Star."

"What is . . . That star, why . . ."

"Oh, yeah. Stunningly poor theme choice, isn't it? The student council picked something else, but Mrs. Cronick overruled it. The principal," she said.

"Unbelievable. 'Catch a falling star?' They know, don't they? About asteroid? This is joke?"

"No, this is high school administration. The decorations were like eighteen dollars cheaper than the ones the student council wanted."

He stared at her.

"She did" —he swept his arm across the room— "*this*, to save eighteen dollars?"

"Don't try to understand high school administration. Your brain isn't big enough," Dovie said, pulling on his arm. "Come on, they're dancing."

And they were. A middle-aged DJ with a huge mustache smiled genially from the stage. His playlist was a little old, Yuri thought, as he'd heard the songs before, even though he couldn't identify most of them. Dovie led him to a collapsible table covered with a disposable white cloth, holding a plastic punch bowl and a stack of clear plastic glasses.

"It looks like spiral galaxy," Yuri said, nodding toward the swaying dancers.

"Yeah," Dovie said. "I noticed that, too."

Yuri didn't catch the sarcasm.

"And that big guy surrounded by girls over there could be Saturn, except he's missing one moon," Yuri said.

She handed him a cup of startlingly blue punch.

"He's missing more than that. That's Kyle Davidson, the quarterback of the football team and a huge jerk."

"What's wrong with him?"

"He's ar-ro-gant."

"Is he good?"

"Yeah. He's really good."

"Then maybe he has reason."

She looked at him for a long moment.

"Drink your punch," she said.

He drank.

"This is appalling," he said, and meant it.

"But it's blue, and that's what counts."

He swiveled his head. "Is Mr. Pisotto here?"

"No, he chaperoned homecoming, so he got out of this. Mr. Reynolds isn't here, either."

Yuri tossed his cup in the pressed-metal trash can at the end of the table. Dovie put her hand on his back and began to push him gently forward. He turned and held Dovie's elbow, her flesh warm under his fingers. He could feel the pulse in her brachial artery.

"We are going to dance," she said.

"I don't dance."

"Not even for me?"

He hesitated. He didn't know any of these people and would never see any of them again.

"I guess I can sway awkwardly."

She led him past a dozen gawky, angular guys leaning against the wall under the caged windows. They looked like they'd been put together from a kit of irregular parts. Dovie stopped at the edge of the crowd, where it thinned into space filled with pastel dancers with tuxedoed dates, all in irregularly shaped orbits. It would have driven Kepler mad.

He put his right hand against her warm fingers, placed his left palm on her lower back and pressed her close enough that her dress brushed over his shoes, back and forth, and he wished he had sensory receptors in his footwear. Then he realized he didn't need them. He was aroused just thinking about her hem swishing rhythmically over his shoe leather. And that couldn't be normal.

He risked a sideways step, and after a brief hesitation Dovie followed. Problem was, her legs were covered by billowing pink silk, so any move she made looked graceful. Who knew what her feet were doing under there? She could get away with virtually anything. He stepped back to where they'd started. Figured he could get away with the side-to-side thing for a while.

"I can't talk about my work," he said, "but I'm having problem with two colleagues. I don't know what to do about it."

"The guy who wants to make you stay?"

"No. Guys I'm working with."

"Hmm. Can you tell me more?"

"Not really. I shouldn't have said anything at all."

She bit her lip and it rose around the glistening bottom edge of her teeth. She narrowed her eyes at him, thinking.

"So I have to give you advice without any idea what you're talking about."

"Yes."

"In that situation, I always turn to Immanuel Kant."

He blinked.

"Kant said, 'Do what is right, though the world should perish.' Of course, he said it in German, which probably sounded cooler."

"Except if he got it wrong, world wasn't really going to perish."

"The world perishes for everybody, Science Boy. That concept is the foundation of religion and cosmetic surgery."

She twirled away from him, still holding his right hand with her left. He reeled her back in and caught the scent of the flowers in her hair.

"I was thinking about that other guy," she said. "The one who wants you to stay."

"Who wants to *make* me stay."

"Yeah."

They shuffled in a small arc, surrounded by other couples, Yuri trying to avoid bumping into anyone. He wasn't superstitious, but he thought it best to avoid collisions.

"Would it be so bad to live here? I mean, it's a big country. You could find a good place to work."

"I used to think about living in America. That maybe I would someday. But they should *ask* me," he said, leaning forward so he could talk directly into her ear. "It should be *my* decision."

"You'd stay if they asked?"

"No. I don't have much of life in Russia, but it's still my life." He thought for a moment about Fyodor Laskov in his office and pushed the image from his mind.

Dovie nodded, and her hair brushed the side of his face. He wondered if he should kiss her ear. Tiny, soft hairs, almost invisible, rose from its pink curve.

"Dovieee!" Mary and another girl stood there in shimmering fabrics, their dates—James and another guy—shifting awkwardly behind them.

Dovie hugged the girls, then the guys. It occurred to Yuri that he should have practiced some other expressions in the bathroom mirror. How did you move an eyebrow to convey *your hands are a little too low on my date's back and also this hug is taking too long*? Still, they'd stopped dancing in order to talk, and that was worth something.

"Yuri, you know Mary and this is Rique, and this is Jen, and of course, James."

"Hey, Crash," James said, sticking his fist out. Yuri bumped it.

"I have gym with her," Jen said. "I am so sorry I missed Jake Bortell's crash. I skipped to get a manicure." She waggled silver nails at them.

"So are you going to come here?" James said to Yuri.

It took him a moment to realize what James meant. "Oh. Um . . . no." How could he explain what he did, and why he was there, without sounding pretentious? James needed to work on his speed-hugging skills, but Yuri had no need to flash his credentials in the guy's face.

"Oh."

"I'm so glad you brought Dovie," Mary said, twirling a finger at her. Dovie obediently turned to display her dress from all angles. "We couldn't believe she didn't have a date."

"I couldn't, either," Yuri said.

Dovie shrugged, and the pink silk rustled. "Guys think I'm weird."

Yuri hesitated for a moment, and she punched him lightly in the shoulder.

"Oh, crap. We gotta go," Mary said, looking over Dovie's head. "Maybe we can all dance later or something." She dragged her date off, and Jen grabbed James's hand and pulled him away, too.

"Dovie Collum," a woman's voice said.

Dovie stiffened beneath Yuri's palm, as if she'd suddenly dehydrated. It was the principal she had pointed out earlier, a small woman with a severe mouth. Yuri wondered what the tensile strength of her vocal cords was. Probably pretty impressive.

"Who is your date?"

Dovie wriggled out from his palm and dropped his hand.

"Um, this is Yuri Strelnikov. He's a friend."

Mrs. Cronick looked at him but spoke to Dovie.

"And is he a student here?"

"Um, no."

"Uh-huh. And do we allow students to come to prom if they don't attend Edmund Andros High School?"

"Um, I know there's a form to fill out . . ."

"Did you do it? Because I don't have a form from you."

"I guess I didn't." Her voice was soft, defeated. Kyle Davidson pointed at them from his perch by the punch bowl, and the girls around him whispered.

"I'm sorry, was it Yuri? You'll have to leave."

"Why?"

"Miss Collum didn't file the necessary paperwork," the principal said, tilting her head slightly as she spoke. Yuri got the feeling she could spin it all the way around if she wanted, using her nose as a fulcrum.

"I'm sure she'll know for next time," he said. "I'm working with NEO Program at JPL." Maybe James didn't need to know that, but this principal did. "We only met recently."

The gym rustled with interest. He took Dovie's hand and started to move away.

Jen, her black curls skimming a sequined peach dress, threw her arms in the air and shouted, "Dovie bagged a Meteor Man! Whoo-hoo!"

Laughter bounced through the gym.

"You don't work at JPL," Mrs. Cronick said, stepping in front of them. "You're a teenager. But I don't care who you are or what you're doing. She didn't follow my rules."

"I asked her to come to dance rather late. Was my fault," he said, flashing what he hoped was a charming smile.

"Irrelevant," Mrs. Cronick said. "Out."

He stared at her.

"Come on," Dovie whispered.

No, he would not come on. There was supposed to be more freedom in America, but guards trailed him at work and now this petty administrator was ruining Dovie's night. He thought of her painting, of the girl trapped in the rectangles. This woman was starting to piss him off.

"Do you run high school this way? Arbitrary bureaucratism?"

The principal's mouth tightened, her red lipstick slowly rolling under like a submerging submarine.

"Out."

Dovie tugged at his hand.

"You lock hundreds of teenagers together in building, treat them like criminals, and can't figure out why your education system doesn't work?" The gym was silent. "What do you people hope to get from this experience? Seriously?"

"What high school do you go to?" Mrs. Cronick said.

"I don't go to high school. I graduated already."

The principal's tight mouth curled up.

"You're over eighteen? That's another infraction, Dovie Collum."

"I'm seventeen. But I graduated high school when I had twelve years."

"Sure you did," Mrs. Cronick said. "You little jackass."

"Whooo!" Kyle Davidson yelled appreciatively.

"That's Doctor Jackass to you," Yuri said, then turned his back on her. "Dovie, do you want to dance more?"

"No, thank you," she squeaked.

"Let's get some punch before we leave, then."

He took her hand and walked past Mrs. Cronick, shielding Dovie. Their shoes clicked on the golden boards of the gym floor. Yuri poured a cup of the blue punch, and in the silent gym the gurgle reverberated past the iron basketball rims. When he handed it to Dovie, she took the drink with both hands. As Yuri reached for another cup, Kyle Davidson stepped sideways, blocking him.

"Think you're hot stuff, don't you?"

Yuri glanced at Dovie, unsure of the idiom.

"I can hit a receiver in the hands from seventy yards. What do you think about that?"

Yuri shrugged. "That's good."

"Damn straight that's good."

"Move, please. I want to get another cup."

"I'm not moving for you."

"Why?"

Kyle hesitated for a moment.

"I don't have to."

"No, but would be courteous."

Kyle glanced at the girls around him, shifted, then set his jaw.

"Yeah, well, I'm not moving."

Yuri shrugged.

"I think that punch is poison, anyway." He took Dovie's empty cup and tossed it in the trash can. "How do you say, it's your funeral?" He locked his fingers with Dovie's and moved toward the exit, his-and-hers heel clicks on the lacquered floorboards. He stopped in the doorway.

"Hey, Kyle. You know what I can hit?"

"What?"

"Asteroid traveling at seventy-one kilometers per second. And if I can't, you're dead."

And then he let Dovie lead him back up the stairs and into the parking lot.

CHAPTER 18

HOPING IT WAS MURDER

"So here's the thing," Dovie said, guiding the steering wheel with her inner wrist. "My parents want to get a picture of us, which is totally lame, but they wanted us to stop by the house after the dance. If you have time."

"Sure, but that guy took picture at school."

"I don't know if I can get that, since we got kicked out."

"Sorry."

"Not your fault."

Dovie accelerated through a yellow light.

"Hey, Yuri?"

"Yes?"

"If the asteroid hits Earth, will it be bad? I mean, really bad?"

"Yeah. It'll devastate California."

She turned to stare at him. He glanced from her bulging eyes to the road ahead.

"I'm sorry. I shouldn't have told you."

"Oh my God." She was silent for a moment. "What do you think it will be like?"

"Um . . . I don't think human vertebrae can withstand concussion, so I think it will be whole lot like being dead."

Dovie's eyes glistened.

"Will it knock the planet apart?"

"No, that's impossible . . ."

"I wonder if water will flow from the ocean, right off the edge of the world."

"The atmospheric . . ."

"Shut up, Science Boy. And pirate gold will spill out, doubloons clinking, and *T. rex* bones will tumble into space and float there. Oh! They may get caught by the gravity of some planet. That could happen, right?"

"Well, yes, but . . ."

"And there would be skeletal *T. rexes* marching around a planet, deathless sentries from a dead world. And some day it'll freak out aliens flying by. They'll press their little green faces to the windshield and say, 'What the hell, Zork! Look at that!'"

"You know, you don't have to try so hard to be different. You *are* different."

"Um, thank you?"

He grimaced slightly. He'd always assumed he would be smooth with women. Experimentation was proving that hypothesis wrong.

"I mean, you're artist. Life is your canvas."

"Wow. That's actually very nice."

She turned onto her street.

"I'm very nice guy. But don't worry about planet breaking apart, okay? Wouldn't happen with biggest asteroid you could find." He didn't add, *It wouldn't have to break apart for us to die.*

Dovie parked with three wheels on the driveway, and they walked to the front stoop with hooked pinkie fingers. The door was unlocked and as Dovie opened it, warmth and light and the smell of burnt cinnamon spilled out.

"Hey, it's the Spockovskii!" Lennon called, splitting his fingers in a Vulcan salute. He'd taken the wings off his chair, but had left the bat-signal flashlight underneath it.

Yuri nodded to Dovie's parents, who were washing dishes together. "'Skii' is ending for adjectives," he said. "I'm noun."

"Knowing that is proof you're the Spockovskii."

Mr. Collum dried his hands and tossed the dish towel over his shoulder. He grabbed a camera from the kitchen table and motioned Dovie and Yuri in closer together. Yuri put his hand lightly on her back, awkward now—her house, her father. Mr. Collum clicked the picture, then turned the camera on end, his elbow jutting out as he shot again.

"Got it!" He put the camera down. "You're home early."

"Mrs. Cronick kicked us out," Dovie said.

"Did you visibly enjoy yourself or something?" Lennon asked, without looking up from the television.

"Something like that," Dovie said. "Yuri told her off."

"God bless you," Mr. Collum said. "Any chance you could get the asteroid to land just on her?"

"Um, probably not."

"Yeah. That's a shame." Dovie's father grabbed a newspaper and disappeared down the hall.

Yuri waved a hand to Lennon and Mrs. Collum, and then stepped out on the stoop with Dovie. The night air was soft and warm, and they could still smell cinnamon, wafting out through the open windows. He put a hand on Dovie's back, where the soft silk gave way to softer skin. He wasn't sure he'd ever been so happy.

"Is it okay to kiss you?"

"Totally."

"Would you be willing to remove your tongue stud first?"

Dovie stared at him. "*What?*" She narrowed her eyes.

"It might scratch me. I could get infection."

"What do you care if you get an infection?" Lennon shouted from the living room. "You're suicidal."

"I am not. But it could be painful. There could be unpleasant discharge."

Dovie snorted.

"You'd be embarrassed for the undertaker to see it?" she said.

"He'd see your skinny ass, too," Lennon shouted. "That ass is a good reason not to kill yourself. Seriously, dude, you need to work out before you do yourself in."

"I'm not suicidal. I *slipped.*"

"You could get implants," Delinda Collum called.

Yuri put his hands on his backside and shut his eyes to kiss Dovie. Her lips seemed firmer, less yielding, and when he tried to nuzzle them apart they pursed tight. He opened one eye to find her glowering at him from an inch away. He felt like a grass-eater on the savannah.

"This is where I apologize?"

"Yep."

"I'm sorry I'm afraid of your tongue stud. May I kiss you anyway?"

She appraised him for a moment.

"Okay."

He leaned in and kissed her, and she threw her arms around his neck. He brushed the sides of her breasts with his palms as he encircled her. Figured he could claim it was an accident if she protested, but she was busy gnawing on his lip, and he tasted the blue punch. Then she brought her tongue stud up and tapped the back of his front teeth.

"Gotcha."

He smiled at her, and they held hands as they walked to her car.

"Dovie? Is your door different color because it was inexpensive used part?"

"No. I was experimenting with people's perceptions of color appropriateness. Whether analogous colors with the same saturation and finish nevertheless produce an anxiety response when found in unexpected visual environments."

He swung in and fastened his seat belt.

"Really?"

"No. It was just the cheapest door that fit."

"Oh."

She pulled out of the driveway and the back wheels bumped up over the neighbor's curb, her headlights pointing down to illuminate cracks in the street. Then they bounced off and swung back to the feeder street that would T with an artery that would merge with the highway that would take them back to his hotel.

They rode a few minutes, Yuri lost in thought, unconsciously tapping his fingers on his knee in rhythm with the rattling of the car.

"You thinking about those guys at work?"

"Hmm? No. Maybe."

"You're very grave."

"I'm always grave about gravity." He grabbed the door handle as Dovie noticed a stop sign and slammed on the brakes. "Is that funny in English?"

"No, it's really not. Are you funny in Russian?"

"No."

She laughed.

"That's funny?"

"Yes. Yes, it is."

Yuri sighed. The windows were down and the air was still warm and it washed over his face, bringing with it the smell of exhaust. They drove by a row of gas stations and convenience stores and a secondhand clothing store, glare from the streetlights bouncing off Dovie's green hood.

Yuri thought of full pink skirts and the geometry of high schools and the clink of a tongue stud behind his tooth, and my god, how could that be so sexy? Dovie accelerated through a yellow light. Yuri fingered his seat belt strap.

"I think I just discovered something that moves faster than speed of light."

"Me?"

"Yeah. You know, light might be common ground for us."

"I try to capture it in oils, while you regale me with stories of the little photon that could?"

"Something like that."

They could see red and blue wash over the front of the hotel as they approached, coming from two cruisers parked, noses pointed out.

"That doesn't look good," Dovie muttered.

"Maybe was murder," Yuri said, trying not to sound hopeful. Then he noticed the dark NASA car service vehicle parked between the police cars.

Dovie stopped in the restaurant lot and Yuri kissed her hand as he left, but he was already thinking about the flashers. Something had happened. He caught her eye and smiled tightly, then closed the door, slipped through the trees between lots, and walked toward the front entrance, trying to look confident, and innocent.

"Dr. Strelnikov?"

It was the driver. Same guy who'd driven him in that morning and back to the hotel four hours ago.

"Yes?"

"I have orders to get you to JPL immediately, sir."

The driver held the door open. Yuri ducked in and the man punched the accelerator, following one cruiser, leading the other, their lights still rotating.

"What's going on?" Yuri asked.

The driver was silent for a moment, then said, "I don't know." He looked at Yuri in the rearview mirror, as though maybe he'd explain it.

Yuri fidgeted all the way down Oak Grove Drive, past the guard gate, the California hills getting taller, the JPL buildings rising, bright, ahead of him—fully lit this late in the evening. He could see people move past office windows. The place was humming.

Yuri mumbled Nobel winners under his breath to calm himself. He was up to Arthur Holly Compton when the driver pulled up to the entrance. Yuri jerked the car door open and bounded out without looking back at the man or thanking him for the ride. He trotted up the steps and ran into the lobby, walking quickly to the conference room.

Someone had taped up a piece of computer paper beside the marker boards holding the equation. The scrawled header read, "Who I wish was here right now." Underneath, the same hand had written, "Isaac Newton," and someone else had added "x2." Below, in black ink, a different hand had written, "Einstein," and below that it read, "Niels Bohr," "Aristotle," "Stephen Hawking," and "Galileo," and below that, in the director's precise script, "Yuri Strelnikov."

Yuri's face burned. It wasn't a compliment to his abilities, ranking him with Newton and Einstein. It was a sarcastic remark about him going AWOL. Yuri turned, headed across the conference room toward Fletcher's office, and caught a hostile stare from a couple of orbital dynamicists. There must have been a meeting, everyone gathered back from their offices, something announced— and his absence noted.

Yuri tucked his head down and caught sight of the drooping alstroemeria bloom in his buttonhole. He gently dislodged it and put it in his jacket pocket. He stepped into the hallway that held Fletcher's office. The janitors walked down the corridor, setting up cots. The oldest one caught sight of him and tucked his head down as he unfolded another cot, taking care not to let the metal tubing clank against the wall.

Something was very wrong.

CHAPTER 19

THE MOTHER OF ALL
NIGHTMARES

Yuri knocked quietly on Fletcher's office door.

"If you're not Yuri Strelnikov, you can go screw yourself," Fletcher yelled.

"I'm Yuri Strelnikov."

There was a pause, and then the door flew wide.

"You can still go screw yourself. Where were you?"

Yuri flushed.

"I took walk . . ."

"Save it." Then Fletcher laughed, a tense noise, vocal cords vibrating tightly. "Save it. That's good."

Yuri looked at him curiously.

"We'll walk to your office so you can get right to work, after your own special briefing."

"I'm sorry."

Fletcher waved him off.

"We got more data back."

"Yeah?"

"It's an unusual asteroid," Fletcher said.

"Because of speed," Yuri said. "Which is partly because of retrograde orbit. Instead of coming up from behind Earth, like asteroids normally do, it's coming from front, so Earth's orbital speed adds to total. Like head-on car collision."

"Yeah," Fletcher said as they rounded the corner. "That's why this is so much faster than most asteroids—because we're heading into it."

"We already knew this," Yuri said.

"But that's not what makes it so unusual."

Yuri looked at the side of his face, at the high forehead. There was something brittle about him, as though he'd been dipped in liquid nitrogen and if you touched him he might shatter. The director went on. "We had to figure its orbit first— would it hit—and how fast it's moving. How long we have to work."

They were at Yuri's office. He stopped outside the door, still not sure where this was headed.

"We just got the spectral analysis back."

Yuri looked at him, not getting it.

"It's red-sloped."

Yuri felt the hairs on the back of his neck prick up.

"No. It's S-type. Silicaceous. They can look reddish."

"We got the analysis. It's red-sloped but featureless spectra," Fletcher said.

"Is mixed composition, maybe?" His voice pitched high, and he hated himself for it. "Silica can have nickel-iron mixed in."

Fletcher gave him a sober look. "It's an M-type. Metal. There isn't any question about it. And it's almost uniform. Looks like a little palladium and iridium, but it's almost all iron."

They were silent for a moment. Yuri felt a sense of great quiet, of stillness, as though the barometric pressure had just plunged.

"We can't do it," he whispered. "Our plan to pulverize it. This thing's mass must be—it's not going to work."

"No," Fletcher said. "It's not."

Yuri stared at him.

"We have to come up with a new plan, and we have almost no time. And the weapons team will need some of that little time to deploy whatever we decide to use."

"What are we going to do?"

"Die," Fletcher said. "Unless one of you can come up with a better idea."

Yuri ran his hand over his mouth. "M-type."

"M-type in retrograde orbit," Fletcher said. "The mother of all nightmares." He scratched the back of his neck. "Meeting in the conference room in twenty minutes. We have to agree on a new strategy then, because we'll need the rest of the time to implement it."

Yuri stared at him. Twenty minutes?

Fletcher started to walk away, then turned.

"Another thing. Everybody stays here. Eat while you work. No showers. If you start to fall asleep, move to one of the cots.

Someone will wake you in twenty minutes." Yuri nodded. "No walks."

Yuri stared after the director for a full minute after he'd rounded the corner. Then he entered his office and caught the pale smudge of his face in the black window glass, and shame tasted like vomit in his mouth.

The world was ending, and he'd gone to prom.

He looked on his desk for a briefing and found nothing. They were starting over, here, shortly before midnight, six days before impact. There was nothing to report. All their work had meant nothing. His arguments with Simons and Pirkola—pointless. Nothing they had been calculating had ever had a chance, because something unfathomably fast and cold was rushing in, and they hadn't recognized it. It was a failure of understanding.

Could this hurt his chances for the Nobel?

It was a full second before he realized that if life on Earth was wiped out, it would include the Nobel committee. It was another second before he realized that it didn't matter anymore.

In those two seconds, the BR1019 came 142 kilometers closer.

Yuri ran back through a printout of his previous work, looking for bits that could be salvaged, then brushed it off his desktop with the back of his hand. He pulled out a clean piece of paper and wrote in Russian: *Make it stop. Shove it sideways. Move Earth out of the way. Blow it up. Make it disappear.* He wrote a dash, and *Impossible*, after each of the first four possibilities. Then he stared at the last one, and chewed on the pencil eraser.

He hadn't been tired, but he now ground the heels of his palms into his eyes. There had been time before. He had finished the calculations, come up with the answers his team needed, and done it easily. He might have had time to persuade Simons and Pirkola, too. Now their difference of opinion didn't matter, because while they would have been able—just barely—to blow up a rock of BR1019's magnitude, all the nuclear weapons in the world put together wouldn't blow up a hunk of iron that size.

It wasn't a matter of switching out a few numbers, calculating for a new mass. It would require a whole different approach. There might not be an answer. Nothing might work.

Yuri was on his second pencil eraser when a woman he didn't know shouted down the hall that it was time for the meeting, and everyone should go down to the media room. Yuri stared at his desk. He had a piece of paper scrawled with five potential approaches, four of which were impossible and one of which was crazy. He flipped the paper facedown and bent forward, resting his forehead on it, his eyes squeezed shut.

Then he stood and followed others to the media room. It was large, filled with dark blue seats like a movie theater, but with no cup holders. Most of the seats were already taken, and Yuri got swept in by the shuffling scientists, seated by default next to a young woman who was an expert in dense stellar systems. The anxiety in the room was palpable.

Fletcher walked to the front and stood where the screen would be if they'd lowered it.

"I'm not introducing myself or anyone else," he said. "You all know who I am, and I don't give a goddamn if you know your neighbor. A few hours ago, after we got the spectral analysis back, I asked you to go to your offices and brainstorm. I don't know how we're going to beat this thing, and if we do come up with a strategy, we may not have time to implement it. So keep it short, and talk fast. What have you got?"

No one spoke for a moment, but it wasn't silent. Papers rustled in reluctant hands, necks rubbed against collars as people looked at each other, waiting for someone else to speak.

"Seventy-one kilometers a second, people!" Fletcher bellowed.

A tall man with a scholar's stoop stood to the left of the room.

"I'm Dan Kilpatrick, usually at Goddard." He caught Fletcher's expression and ended his intro. "This thing's kilometers across. We had a chance at blowing up a rock that big, but iron isn't going to react the same way. We all know it won't work, and if we do manage to blow it into a few pieces, they'll still be too big to burn up on entering the atmosphere. We'd just be creating multiple impacts of a catastrophic nature."

"There's no viable alternative," an older man called from the right, without bothering to stand. "We may as well try it—nothing else has a chance."

"We may as well do nothing," Kilpatrick snapped. "The only reasonable strategy is to try to deflect the asteroid, just punch it to the side as it goes by."

"It'd be like punching a skyscraper with your fist," the woman beside Yuri whispered to him. "You can punch, but it ain't moving."

He nodded. She was right.

"Dan, what's your thought on the deflection process?" Fletcher said.

Kilpatrick fanned his fingers out.

"We use everything we've got. Throw it up, detonate simultaneously along one side."

A general murmur rose in the room.

"It won't be enough," a small woman called from the front. "Anyway, they'd have to touch. No air in space, no concussion. Every single nuke would have to touch the asteroid, and with simultaneous detonation, they're as likely to destroy each other as they are the 1019."

"So what do you want to do, Amy?" Kilpatrick asked.

"What if we send them up in sequence, one at a time, and try to chip away at as much of it as we can? Place the detonations so that we break off what we can, and make the remainder as small as possible."

"That would reduce the blow, but it would still be catastrophic," Fletcher said, frowning.

Amy rose to look at them. She was a spark plug kind of woman. Yuri wondered if she might once have been a gymnast. "We're not going to push it aside, not this late, not with what's available now. We're not going to break it into small-enough pieces to avoid multiple regional devastations." Someone started to say something, and she talked over him. "Come on, this is a ten on the Torino Scale. What we can do is make it a smaller catastrophe, so that a million years from now life might rise again from the permafrost."

A hush fell over the room, heavy and impenetrable. The silence filled Yuri's nose and mouth and stuffed his trachea. His chest contracted in shallow heaves that drew in no air.

"Maybe we don't get to save it for ourselves," Amy said, her tone softer. "Maybe all we can do is save it for someone else."

Her words floated over the room and settled like ash. Finally Fletcher spoke.

"Are we redefining our mission, then? Instead of trying to save life, are we trying to save the possibility of life at some point in the future?"

Yuri felt sick. The future was supposed to be his, not someone else's. He hadn't lived long enough to turn life in, like a piece of lab equipment checked out and then returned so others could use it.

There was silence for a moment. Then the tall guy, Kilpatrick, said, "I'm not ready to give up. We may as well try to punch it away."

Fletcher sighed, and his whole body seemed to deflate.

"Does anybody have an idea that has a chance—a real chance, Dan—to save us in the here and now?"

"It's metallic," a man shouted out. "What if we launched an enormous magnet and drew it . . ."

"You got a magnet that size?" Fletcher snapped.

Yuri thought the director might have a better chance of getting people to speak if he didn't yell at them when they did.

"Okay, give me a quick show of hands on which is better, trying Dan's deflection or Amy's breaking it up as much as we can. Understand, the bomb placement will be different. We can't do both." He gave them a moment. "Okay, raise your hand if . . ."

Yuri stood.

"Um, is another possibility," he said. "Doctor . . ." What was her last name? "Amy's idea to blow it up would work if asteroid were smaller."

Fletcher paused. "You want to use your antimatter."

When he said "antimatter," a collective groan rose from the assembled scientists.

"There's no way to contain antimatter," someone shouted. "You know that. If it comes in contact with its container, they both go poof."

"Poof?" someone said.

"Math is extremely complex," Yuri said. "But I've already done it. We launch high-flux antimatter accelerator, park it next to asteroid. Shoot pulses to create matter-antimatter reaction, in which particles annihilate each other. Then antimatter is gone—no loss to us—and part of asteroid disappears with it. Not invisible—just gone. And each burst creates push, too, like jet engine. Will push asteroid farther away with each shot."

Simons rose. "We don't just need to contain the antimatter. Maybe you have got that figured out—hooray for you if it really works. We don't have time to find out if you know what you're talking about."

"In Russia, is already prototype . . ." Yuri said.

"But even if you *can* contain it," Simons said, talking over him, "you'd have to accelerate it in a tight beam over a long distance. Because we'd have to park the accelerator at a safe distance, and that's gonna be a few *kilometers* away."

"Yes . . ." Yuri said.

"The antimatter will want to spread . . ."

"I know," Yuri said. "Was very hard problem. I can show you . . ."

"You can throw any damn numbers you want up there," Simons said, gesturing vaguely toward the raised screen. "It doesn't mean they're right, and it doesn't mean they'll work."

"This is our best chance to stay alive," Yuri said, leaning forward. He looked around at all of them. "This is our only chance to stay alive."

Amy stood.

"We've got a bigger problem than keeping it in a tight beam."

Simons threw his arms up, as though that somehow proved his point.

"What?" Yuri said.

"We have to park the accelerator by the asteroid, right? To match velocity?"

"Yes."

And then Yuri understood. "Asteroid is traveling at 159,000 miles per hour." He felt gut-punched. "Humans can't launch anything approaching that speed."

"No," Amy said. "We can't."

The room was absolutely silent. Could this be it? Could they be so close and lose their chance to fight because they couldn't attain the proper velocity? All the desire for speed, the millennia of races by foot, then horse, then car, every toddler in the world pushing a toy, saying *vroom*, and grinning—was it all for this moment? Was there a biological urge to speed, for this? And they'd failed?

"Okay, people," Fletcher said. "Dig in. How do we do this thing?"

"We shoot at it as it's coming toward us," Amy said. "We launch the accelerator, and shoot as it approaches the BR1019, and as it passes by. Like a cowboy shooting from the hip."

"This is insane," Simons said. He pushed his glasses up with his thumb. "We don't know that an antimatter approach will work at all. It probably won't. We have to go with what we know has a chance."

"Which is what?" Fletcher said. "You forget this is an M-type?"

"We throw everything we've got at it," Simons said. "Try to blow it up or push it sideways."

"Zach, you're a brilliant man," Fletcher said. "So stop being stupid." Simons stared at him. "We're going to try Yuri's antimatter."

"If it doesn't work, that asteroid is going to hit us head-on." Simons jutted his index finger at the ceiling, his arm extended. "*No* reduction in mass, *no* reduction in speed. *No* pushing it aside. A head-on with an M-type."

The room was silent.

"Our problem," Fletcher said, "is that with conventional weaponry and approaches, we'd still have a head-on with an M-type. Look, I'm not making the call here." He ran his hand over his scalp. "We've got brains, and I'd like to think we have wisdom in this room. This is too big a decision for any one person. So how many of you want to launch the high-flux antimatter accelerator, and shoot at the asteroid as it comes in and flies by?"

"We got any backup at all?" Simons asked.

"No," Fletcher said. He hesitated. "We could launch a bunch of nukes at it, to hit after the final antimatter shot. If we're able to erase some of the asteroid, they'd just explode off in space."

"Goodnight Moon," someone said.

"Yeah," Fletcher said. "We'd have to watch that."

"The nukes won't do anything," Amy said.

"No, they wouldn't," Fletcher said. "But they'd be visible from Earth, at least for a little while. They'd give people hope for a few moments. This show is going to be visible from backyard telescopes."

"The speed, though," Dan Kilpatrick said.

Fletcher sighed. "Yeah. That's why we're not launching any nukes. If the antimatter doesn't work, that thing will be on us too fast."

Yuri cleared his throat. "Um, is one other issue." He gestured toward Amy. "We'll need to shoot at BR1019 as it comes in, and as it goes by. But that won't be enough. We'll need to send one final, enormous pulse backward as it passes. So almost one hundred eighty degrees from first shot to last."

Fletcher stared at him. "Back toward Earth?"

"Are you insane?" Simons's face was turning purple. "Are you completely insane? You want to shoot a massive blast of antimatter toward Earth? Toward *us*?"

"Talk about calling in a strike on your own position," Dan Kilpatrick said.

Amy looked at him, her eyes narrowed but unfocused. She was seeing the shot. She let out a low whistle.

"That beam will miss the asteroid and hit us," Simons said. "The antimatter will spread out the farther it goes, like a flashlight beam." He punched an index finger at Yuri. "You'll bathe the Pacific Rim in antimatter, and it'll just be gone. Down to the bedrock."

Fletcher shook his head. "This is too dangerous. I'm all for trying to reduce the size of the asteroid, give it a little shove sideways if we get lucky. But I'm not calling for an antimatter pulse aimed directly at us."

"Asteroid will be between accelerator and Earth at that point," Yuri said. "Beam will hit asteroid."

"What if it does a great job, and goes all the way through the asteroid? Or misses off the side?"

"Then we lose some of California but save Earth," Yuri said. "But it won't . . ."

"Spoken like a guy from Moscow," Simons said.

There was a stir in the room, and Yuri flushed. *Svoloch.*

"I'm right here," he said, jabbing both index fingers at the ground. "I'm here, too." He exhaled sharply. "Look, if we're going to do this, let's do it right. We need final, massive backward shot to reduce asteroid mass, and to produce sideways thrust. Maybe asteroid will just hit us glancing blow, or miss entirely."

"Maybe the accelerator does its job beforehand," Simons said, "and we would be fine. But then we take an unnecessary final shot. You know how many things could go wrong with that last pulse?"

Yuri looked to Amy, but she shook her head slowly and stared at a seat back.

"The rest of you may not be aware of this," Fletcher said, "but as Yuri said, the Russians have a prototype going. They say it's for energy production." He shot a glance at Yuri. Yuri nodded. It *was* for energy production. "We know that the kid's math works, at least in those circumstances."

"Those circumstances," Simons said, "are a helluva lot different than space conditions."

"Yeah," Fletcher said. "But I'm saying there's been some testing. His math holds up."

Simons turned to Yuri. "You ever use a high-flux antimatter accelerator to destroy an asteroid before?"

"No," Yuri said. "You ever destroy M-type in retrograde using another method?"

Simons snorted and turned away.

"Look," Fletcher said. "I'm thrilled we have the hardware, and you have the math, to be able to take a shot at this bullet coming at us. But there's no way I'm authorizing a shot toward Earth." He looked around. "Anyone here disagree?"

The room was silent. Yuri raked his fingers through his hair.

"You know," Fletcher said, "the accelerator gets programmed before it's launched. Once it's up there, it's out of our hands. So if we hit it too hard with one of the earlier pulses and break it apart, a final shot could go right between the pieces." He smiled thinly. "Zach's right. Too many things could go wrong."

Fletcher crouched for a moment, rocking back on his heels, his fingers laced over his head. He sucked in air and blew it out. Finally he stood. "Okay. We're launching the high-flux antimatter accelerator, programmed to shoot at the BR1019 as it comes in and as it passes, but not after it's passed. All in favor, let's see your hands," Fletcher called, and hands flew up all around the room. "Okay, it's settled. You," he said, pointing at Yuri, "get to work. You're the only guy who can do the math." He threw an arm out, encompassing the room. "The rest of you get busy working on launch time, the number of pulses, how far away we park the accelerator, all the rest . . . You know what to do."

"If you do it this way, it won't be enough," Yuri said, his voice higher than he wanted.

"I won't call a strike down on us," Fletcher said. "If we die, it won't be by my hand."

The assembled scientists began to filter back to their offices, heads down, not talking. Yuri stood for a moment, watching them go.

He was still at odds with every other physicist in the world. Unbelievable.

CHAPTER 20

ANTACID

Back in his office, Yuri worked in a caffeinated blur as night moved to morning. He chewed all the erasers off his pencils, called the front desk to ask for more, and within a minute a middle-aged man showed up at his office with three dozen new pencils. If the circumstances were different, Yuri would have enjoyed that a lot. He was scribbling longhand more than using the computer, with a spare pencil over his ear that he took out to nibble as he thought.

He kicked his shoes off, then his socks, and grabbed at the carpet with his toes while he worked. It had a short weave and he couldn't quite grasp it. He pulled his fists through his hair until his hair looked like horns.

He made progress but felt he would go mad sitting. Physical inactivity was one of the hardest parts of his lifestyle, and always had been. When he'd complained about it once to Gregor Kryukov, his advisor had told him to use the gym—as though walking on a treadmill once a day made up for the immobility of adult life. Some days Yuri needed to move so badly that he ran in place at his desk. Some nights he woke, writhing in bed, and couldn't sleep again until sweat ran down his back from shadowboxing the moon.

Now he used the men's room, just for the change of pace. It was quiet, even for a bathroom. No one talked, not in the hall, not at the food tables in the conference room. As if in the face of extinction, speech became a lost power. Civilization was collapsing inward on itself, as the universe might someday do. Humans wouldn't be around to see it.

Yuri worked on, sometimes standing, one leg extended on the desk to stretch his hamstring. He'd switch legs, then run in place, slowing as he needed to jot something down. He lined rows of Styrofoam cups on the left side of his desk. They rounded the corner, but he slowly destroyed the first by digging his thumbnail into it, leaving crescent moons in the foam. Then he pulled a cup apart, shredding it as small as he could. The next cup he ripped apart with his teeth and growled, then moved the line of cups back so it always started at the back left corner of his desk.

He worked through the day, fidgeting, but always moving forward with his calculations. When night fell no one moved to the west wall to watch the sunset. Yuri walked barefoot to the conference room. Someone had brought food up from the cafeteria and set it out on tables. It saved them a minute going downstairs—worth the trouble. Every minute the cold metal edge of the asteroid came 4,260 kilometers closer.

Yuri was still in the gray suit pants he'd worn to Dovie's high school prom. He realized he'd probably die in that suit, and decided to put the jacket back on when the time came. Irrelevant, of course, but it seemed the right thing to do. It would add a proper solemnity to the occasion. Why had no one written *An Atheist's Guide to the End of the World?*

He stuffed his hand in his pocket. His fingers brushed something soft and he pulled it out. It was the withered alstroemeria bloom from his lapel. He smiled faintly, like an old man recalling his childhood, pushed it back in his pants, and carried a sandwich to his office.

He noticed something on the way—other people were on the cots, sleeping. A guard with a clipboard roamed the hall, watching when each lay down, scrawling down the time he should wake him. He was gently shaking an older man as Yuri approached, and the man sat up, swung his black socks to the floor, an inch of hairless white skin showing below his pants hem. The man seemed confused for a moment, and his eyes were watering. And then Yuri realized he was crying. Yuri flicked his eyes away, embarrassed, and kept them lowered until his office door clicked shut behind him.

He was the youngest person in the building. He'd seen the Chinese guy a couple of times, and he wasn't too old—mid-thirties, maybe—one of three or four physicists that age. The rest were at least a decade older, and most were mid-fifties and -sixties. Which meant that while he might be the only person at NEO to be late because he'd gone to prom, he was also the only one who could stay up for three days. He could keep working while they napped, and he could work while they rubbed their bunions, or whatever it was they did. He might have to squirm around, to stretch out and run in place while he did it, but he could stay awake and make up for the evening he'd lost.

He spent the second night at his desk, sitting on occasion, but mostly leaning over, fidgeting, grinding the heels of his hands into eyes bruised by numbers, and thinking about the speed of light, and the speed of death. Thoughts came unbidden. He wouldn't have a casket. None of them would, and though there would be no one left to notice, it still didn't seem right. He would have liked a blue lining cloth. He looked good in blue.

He blinked the thought from his mind and couldn't stop the mental calculation—the asteroid had hurtled 24 kilometers closer to the bridge of his nose during his blink. He blinked again, and again. Twenty-four. Twenty-four. He refocused, punching numbers into his calculator, and realized he hadn't double-checked himself in hours. What if he messed up because he forgot to carry the one? That would actually be funny. He started to laugh and couldn't stop, laughed while tears streamed down his cheeks and his stomach muscles began to burn. Then the tears were real and he was crying, and he kept his pen moving, kept tapping on his calculator while wiping his cheeks with the side of his palm.

He would never win a Nobel. Never feel the heft of the medal in his hand, never run his finger over the engraving of Science pulling the veil from Isis's face. The stars would not align for him.

He put two Styrofoam cups upside down on the floor and jumped on them, landing with his heels. He looked at the broken shards and thought of Dovie and her fear that Earth would splinter.

"It won't break apart, Dovie," he whispered. "But we'll still die."

When he had been awake for sixty hours, he had scribbled down the math to contain the antimatter, to focus the beam, to make each pulse small enough that it didn't break the asteroid apart, causing the next shot to miss. He had done everything he was supposed to.

He allowed himself a celebratory fruit cup and then bent again over his desk, because he had one more thing to calculate: the final, long backward shot toward the BR1019 after it passed the high-flux accelerator. The shot aimed at Earth. Because the first streams of antimatter would reduce the asteroid's size, but not enough. There would still be a huge body hurtling toward them—flattened on one side, and pushed a little farther away. But not enough. Without the last, huge pulse, the BR1019 was still a planet killer. The job had to be done his way if it was going to work, and there would be no second chance.

When he was done, he took two sheaves of paper, a thick one with his work on the first shots, and a thinner one with scribbled notes for the long last shot, and walked to Fletcher's office. The director was awake, but his eyes were red and crusty at the corners. He smiled at Yuri and pointed at the papers.

"You got it?"

"Yeah."

"I'd have somebody double-check it, but there isn't anybody who can do it. Damn bad break that it hasn't been published yet."

Yuri shrugged and scratched his forearm, deeply grooved from angling against the desk edge for dozens of hours. He handed Fletcher the top sheets of paper.

"It's right. This is, too."

He handed over the last bit of work he'd done.

Fletcher frowned. "What's this?"

"You know."

Fletcher rolled his head back and looked at the ceiling. "I wish to hell everybody agreed on an approach."

"I ran the numbers. The first pulses won't be enough."

"We already decided . . ."

"You know it's true. I'll bet you had somebody else run it, too. They can calculate that much." He saw in Fletcher's face that he was right.

"He wasn't sure," Fletcher said flatly. The director pushed the second sheaf of papers back at Yuri. "We're only using antimatter at all because we've got no choice. But I will not call for a strike directly on Earth—on our position." Fletcher leaned forward, and stared at Yuri from under his crusty red lids. "I will not be the man who condemns the planet."

"Then you just did."

Yuri didn't take the papers, so Fletcher laid them on the edge of his desk. Yuri cocked his head back and squeezed his eyes shut. He wanted to hit something. For a moment, he considered punching Fletcher. What difference would it make? He'd just die with a broken hand, and Fletcher with a sore jaw. Yuri let the urge pass and opened his eyes. Fletcher's wall clock faced him. The second hand was ticking, parsing time into seconds, each the same as the last, like a man who doesn't break his stride as he walks over a cliff.

"Come on," Fletcher said. "Everybody's finished. I've been writing the work up on some marker boards."

"I saw them when I got sandwich . . ." Yuri hesitated. "Yesterday, I think." Or was it the day before? He picked up his papers off Fletcher's desk.

"I'm gonna write your data in, let everybody look at the whole thing. I want to see if anything jumps out at anybody. Any simple mistake. We're all exhausted—it could happen."

Fletcher sent someone to roust the napping scientists, then walked with Yuri to the marker boards in the conference room. Yuri held up the paper with his antimatter work, and Fletcher glanced at it as he scribbled the math in with a foul-smelling black marker. Yuri held up his second paper, the one on the final shot.

Fletcher shook his head. "Nice try." His gaze held Yuri's for a moment. "If you were me, would you use it?"

Yuri leaned forward. "Yes."

Fletcher snorted softly. "You think you're the smartest guy in this building?"

"No. I know I'm not. I'm just right about this."

Fletcher sighed. "Too many things could go wrong. And every one of them would be catastrophic."

"We have to try."

Fletcher capped his pen, but the stink still lingered. "We

may have just found a creative solution to the Mideast peace problem."

Yuri nodded numbly. "I'm going to men's room. I think I'm going to be sick."

Fletcher gripped his bicep. "You did good work." He shook Yuri's arm, then let it go. "You know the telescope guys are going to give us a live feed."

"We'll actually see it?" Yuri felt a new wave of nausea.

"If we see the accelerator take too small a bite out of that big iron apple," Fletcher said, "you'll have several minutes to tell us that you told us so."

Yuri clenched his fists behind his head, hair spraying through his knuckles.

"Is okay if I call couple of people? To say good-bye?"

"Sure."

Yuri went back to his office and laid his forehead on the desk for a moment. He sighed and sat up and got the woman at the front desk to put a call through to his mother. The hospital receptionist told him that she was in surgery. He smiled as he hung up. She was doing what she did best. He'd never thought of it that way before.

He tried Gregor Kryukov, his advisor, but the office phone just rang. Yuri could see it, sitting on Kryukov's desk beside his stainless steel pen cup, ringing in the old man's office in the physics building on Lebedev Street. He felt a moment of panic, wondering if they'd already pushed Kryukov out, if his advisor had defended Yuri's authorship of his work and been penalized for it. Then he realized what time it was in Moscow—Kryukov would be in bed. That meant his mother was doing an emergency surgery. He squeezed his eyes shut for a moment and thought of her, electronic scalpel in hand, saving someone's world. He didn't know her very well, and didn't always like her, but he was proud of her.

Then he called Dovie.

"Hello?"

"It's Yuri."

"Hey. Is everything okay?"

"Um, no." He hesitated. What was he going to say? And why hadn't he thought about this before he picked up the phone? "I'm sorry I didn't call after dance. We got busy here."

"Yeah, I heard. They said the asteroid's worse than they thought because it's metal, but I don't really understand why."

"Who told that?"

"The TV news. It's all they're talking about."

"They released that? They told people it's iron?"

"Yeah."

He wondered if people in Russia knew, too. Did his mother know that while she was scrubbing in, standing in a cold hospital corridor in the night, next to a rack holding boxes of suture line?

They were silent for a moment.

"My Dad's upset because they're selling these T-shirts," Dovie said. "They say 'I survived the BR1019 asteroid.' Dad's mad because there'd be no way to get a refund. You know, if we don't survive."

Yuri laughed. "That sounds like your dad."

Dovie turned serious. "Why is this so much worse? Than before?"

"Iron is very heavy. It has huge mass. If your refrigerator were solid iron, it would weigh almost 30,000 pounds."

"Get out!"

"Um, pardon?"

"You know, it probably does. Some of Mom's banana bran muffins are in there."

Yuri laughed.

"So there's a big iron thing coming for us. Yuri, it's a cannonball!"

He blinked. That hadn't occurred to him.

"It's like we're being attacked by giant space pirates!"

Yuri could hear Lennon's voice in the background say, "Space pirates? You have my attention."

"I'm going to have to go in minute. There's more to do here."

"Okay," Dovie said, and her voice sounded suddenly small.

"Dovie? Are your bangs sticking up?"

"Yeah. Up and at a rakish angle to the side."

He visualized it and smiled, but his mouth twisted, and he ran a hand over his eyes.

"Are we going to be okay?" Dovie whispered.

"I'm not sure. I'll try to call again later, okay?" he said.

"Yeah."

They didn't say good-bye.

A few minutes later, Karl Fletcher knocked on Yuri's door, and stuck his head in. "Grab your work," Fletcher said. "Time to go down to the lion's den."

"Um . . ."

"The computer programmers." Fletcher handed Yuri the sheaf of papers he had copied to the marker board. "I photocopied this," he said, "just in case someone drops pizza on it and we can't read it. Wouldn't that be something."

"I won't get it anywhere near pizza," Yuri said, unable to keep the offense out of his voice.

"Oh yes, you will. You're going to be on their turf now, and trust me, there will be pizza." Fletcher led him into the hall. "Communication is going to be the key here—they don't know our job, and we don't know theirs. They know how to turn the math into an algorithm that can control our flux accelerator. We don't. But they don't understand what they're working with. They won't get why your numbers are what they are." Fletcher gave Yuri a lopsided grin. "Hell, I don't, either."

"They won't really understand what they're seeing?" Yuri asked.

"Not a chance. You'll think they're a bunch of idiots. Honestly, their first attempts will make you want to tear out your hair. Resist the impulse." Fletcher ran a hand over his smooth scalp.

He took Yuri down to the second floor, and paused outside a closed door. "By the way, don't call their computers 'computers.' They're workstations."

"Okay. How is it different?"

"If you asked them that, they'd turn purple and start telling you about all their gadgets and generally bore the hell out of you, all in an incredibly condescending tone. It'd make you miss Zach Simons."

"Workstations," Yuri said. "I'll remember that."

Fletcher opened the door to a large room filled with computers in what had been cubicles in facing rows. The cubicle walls were gone, stacked against the right wall near the servers. Fletcher saw him looking. "The barbarians dismantled them."

A fleshy man with glasses walked toward them and stuck out his hand. "Mike Ellenberg," he said. "I'm lead here." He nodded toward the cubicle walls and grinned. "We live by our own rules."

Fletcher sighed.

Yuri glanced around. Wires exploded from the front of the metal server racks, and cables stretched across the floor and ceiling. Laptops were scattered around on tables and open metal shelving, along with printers and unidentifiable bits of outdated equipment. A flat screen was mounted on the wall with the door, and a white marker board stretched across the facing wall. In the upper-right-hand corner someone had written the wireless password and the phone number for Antonio's.

"We've got the best computer programmers and program managers in the country right here in this room," Fletcher said, gesturing sideways with his hand. "It's still gonna be tough to reduce the math to a programming language. It usually takes a butt load of meetings to get it worked out, and we don't have time for that."

Mike Ellenberg moved away and Fletcher whispered to Yuri, "They never really understand the math. Humor the hell out of them anyway."

Yuri nodded. Humor them. Tell them a joke? Seriously?

Fletcher nodded to the papers in Yuri's hand and spoke loudly, addressing the room. "This is what we've got. You need to turn it into something the computer's gonna like, and you have to do it fast, and if it's not perfect, you die. So, I'm parking The Brain right here. You're not sure what he means by something, you ask."

Fletcher pushed a padded swivel chair against the wall, and swept his hand toward it. "Your throne."

Yuri looked at him. "I just sit here?"

"Oh, they'll have questions. You'll be up and down constantly."

Ellenberg walked over and Yuri handed him the sheaf of papers. Fletcher clapped the program manager on the back, nodded to Yuri, and left. Ellenberg flipped through the papers. The programmers threw curious glances at Yuri. He felt exposed, sitting in a chair by the wall. He wished he had a desk.

"You wrote it out by hand," Ellenberg said.

"Yeah."

"In Russian."

"Yeah. I think in Russian."

"That's lovely," Ellenberg said. "But I don't speak it."

"I translated," Yuri said. "See? I made little notes in margin, so you'd understand."

"Ah. These cramped scribbles?"

"Yes." Yuri smiled.

"Your graphs are hand drawn."

"They're estimates," Yuri said. "The equations are all there."

Ellenberg scratched his head. "Oh, joy. Give me a minute with my people, okay?"

Yuri nodded and sat in the chair. Ellenberg took the papers and huddled with his programmers, and Yuri watched them. He thought about them not understanding what they were seeing, and a stillness crept over him.

"Um, anyone have question right now?"

"We just got it," a woman said. "Give us a minute, okay?"

"Holy crap, this is complex," a man said.

"I just thought I'd run back to my office. Maybe get something to read," Yuri said.

"Go ahead," the woman said, without looking up.

Yuri walked quickly back to his office. He picked up a sheaf of papers from his desk—his work on hitting the asteroid the way he wanted, with a last, huge shot back toward Earth. He rolled it and stuck it down the back of his pants, and was at the bookshelf, searching for something that might keep him awake, when Fletcher stuck his head in. Yuri turned quickly to face him.

"What are you doing in here? You're supposed to be down with the programmers."

"I thought I'd get something to read," Yuri said.

"My speech on communication, fate of the world, all that? You get that you have to be in the room to make that happen?"

"Right," Yuri said, flushing. The director didn't move, making Yuri slide by him to get out of the office. Yuri put a hand on the rolled printout so that it wouldn't catch on the doorway, then brought it in front of his body, under the text he'd pulled from the shelf. Fletcher didn't seem to notice.

Yuri kept walking, resisting the urge to look back. When he made it to the stairwell and turned, Fletcher was still standing by his office, watching him go.

Yuri could hear the programmers complaining as he opened the door, but they fell silent when he entered the room. He smiled tightly and sat in the chair, opening the book at random so that it covered his papers. Then he looked up.

"Um, I'd like to know something about your process. Are you all doing same work? Or do you work on separate parts?"

"We work together," Ellenberg said. "Everybody's got their job, but we work together."

What did that mean?

"I need you to split them," Yuri said. Ellenberg frowned. "There are two sets of data that need algorithms." Yuri showed him the second sheaf of papers.

"Fletcher didn't say anything about this," Ellenbeg muttered. "I better call him."

"He knows about it. He needs the option to go with second set."

Ellenberg held Yuri's eye. "Jesus H. Christ. You guys haven't made a decision, have you?"

Yuri paused for a moment. "We need both sets of data put in programming language."

Ellenberg walked to the marker board ledge and picked up an

aqua bottle of generic antacid. He took a slug directly from the bottle, recapped it, and put it back in place. He wiped his mouth with the back of his hand, but he still had chalky lips when he returned to where Yuri was standing.

"We do them one at a time," Ellenberg said. "We may not have time for both. Which one's the primary set?"

Yuri pulled out the bottom papers, the set he'd retrieved from his office. "This one."

CHAPTER 21

RAINBOWS

Mike Ellenberg's people huddled around him. Yuri slumped in the chair by the wall, aware suddenly that he was desperately tired. He thought he might nap, but then the barrage of questions began.

"Hey," a woman said. "Is 'lambda' the same in Russian as in English?"

"Is 'lambda' . . .?" Yuri said. "Of course it is. Lambda is Greek."

"Yeah, okay," the woman said, clearly not embarrassed. "Just checking."

It went on from there.

An hour in, Yuri had answered twenty questions. He was becoming increasingly frustrated.

"What's this mean?" Ellenberg said.

Yuri walked over to him.

"I'm ordering pizza," someone called.

Yuri ignored the phone call to Antonio's and focused on

Ellenberg. "It's . . . see, this is for containment of antimatter. Is very hard thing."

"Yeah, but I don't get . . ."

"You just take this," Yuri said, pointing at the papers in Ellenberg's hand, "and turn it into algorithm, and convert that into computer code, and run code to generate graphs. Simple."

Ellenberg stared at him from behind the glasses. "If it's so simple, why don't you do it?"

Yuri flushed. "Is not my area."

"That's right. You don't know how. If you can remember that, you can have some pizza, too."

Ellenberg pointed to the paper. "So this grubby little equation here is a conditional . . ."

"No!" Yuri stalked to the marker board. He grabbed a marker from the tray and attacked the board with it, but its tip scraped, dry, over the surface. He flipped it across the room into a wastebasket and it rattled in. A rare athletic moment, and Dovie hadn't been there to see it. He pushed her from his mind.

"There are no other markers." He looked around in frustration. "Where do you keep spares?"

"I don't think there are any," a programmer said.

Yuri, Ellenberg, and several of the programmers rooted around on desktops, in an empty copier-paper box full of remote controls and dead batteries, and under the servers. Finally a programmer shouted in triumph. "Got one!" He tossed the marker to Yuri, who caught it with two hands.

"Orange?" Of course it was. Black would have been too much

to ask. Yuri began scribbling at the left side of the board, remembering to put the few words he wrote into English—even the 'lambda.' He was peppered with questions. After a moment, Ellenberg took the marker out of his hand and stepped to the right side of the board, and began to draw a bunch of circles, triangles, and squares, connected by lines and arrows. None of it made any sense. Yuri jammed his hands in his pockets and hissed softly. Ellenberg caught it, and began drawing lines from the shapes to Yuri's individual equations. Oh. That made a little more sense, except Ellenberg had it all wrong. Yuri looked for an eraser, saw none, and pointed out a line to Ellenberg. "That's wrong," he said. "Should be like this." He took the marker back and made a different connection. Ellenberg spat on the side of his fist and wiped out the first line.

The pizzas came, and the room smelled of oregano and desperation. Yuri began spitting on the side of his fist and wiping out half of Ellenberg's work. Ellenberg spat and wiped out Yuri's connections. It was a duel, and Yuri heard a crashing Tchaikovsky score in his head. After half an hour, they both stood back and stared at the board.

"I think I understand this part," Ellenberg said. "You wanta rest for a couple of hours and give us a chance to work on this?"

Yuri nodded and rolled his shoulders. He ceded the orange marker to Ellenberg and turned. Karl Fletcher was in the doorway. Yuri's mind raced over the work on the board. Was any of it different from what the director would expect?

"How's it going?" Fletcher asked.

"I need alcohol-based hand sanitizer," Yuri said, stepping away from the marker board. "Badly."

Fletcher snorted. His eyes followed Yuri. Not looking at the marker board.

"You can have him," Ellenberg called. "We just need time to run with this for a while."

"Good," Fletcher said, smiling. "Because there's a young lady here to see him. I left her in your office," he said to Yuri.

Yuri flushed. "Is that okay?"

Fletcher shrugged. "Sure. If Mike can spring you for a bit, you can have a visitor."

"It is *not* okay," a fortyish programmer said, gesturing with a slice of pepperoni. "Strelnikov's been here for what, two weeks, and he's already got a girlfriend? I've worked here for seventeen years and *I* don't have a girlfriend."

"Let's analyze that, Bill," someone called. Laughter and chatter filled the room.

"They need markers," Yuri said as they trudged upstairs.

"They have a huge budget," Fletcher said. "They buy the latest tech gizmos and forget to spend any of it on paper and markers."

"Oh, and I forgot to tell them jokes."

Fletcher held the stairwell door, his head tilted to the side. "You, telling a joke to those guys—I can't wrap my mind around that." Fletcher shook his head as though to clear it, and took off.

Yuri stopped by the bathroom, washed his hands, then wadded wet paper towels and scrubbed out his armpits. He walked to his office, took a deep breath, and opened the door.

Dovie was sitting cross-legged on his desk. She was wearing yellow shorts and a white sleeveless shirt with a touch of lace. Her bangs were purple today. The lights were off and the window was dark, but the office was illuminated by the warm glow of six candles stuck in ... beets? He stepped in and quickly closed the door.

"Hi," she said.

"Um ..."

"I hope it's okay that I came by. I called and asked, and they said you'd have a break."

"Yes, it's fine. It's good."

"I wanted to see you again. You know, in case ..."

He nodded. "Um, are those beets?"

She smiled and gestured with both hands at the candles on either side of her. "I thought you might be homesick. I was trying to think of something Russian for you, and I thought of beets."

"To hold candles?"

"I sliced off the bottoms to make them level."

"It would be good not to set NASA on fire right now."

"Yep. Oh, and I brought food."

She gestured toward a picnic basket on his floor, on top of a blanket. "And they let me have a TV so we can watch the replay of the Angels game."

"Is that hockey?" Yuri asked hopefully.

"Baseball. This is a merging of Russian and American cultures. You've got the beets and I brought a couple of cabbages, too. I couldn't think of anything else."

"We also have very rude civil servants."

"If only I'd known."

She beckoned to him and he stepped forward and she threw her arms around his neck and kissed him. He put his arms around her, amazed at the warmth of her skin, and stood before her, gnawing gently on her lip. Finally Dovie leaned back.

He helped her down from the desk and they lay on the blanket, propped on their elbows. Dovie used the remote to click on the television on the floor at their feet, then heaped fried chicken and mashed potatoes on their plates. They watched the game while they ate.

Yuri wiped his mouth with his napkin and pointed at the screen. "I don't understand why Americans like baseball. It seems like most un-American sport to me."

"How's that?"

"America is all about equality, right? But on field, it's nine to one. That's not fair."

She sat upright. "Are you kidding me? Baseball's the only game with no time limit. It isn't over until you've done every-thing that needs doing."

"I've noticed. You need shot clock or something."

"No! And everybody gets a turn. In hockey you could just have your best player take the shot every time, right?"

"Sure."

"But in baseball, no one player takes over. At the most urgent moment you could have your weakest batter up, and he has to get the hit. *Everybody gets a chance to be the hero.*"

"What's point in being best player, then?"

Dovie made an exaggerated sigh. "Eat your chicken, commie genius."

He shrugged and snagged another leg. The game wore on. The visitors' manager walked to the mound for the second time that inning, signaling for a pitching change.

"This is excruciating," Yuri said. "No wonder you people do so well in world wars. You're well rested."

Dovie exhaled in indignation.

"And besides, your diamond infield represents geometry, and announcers give many statistics, but calculus seems to be underrepresented."

Dovie laughed. "No one else in the world would criticize baseball for slighting calculus."

He shrugged. The relief pitcher took his warm-up throws.

Dovie tapped Yuri's chest. "Baseball," she said, "is about hot dogs and warm summer evenings."

"Oh. I thought it was about limits of human endurance."

The batter stepped in, grinding his toe into the dirt. The pitcher wound up and hung one over the plate, and the batter sent it over the geysers in left centerfield. The geysers erupted and the camera cut to show them, water gushing up, then running down the fake rocks. For a moment the water created a rainbow shimmering against the desert sun. Yuri had always enjoyed seeing rainbows, had felt special as a young child when he explained the mechanics of light refraction to a couple of teachers and they'd exchanged a knowing glance. He wondered if Dovie thought about their mechanics.

"Dovie? Do you love rainbows?"

"Yeah."

"Why?"

She looked at him for a moment. "Because they start with us, reach up to touch God, and still come back down to be with us. The treasure isn't at the end of the rainbow; it's that the rainbow cared enough to come back."

"You're poet."

"And a prism," she said, waggling her fingers and catching the candlelight in her rings. She was silent for a moment, and when she spoke, her voice was tinged with melancholy. "Yuri? One way or another, this will all be over in a few days, won't it?"

"Yes." He hesitated a moment. "There is this guy in Russia—bad physicist, but his father's very powerful. He's claiming he co-authored my work. I have to get back."

"Wow. I'm so sorry."

He shrugged.

"Would this hurt your chance to get the Nobel?"

"I might have to share it."

"With this guy who doesn't deserve it?" He nodded. "Wow. The ultimate ego fulfillment and the ultimate offense to ego, wrapped together."

He narrowed his eyes at her.

"Did you ever look carefully at the *Pietà*? Michelangelo's sculpture of the Virgin Mary holding the dead Christ?"

"I don't know it."

She rolled her eyes. "It's the best sculpture ever made.

Seriously. And Michelangelo knew it. A few days after it was installed, he was hanging around, trying to overhear compliments about his work. And somebody standing there looking at it told the guy next to him that it had been sculpted by one of Michelangelo's rivals."

"That's terrible," Yuri said. "Michelangelo deserved credit for his work."

"Yeah," Dovie said. "That night he sneaked in with a chisel and on the sash across Mary's chest he carved, 'This sculpture was made by Michelangelo Buonarroti of Florence.'"

"Ha!" Yuri said. "That showed them!"

Dovie looked at him soberly. "It showed them more than he meant. He marred his greatest accomplishment because of his ego. He regretted it immediately, but there was nothing he could do about it."

Yuri shifted on the blanket.

"It's still there for everyone to see—the greatest sculpture in history, scarred by one of history's greatest egos."

"He deserved recognition," Yuri said. "He was sculptor, yes? Not that other guy."

"Yeah," Dovie said. "It was his work. But it could have stood on its own." They were quiet for a few minutes. "So," Dovie said, "if we survive, you're going home?"

"Yes. As soon as I can."

"Then take off your socks."

He blinked. "What?"

"Your socks, Science Boy. Take 'em off."

Was this a romantic overture? He felt a moment of panic. Was there some type of American foot sex he didn't know about? He stripped off his socks. Dovie rolled on her side to reach her voluminous purse, then set it beside the picnic basket and pulled out a bottle of nail polish. She beckoned. Oh. No American foot sex. He hesitated, then put his heel in her lap. On a list of things he would least want done to his body, having his toenails painted had to be in the top five. But his foot was in Dovie's lap, his heel resting in the gentle depression between her thighs. And touching her, there, topped his list of things to do with his body. His heel was a lucky *ublyuodok*.

Dovie shook the little glass bottle, then with three deft strokes painted his right big toenail indigo. She capped the polish and pulled another bottle out and painted his second toe violet. Yuri shut his eyes and concentrated on the feel of her hands on his skin, gently separating his toes, adjusting the angle of his foot. When she was done, he opened his eyes.

"You painted them like rainbow."

"Yeah. I had to start the color sequence over again. It was that or cut three toes off."

"You made right choice." He waggled his feet and admired the polish—red, orange, yellow, green, blue. Indigo, violet, then red, orange, and yellow.

"It's so you'll remember me," Dovie said. "So someday you'll come back." She started to cry softly, and he pulled her into his chest and cupped her head with his hand.

"Rainbows come back," he said. "And now my feet are rainbow."

She smiled up at him, and he kissed a tear on her cheek and tasted the salt.

"You understood."

He nodded. They were silent for a moment.

"I believe I was promised cabbage."

"Oh!" Dovie pulled two fresh cabbages from the picnic basket and held them up, blinking away the last of her tears.

"Did you have plan for them?"

"No. They just seemed Russian."

"They are," he said, taking them from her. "We are cabbage-powered people. It's what gives us strength to stand near walls without leaning on them."

He pulled a leaf off and cupped it over Dovie's head, making her smile, then pulled the others off, one by one, and scattered them over her, over him, over the picnic blanket. The light from the candles flickered softly against the pale green leaves. Dovie lay on her back and he gently placed a curving leaf over each of her breasts. *I will never be able to go down the produce aisle again.*

Dovie tugged on his shirtfront till it came out of his pants, and then she rolled on top of him and unbuttoned his shirt. He put his arms around her and they kissed, her hands exploring his neck and shoulders, then brushing softly over his stomach. He rolled them onto their sides, crushing cabbage leaves beneath them, and circled her breast with his finger.

They lay there for a moment, arms around each other in the candle glow. And then he fell asleep.

C H A P T E R 2 2

BET YOUR LIFE?

Yuri woke to a sharp rap on his door.

"Mike Ellenberg needs to see you again." It was Fletcher's voice.

Right then he hated them both for taking him away from Dovie. Then he came more fully awake and knew she was gone even before he looked. The beet candles were missing, and her bag that clinked with nail polish bottles and who knew what other treasures. The picnic basket was gone, and somehow she'd gotten the blanket out from under him without waking him. She'd arranged crushed cabbage leaves over him as a blanket.

Fletcher banged again. "Strelnikov? You in there?"

"Yeah."

He stood, stretched, and buttoned his shirt.

"Ellenberg! Fate of the world!"

He picked up the leaves and put the stack in a desk drawer.

"Boom!" Fletcher shouted.

Yuri tucked in his shirt and opened the door.

"About time . . ."

Yuri slammed the door shut. He ran for his socks, pulled them on, and had crammed one foot in a shoe when Fletcher opened the door. He looked around suspiciously. "It smells like peasants in here."

"Sweat and cabbage," Yuri said. "You're right, it smells like peasants." He smiled.

Fletcher narrowed his eyes, and pointed toward the staircase.

"Ellenberg said he needs to see you. Said he's ready for the second part?"

Yuri flushed. "Right. I'm giving it to them a piece at a time."

Fletcher grunted.

Yuri grabbed a spare box of disinfectant wipes off his shelf and tucked them under his arm as he walked back down to the programmers' room.

Ellenberg grinned at him when he walked in. "We got it. I'm not kidding, we got the first one done."

Yuri looked at him suspiciously. Ellenberg ran it for him, the graphs, the models. He was wrong, they didn't have it, but another four hours of working together at the marker board and they did. One of the programmers, a heavy man with a pizza sauce stain on his khakis, ran through the room giving everyone a high five.

"He doesn't get out much," Ellenberg said by way of explanation.

Then they tackled the second set of data—the set Fletcher intended to use. Yuri had to have both available—he might yet be able to sell the director on the backward shot.

They'd worked twelve hours straight, Yuri catching occasional catnaps in the chair, when he asked Ellenberg, "How sure are you of work on first set of data?"

"What do you mean?"

"Is it perfect? Would you bet your life on it?"

"Why would anyone ever bet their life on anything? But yeah, if you gotta know. It's perfect."

Yuri gave him a tight smile, and they worked on.

Hours later, exhausted and full of Italian sausage and onion, Yuri agreed with Mike Ellenberg that they had the second data set nailed down. The programming lead ran the models on the whiteboard, without bothering to pull the screen down or erase the orange scrawls on the board. It worked perfectly. The wrong approach, but the models ran. Yuri shook Ellenberg's hand, then went around the room, shaking hands with each of the programmers. He still didn't know most of their names, but he'd come to respect them all.

"Thank you for your work."

The programmers shuffled wearily to gather up their belongings and head home. Yuri took his handwritten notes, and the programming code and graphs Ellenberg's people had generated, and trudged upstairs to Fletcher's office.

The door was open. Fletcher was sitting in his chair, his posture perfect but his head slumped forward. The ceiling light shone off his scalp. For a moment Yuri thought he was dead.

"Dr. Fletcher?"

The director's head came up before his eyes opened. He grunted.

"Guess I drifted off. Mike's guys get it done?"

Yuri stood at the door, gripping the papers. "Yeah. They ran models for both approaches."

It took Fletcher a moment to understand, and when he did, his face turned purple.

"What do you mean, both approaches? Because I'm sure as hell not telling the Pentagon to direct a stream of antimatter straight back at us. If we die, it's going to be because of the asteroid, not because of me."

Yuri didn't trust himself to speak. Fletcher impatiently motioned him forward, and Yuri's legs moved of their own accord. He felt detached, as though he were watching himself from the ceiling. Would Fletcher even know if he handed him the wrong set? The *right* set. Fletcher saw the hesitation and raised an eyebrow, and Yuri handed him the data he wanted, for shooting at the asteroid only as it came toward the accelerator, and not after it passed.

Fletcher laid it beside Yuri's handwritten notes and started reading, slowly. Checking to make sure Yuri hadn't made the switch. When he was satisfied, he looked up and nodded. "No offense. Just checking."

Yuri didn't trust himself to speak.

"There'll be a meeting in the conference room in an hour. I want to show this to everybody."

"Okay."

He left Fletcher's office. *One hour. I have one hour to persuade the others to use my approach, to rally them and force Fletcher to send the Pentagon the right models. And I have absolutely no idea how to do that.*

CHAPTER 23

SUKIN SYN

Yuri walked barefoot down to the cafeteria. The place was nearly deserted—no colleagues to rally to his cause—so he snagged an apple and trudged back upstairs, his crunches echoing in the empty stairwell. He thought about calling Dovie to ask for advice. But what could she—or anyone—say? He needed charisma, and he needed it now.

He walked down to the conference room. The place was filling up with bleary-eyed scientists who had been in the building for the better part of a week, and the odor made his nose curl. Eau de Physicist wasn't going to be in anybody's spring collection.

"Hey," he said, getting the attention of a specialist in the Sunyaev-Zeldovich effect, "have you thought about our other approach to antimatter bursts?"

"The one you suggested, with the backward shot? We decided to go with the safer approach," the man said.

"Yes, but do you understand, backward shot . . ."

"Would be risky as hell. Are you still lobbying for that? It's too late. Fletcher's already entered the data."

"What? No. He's going to have meeting to show models to everybody."

"Yeah, but it's just so we can see it. People want to see it run," the man said. "But he was by here a minute ago and said he already entered it."

Yuri stood perfectly still for a moment.

"Has he sent it yet? To Pentagon?"

"Hmm? No. He wants all of us to see it run—Mike Ellenberg and a couple of his guys, too. Just to be sure, you know? Then he's got to go in his office and push 'send.'" He shook his head. "I don't envy him, doing that."

Yuri was suddenly in a hurry. "You said he was just through here? Where did he go?"

The man nodded toward the back hall, and Yuri saw the director's tall forehead over the crowd. "He's running to his office, but he'll be back after a while. Let me ask you, your research . . ."

Yuri nodded and pushed through the crowd, chasing Fletcher's receding head. People turned, recognized him, and reached out, patting his shoulders, wanting to talk about his work and antimatter containment, but he kept his eyes focused, and by the time Fletcher neared his office, Yuri was right behind him.

Fletcher turned.

"Did you need something?"

Yuri stared at him for a moment.

"Uh, I need bathroom." He pointed to the men's room door. "Have to go every five minutes, seems like."

"Yeah," Fletcher said. "We've all got nerves."

Yuri walked ten feet to the bathroom, pushed open the door and reached for his cell phone. He hadn't made a call with it in the United States—how expensive would that be?—but he still had it on him. The door hinged on the left, which was perfect. Yuri stepped into the restroom, made sure it was empty, and tapped the phone until he had the video function up.

Fletcher snagged a cot from the hall and stood in front of his office, balancing its tubular frame on the toe box of his shoe. Yuri stood concealed by the partially closed door, raised his phone, and recorded the director tapping the number pad outside his office. As Fletcher stepped in, wrestling the cot, Yuri sank back into the bathroom.

He watched the video in a stall thirteen times before he was sure he had the combination.

Yuri sauntered casually back to the conference room. Simons was stationed right inside the door, just standing there, not jostling to examine the math on the marker boards, not conversing in low tones.

"Hey," Yuri said. "Do you know where Director Fletcher is?"

"He's in his office, but don't disturb him. He's taking a nap while we have our last look at this. He wanted to get his mind clear."

"Oh. Well, do you know when he'll be out?"

"He asked me to wake him in half an hour." Simons glanced at his watch. "There's nineteen minutes left."

Nineteen minutes?

Yuri looked at the wall clock and nodded dumbly.

"Um, I'm not feeling so good. I think maybe I'll skip meeting, go lie down in my office."

"The hell you will," Simons said sharply. "You're the man of the hour. Any questions anybody's got, you're the one who's going to have to answer them. You're the last guy who can skip out." Simons squinted at him. "If you disappear again, Fletcher will send the Marines after you. No joke."

Yuri nodded. "I think I'll just use men's room."

His bladder was going to get a reputation.

There was no one in the hall, and he couldn't risk waiting any longer. Would Fletcher be asleep yet? He had to be exhausted. They all were. Yuri tapped in the code he'd taken off his cell phone: 051755. He bet it was Fletcher's birth date. Awesome security, but the director probably felt it was just a formality.

The door popped with a slight click and Yuri eased it open and slipped inside. Fletcher was lying on his side on the cot, his back to the door. His face toward the computer. Were his eyes closed? Yuri shut the door behind him, releasing the knob slowly. The only light came from the glow of electronic devices—green spots on the printer and computer, a red spot on a wall outlet.

Yuri walked past Fletcher's feet. He had seen the computer before, but hadn't paid attention. Last time he broke into the director's office, he was after files. The computer was a normal desktop. No gleaming white case with random lights. No biometric access, either. The screen was dark, and when Yuri tapped the space bar the room instantly brightened. He squinted at Fletcher, but he didn't stir.

Yuri clicked on an icon and a password screen appeared. *Sukin syn,* he thought, *son of a bitch,* but didn't say it out loud. He tried the door code, 051755, and red words flashed, telling him he had two more tries. *Mat' tvoyu.* He thought for a moment. He tried the Fibonacci sequence, 11235813, because it was mathematical, easy to remember, and one of the most common passwords in the world. Red letters flashed. One more attempt.

His fingers hesitated over the keys. Fletcher was a straight-forward guy. Not tricky. The kind of guy who labeled his file drawers and used them, the kind of guy who used his birth date for his office keypad. Yuri lowered his fingers to the keyboard and typed "BR1019," and then hit "enter" with his right pinkie.

A list of files came up. He squeezed his eyes shut and exhaled. Yuri clicked on the file marked "Equation, Final," and there was their work, elegant, pretty even, a whole that was so much more, or so much less, than its parts. He scrolled through, found the targeting information, and used his index finger to hit "back-space" and erase the end code.

He pulled Ellenberg's graphs from his back pocket, folded into quarters, the pages that would direct a final backward shot. He slowly unfolded the papers, but the crackle was painfully loud. Fletcher grunted and Yuri stayed still, crouched in front of the computer. He waited until he heard deep, even breathing again, then counted to thirty before he started tapping keys. It was a lot to enter. Not a short sequence. He resisted the impulse to check his watch.

He entered his data, hit "save," and started to slink out of the room. Six minutes to spare. He allowed himself a grin.

Then he realized there must be a redundant file. No way this went through without a fail-safe. You had to enter your password twice just to make an online purchase. The computer would compare the two files, making sure they matched, to prevent human error. He was sure of it.

He crept back to the computer, found the second file, and deleted the end code all over again. He could go faster this time. He opened the original, highlighted his work, hit "copy," then pasted it into the redundant file. He checked the beginning and end to make sure they were seamless, that he hadn't missed a digit somewhere. He checked for a third file, but it was just the two.

Yuri exited and slipped past Fletcher's feet to the door. He touched the handle, but there were voices down the hall. Someone he didn't know, and Simons.

"I have to wake him in a minute," Simons was saying.

"Yes," Yuri wanted to shout. "One minute. You're not supposed to be here for one more minute."

He could leave the office, but they would see him. There would be questions, and Fletcher would check the computer. Yuri glanced back at it, saw the glow. What if Fletcher realized it should be on screensaver?

Yuri crept back, got into Fletcher's screensaver control and changed the setting so that it came on immediately. Then he did the only thing he could do—as the computer went dark, he crouched behind the desk, where a stack of drawers reached all the way to the floor.

Had the director left anything on his desk?

His glasses. Fletcher's glasses were on the desktop, next to the mouse. Yuri reached a hand up and scooted them to the front edge, close to the cot. *No reason to come around. You can grab them from there.*

There was a soft knock on the door. Fletcher grunted. Another knock, a little harder.

"Karl? It's time."

Fletcher groaned and Yuri heard his joints crack as he stood. It must be hell getting old. He wondered if he'd ever have the chance.

"Yeah, I'm coming. Just gotta find . . ."

There was a light scrape as Fletcher grabbed his glasses, then the office flooded with light as he opened the door.

"Strelnikov down there?"

"He better be. I told him we needed him," Simons said.

Fletcher yawned and the angle of light in the room narrowed until it was a line, then disappeared.

Yuri exhaled, and it was only then that he realized he hadn't been breathing. He waited fifteen seconds, then ran down the hall away from the conference room, turned right, then right again, so he'd join the group from the other side, away from the director's office.

He wandered into the conference room, hands thrust in his pockets. All he felt was relief at having escaped detection, and a sucking fatigue.

Fletcher was up front by the whiteboards, asking if there were questions. He saw Yuri standing at the back and gave a slight nod, and Yuri nodded back, thinking that there was remarkably little security around the computer, particularly considering what was at stake. Apparently it hadn't occurred to them that anyone would try to break in—nobody in the building, anyway. But it had only taken him a cell phone and fifty seconds to hack in—not because he was a genius, but because he was a teenager.

CHAPTER 24

I AM A GNOME-KISSER

Yuri worked his way to the front, where someone had brought in sub sandwiches, snagged a roast beef, and returned to his spot. He stood by the back wall of the conference center, feeling his heart rate return to normal, paying more attention to the sandwich than to what Fletcher was saying as he gestured at the screen they'd set up. There weren't many questions—it was too late for that, really.

"Reflect on the enormity of what you've done here," Fletcher said. "I'm not much for speeches—you know that. But I want you to know that I'm proud of you, and your selfless efforts, regardless of the outcome." He pointed to Yuri. "And I'm glad we brought a physicist into our astrophysics club. It'll be interesting to see what happens up there."

For a moment everyone turned to look at him, and there was a smattering of applause.

A drop of mustard dripped out of Yuri's sandwich and hit the blue carpet. It was mild American stuff, bright yellow. It made him think about accidents, and mistakes. He shifted his foot to cover the stain.

"I'm going to go send the models now," Fletcher said. That brought Yuri's head up. "They're going to need some time to do the inputs and get the missiles ready. God have mercy on us all."

The director walked through the assembled scientists and they parted for him, clapping softly. He acknowledged them with a slight bow of his head, caught Yuri's eye and gave a wan smile. Yuri wondered if he would review the work before hitting "send." Surely it was too long, too complex? But if he did, would he catch the switch?

And if the asteroid did hit, how far out would the initial impact kill? Yuri wondered if his mother would notice that the world was out of control. Probably not. She never had before.

Would the collision be enough to knock people's clothes off? He knew an overinflated tire could explode with enough force to blow fabric apart, not from any practical experience with cars, but from an ill-conceived elementary school science project, and one very angry teacher. Would girls get horny as Earth shuddered in its orbit? Would there be a few hours of orbit orgy? Would it be wrong to hope for that?

Fletcher reentered the conference room.

"It's done."

An awful silence fell on the room. Somewhere in the Pentagon someone would be shouting orders. At some installation, engineers would be scrambling to take their computer code and put it into guidance for the high-flux antimatter accelerator. Somewhere people had just gotten real busy. But not at JPL.

Most people loitered in the conference room, making feeble jokes to ease the tension and pass the time until launch. Yuri went back to his office, sat on the floor and leaned his back against the desk, and called Dovie.

"Speak."

"Um. Pardon?" Yuri said.

"Hey, it's the Spockovskii! How you doing, man?"

"Hey, Lennon. We're done working here. Just thought I'd call."

"Yeah? So are we gonna live?"

"It's going to be spectacular show, but yes, I think we are."

"Hot damn! Spockovskii says we're good!"

"Hot damn?"

"That's just happy swearing, man. Don't you know how to happy-swear in English?"

"They didn't teach much swearing in my English classes, and your sister refused to explain it."

"You have an incomplete education, my man."

"That's true. I'm specialist. I've never had any course in art or literature."

There was silence on the line for a moment.

"Never? Not *Hamlet*? Not even Pushkin?"

"No."

"Pushkin's your national poet, dude. Even I know that."

"I know. I just don't know what he wrote."

"Okay, this requires real swearing. Repeat after me, 'Goddammit, I am a gnome-kissing monkeyfucker who doesn't appreciate my national poet.'"

Yuri stretched a leg out and pushed his door shut with his toes. "This is bad words, yes?"

"Yes."

"I don't think I want to say this. May I speak to Dovie?"

"Not until you admit to being a gnome-kissing monkeyfucker who doesn't appreciate your national poet."

"I didn't say I don't appreciate . . ."

"Say it."

"I, apparently, am gnome-kissing monkeyfucker who doesn't appreciate my national poet."

"Hmm. All right, apology accepted on behalf of normal people everywhere."

"I wasn't apol—"

"Now, English has three basic swear words: 'damn,' 'shit,' and 'hell.' The fourth is the f-word, or 'fuck.' That's nasty stuff, man. You shouldn't go around saying that one."

"Didn't you just have me—"

"No, you said 'monkeyfucker,' which is just a disgusting thing to say. Never appropriate. Shame on you, man. You kiss your mother with that mouth?"

"Not in years."

"Okay. I think a guy who doesn't want his underwears to show would stick to a classical swearing style. If someone tells you to do something you don't want to, you say 'Hell, no!' If something bad happens, you say 'Shit,' kinda dejected-like. If the situation doesn't seem quite right for either of those, just say 'Damn.' That's simple and elegant. 'Damn' is an all-purpose swear word. You really can't go wrong."

"I'll remember that."

"And if you're really surprised, or you want to lighten things up a little, you can say 'Holy shit!'"

"What's holy about it?"

"I don't know. Maybe it's angel shit."

"I'm atheist."

"So you believe in the shit, but not the angel?"

"Something like that," Yuri mumbled. "Is Dovie there?"

"Ask for her with your new skills."

"Pardon?"

Yuri could hear Lennon breathing. Waiting.

"Damn, may I please speak with your sister?"

"Eh. You're not fluent yet, but it's a start. Dooovie," he shouted. "Phone for you."

Yuri rolled his shoulders against the desk and sniffed his armpits while he waited. How many days had it been since he'd showered?

"Yuri?"

"Hey." And then he could think of nothing else to say. All that came to mind was "damn," "shit," and "hell." Dovie saved him.

"So Lennon taught you to swear?"

"Yes."

"That's good. Now or never, right?"

"We're done, Dovie. We're going to be okay."

"Because that thing is actually casting a shadow."

"Oh. I guess it would."

"You guess it would? And you're the guy who's supposed to shoot it down?"

"Well, one of them. I just haven't been outside in days. Not since prom. I forgot to ask if you got in trouble because of me."

"No—school's out."

"Oh. What have you been doing?"

"I painted some, and I played Lennon's video game with him. Mom made a sugarless tofu cheesecake."

"Ouch."

"Yeah. We're not sure we'll survive long enough to get smashed by the meteor."

"Hey, Dovie? If it doesn't work—if we miss asteroid—will you have sex with me real fast before it gets too cold?"

"No, you perv."

He sighed. "That's incredibly depressing."

She laughed, and clicked her tongue stud on the mouthpiece.

At 9:45 p.m. the scientists attached to NASA's Near Earth Object Program, located at the Jet Propulsion Lab, assembled in the media room with its banked rows of seats. Yuri slipped in next to Simons.

"Pirkola went to the hospital. He had no reason to stay now," Simons said.

"Oh."

The screen at the front of the room was the size you'd find in a movie theater. It showed a distance view of a heavy concrete missile silo lit by huge floodlights. There were a few tiny humans in coveralls in the picture, but they didn't seem to be doing much. Yuri guessed the real action was going on underground, inside the silo. Fletcher sat in the front row without saying anything. Somehow Yuri had expected a speech. Something.

At five minutes until 10:00 p.m., the sound came on, and voices from the silo filled the room. A minute later, a man's voice said, "Understand we have NEO with us. Hope you've got us pointed in the right direction." Then the voices went back to their own discussions.

A countdown began at sixty seconds, which seemed like a long time for a countdown. At ten seconds Yuri leaned forward, along with everyone else, as the room's mass distribution shifted toward the screen.

Five.

Four.

Three.

Two.

One.

For a moment nothing seemed to happen, then the flux accelerator was in the sky, sleek and thin and fragile-looking. Yuri never saw its nose exit the silo; it was just suddenly in the air, white fire behind it, thrusting it up to defy Earth's gravitational pull and escape its orbit. The assembled scientists clapped, a tired kind of applause, polite almost, like something you'd hear at a piano concert. Yuri tried to get in rhythm and after a moment realized they weren't falling in together. The Americans were all clapping to their own beat. He gave up and dropped his hands.

The camera pulled back to show the accelerator streaking across the sky, stars providing the reference points by which to check its progress against the night.

"This is it," a sixtyish astrochemist behind him said, and Yuri swiveled to look at him. "Of all that humans have ever flung into battle—old Scandinavian berserkers, Zulu spearmen, doughboys in trenches—this is it. The last front. The final armada."

Yuri stared at him.

"If we survive, there'll be more wars," the man next to him said. "Nobody will learn anything from this."

"Yeah, I suppose so," the astrochemist said. "Not sure which scenario is more depressing." He paused. "It seems wrong that it's just one accelerator going into battle by itself. Such a lonely sight."

The other man shrugged. "It has all of us behind it. Every person here has a hand on that accelerator. We're wielding it together."

No, Yuri thought. It's just me. Only one hand, only one weapon. Only one chance.

As they filtered up the stairwell, Yuri whispered to himself, "The final armada." Lennon would claim that they were off to fight the space pirates, but the thought of it didn't make him smile.

CHAPTER 25

I AM THE ASTEROID

Yuri dragged a cot into his office and slept like a stone dropping through water, or a rock falling through space. His sleep was heavy and dreamless, but he woke repeating a phrase in his head: *I am the asteroid. I am the asteroid.*

There was a knock at his door, and he realized it was the second one. He stood and stretched his arms over his head. It was light outside—already morning on June 9. Impact was at sunset, which meant that he had just slept through the last sunrise. He opened the door. A guard stood there, and behind him he could see Lennon sitting in his wheelchair, holding a book.

The guard looked uncomfortable.

"This guy says he's from the bookstore, that you asked him to bring you a book."

Lennon raised his eyebrows and nodded at Yuri.

"Um, yes. Bring it in, okay?" he said, motioning Lennon inside.

The guard shifted his weight.

"I can let him back out," Yuri said. Lennon tossed the volume on the desk chair.

The guard looked at the book, then at Lennon. Finally he shrugged and left.

"They made me sign in," Lennon said.

"How did you get out here? Did Dovie drive you?"

"No, I took a taxi. By the way, you owe me thirty-seven fifty."

"For small paperback?" Yuri said, indignant.

"You should cover my cab fare, too," Lennon said. "Seems only right after my thoughtful gesture."

Yuri stared at him, then forked over two twenties.

"That's not much of a tip," Lennon said.

"I didn't order any book," Yuri hissed.

Lennon shrugged and looked around the office.

"So this is where you've been working?"

"Yeah."

"Smells like sweat."

Yuri shrugged.

"Wasn't time for shower." He decided to change the subject. "Why didn't Dovie give you ride?"

"I kind of didn't want her to know I was coming out here. It's sort of a private visit."

"Oh." He waited.

"I need a favor," Lennon said. "That's why I brought the book—as a favor to you, too. Well, and as cover to get in."

"You made me *pay* for it," Yuri said.

Lennon shrugged. Yuri sighed and waited.

"Thing is," Lennon finally said. "I've been thinking about the asteroid. If it hits, it'll be pretty bad, right?"

"Right."

"And it'll knock everything around?"

"Yeah. Stay away from glass." *Like it would matter.*

Lennon stared at the sliver of blue carpet between his footrests. He whispered.

"I'm afraid of getting knocked out of my chair."

It took Yuri a moment to understand, and then he tossed the book on the floor and sat in his chair, scooting it toward Lennon, so they were sitting facing each other.

"From impact?"

"Yeah. I'm helpless without my chair, man. I mean, I keep imagining pulling myself around with my arms, and buildings collapsing around me. Rocks falling from the sky, everybody's running, and I'm dragging myself along." He swiped angrily at his eyes. "It would be humiliating."

Yuri nodded. Two guys talking, both staring at their feet.

"I get that I won't be able to climb over rubble. If the house catches fire or something, I'll have to sit there and roast. But I want to do it in my chair."

"Yeah. That makes sense." Yuri cleared his throat. "Um, what can I do?"

"I was thinking you could make some kind of seat belt for me. Some good kind, like NASA-proof or something." He risked a glance into Yuri's face.

"Sure," Yuri said, thinking of the rocket ship seat Simons was making for his grandson. "I've never done anything like that, but I think we can rig something up."

Lennon nodded.

Yuri put his shoes on, called the front desk, and made a couple of inquiries, and then he led Lennon outside. They crossed the street and went down a couple of buildings. It was strange to be outside, to feel sun on his skin. How long had it been?

"Did you see the shadow?" Lennon asked.

"From asteroid? No, I've been inside."

"It was like having Death pass his hand over your face," Lennon said, and a shiver ran up Yuri's back.

Nobody asked what they were doing in the lab building. It wasn't part of the Near Earth Object Program's facilities, but nobody cared.

In a few hours, the accelerator would destroy the asteroid, or it wouldn't. The building was deserted—everyone was home with their families. The labs were locked, but there was a junk room filled with all sorts of crap, including a couple of harnesses used to secure dummies into capsules for velocity experiments. Yuri took the smaller one, untwisted the black straps, and looked it over. It looked like regular seat belt material to him, like the kind of harness that keeps a kid in a car seat.

He held it up.

"Made of maximum-strength, NASA-grade Einsteinium, with titanium threads for extra durability."

Lennon rewarded him with a whistle.

Yuri slipped it over Lennon's arms, tried to straighten the belts out, then removed it and made a second attempt, passing it over his head.

"You sure you know what you're doing?"

"Of course. I took advanced biometric restraints at Moscow State University," Yuri lied.

The front worked now, with Y-shaped straps over Lennon's shoulders, connected to a belt around his waist. There wasn't a way to fasten it in the back, though. Yuri rummaged through a cardboard box and found a spare buckle, threaded it onto the straps and fastened it behind the chair.

"Can you get out from front? Unsnap front buckle?"

Lennon tried it and grinned.

"Yeah."

He refastened it.

"Yeah, man, it works." He punched Yuri's shoulder. "Thanks."

"Sure."

Yuri rifled through the boxes.

"What are you looking for now?"

"Um. This is all private, right?"

"Yeah," Lennon said.

"From Dovie?"

"Yeah. She doesn't have to know everything."

Yuri found what he wanted, and pulled up a long piece of thin black rubber tubing. He started to thread it through his belt loops.

"I got to thinking earlier about concussions blowing people's clothes off."

Lennon's eyes grew huge.

"No shit! Is that gonna happen? 'Cause I gotta get down to Hollywood if that's gonna happen."

"No, it's not. But . . ."

"Are there gonna be naked actresses blowing around?"

Yuri paused for a moment, visualizing that. "No, but I suppose guys can dream." He tied the piping and tucked the knot behind a belt loop. He knew the belt would last longer than his pants—or his skin. But he'd hit the line where his scientific expertise took a backseat to fear of exposing himself. "I know it's not going to be my biggest problem, but if my belt breaks, I don't want my pants to fall down."

"Ah. Don't want the naked actresses seeing your skinny ass."

"Exactly."

"Gimme some of that, too, would you?"

"You're sitting down."

"Still," Lennon said.

Yuri fished through the boxes and found more rubber piping. Lennon threaded it under the belt loops on his jeans and grinned.

"Prepared for all emergencies."

"Yeah," Yuri said.

He walked back to the NEO building beside Lennon.

"You guys probably have a pretty good telescope to watch this thing come in?" Lennon said.

Yuri glanced sideways at him. "We won't need telescope," he said quietly. "It's heading straight for us. We'll see it in sky. Soon."

"Yeah," Lennon said, "but the antimatter just makes it

dissolve, right? So maybe we'll see a speck up there, and then it's just gone."

Yuri smiled ruefully. "Antimatter isn't going to dissolve all of it. There's just way too much iron."

Lennon's eyes bugged out. "Something's still going to hit? It's still going to hit?" He fingered the buckle of his new harness.

"Idea is to annihilate much of it. Antimatter bursts will also push it to side some. Final strong burst will dissolve big piece and push it enough that rest will scrape by—not hit. Maybe."

"I like the it-disappears-entirely-a-long-way-from-here scenario better," Lennon said.

"Sorry," Yuri said. "Wasn't option for us."

"So how close exactly is this thing going to get?"

Yuri took a breath. "It'll be good thing you're sitting down."

"A wheelchair joke?" Lennon said. "Really?"

Yuri held his eye. "No joke."

"Aw, crap."

"They're grounding airplanes. You heard that, right? Is because asteroid will come close enough it could smash them. Also if leading edge does touch atmosphere, wind may get very turbulent."

Yuri held his eye.

"It's going to be huge in sky. And it's going to be very, very fast." They stopped in front of the NEO building. "You know Hubble telescope, yes? It crosses United States in ten minutes, traveling at eight kilometers per second." He looked out into the sky. "Asteroid is coming at seventy-one kilometers per second."

"Aw, crap," Lennon said.

"Yeah. Anyway, I have to get back now."

"No kidding," Lennon said. "I want to go sit in the basement."

His taxi was waiting in a parking lot down the street. The guard who had brought him to Yuri's office was stationed outside the building, not looking at either of them.

"You want me to go get driver for you?" Yuri asked.

"No, I got it," Lennon said. "The driver's been waiting a while, though. I should probably give him more money."

Yuri pulled his wallet out and fanned it sarcastically in front of Lennon, who ran his fingers through the bills, then plucked out two twenties.

"That was expensive book," Yuri grumbled.

"You'll love it," Lennon said. "You'll use it for years."

Yuri shot him a suspicious glance as Lennon wheeled himself to the taxi, and then the driver was out and helping him with the chair. Yuri waved but didn't stay to see him off. He walked back to his office and picked the book off the floor. He flipped it over to look at the cover. *Techniques for Self-Gratification in the Male: An Illustrated Guide.* He was going to kill Lennon.

CHAPTER 26

SHOWTIME

Yuri got permission to go back to his hotel to shower and took the car service. The driver glanced at him repeatedly in the rearview mirror. Yuri knew he wanted a word of reassurance, to have someone who really knew tell him it would be fine. Yuri was exhausted and didn't know what to say. *I found the math, dammit. Let somebody else find the words.* He got out without looking at the man.

He showered slowly, like a ceremony, and once he was clean he stood under the water and let it rain down on his skin. He couldn't shake the driver's eyes, haunted with their question: have you saved me, or have you killed me?

He finally turned the water off, ran the towel over his head, and realized the phone was ringing in the bedroom. He dived for it.

"It's me," Dovie said, and he smiled. "I wanted to apologize for telling you about Michelangelo. You know I want you to win the Nobel, right? Since that's what you want?"

"Yeah," Yuri said, piling the pillows up and sinking deeply into them. He hesitated. "My father died when I was very young. Little later, my mother read in newspaper about that year's Nobel winners, and she said, 'They're immortal.' And I thought if I could win one, my father might not be dead—because we share name, see? Like I could trick Death. Eventually I figured out that wouldn't work. But I can still make his *name* immortal."

"Oh," Dovie said. "Wow." He could hear her breathing in the phone. "Do you believe in an afterlife?"

"No."

"But you've spent your childhood trying to create one for him. To *be* his afterlife."

"I suppose that's what children are," Yuri said.

"It might be easier to believe in heaven than to win a Nobel."

"Not for me. Next year, when little kids recite list of Nobel physics winners, Strelnikov will be on that list."

"You get that normal kids don't do that, right?" She was silent for a moment, and Yuri was teetering on the brink of sleep when she spoke again. "Is that still why you want it? For your father?"

"No. I'll think of him when I see our name on program. But I can't even remember him. I want it for me."

"Yeah," Dovie said. "That's growing up, I guess. Leaving some things behind."

They got off the phone and he burrowed into the pillows and shut his eyes. He'd lost count of how many hours of sleep he'd lost—how many nights—and now he slept instantly and deeply, a pillow clutched to his chest.

Hours later he dreamed that Hitler strode into his room, boots shining. His face was an alarm clock with that ridiculous little mustache, and he used his arm salute to try to make Yuri get out of bed.

"Go away, Hitler," Yuri mumbled, but the führer's face kept ringing. Yuri finally lifted his head, and it wasn't the alarm clock but the phone that was clamoring. He glanced around quickly to make sure Hitler was gone, shook his head sharply to clear it, and picked up the receiver.

"Hello?"

"Dr. Strelnikov, we have a car waiting for you downstairs. It's showtime."

It was the Dial 1 woman. Time to go back already? How long had he slept? Yuri dressed quickly and trotted downstairs. He hoped he would have the same driver he'd had that morning. Then he could speak to him, say something of comfort. And it was the same man, in the same clothes, his face more drawn, his eyes large and luminous. Yuri had only seen eyes like that before in pictures of Holocaust victims. It was good of the man to leave his family and stay on the job in what could be his last day alive. Yuri should say something about that, too, some word of thanks as well as comfort.

The driver pulled through the checkpoint and stopped in front of the NEO building. Yuri got out and hesitated, his hand on the frame of the open window. "Thanks for ride."

"Yeah," the man said, and pulled away.

Yuri stood watching him go. *I may not be a people person.*

His heels rang across the empty lobby. No one was in the conference room, either, although the coffeepots and tepid water for tea were still there. Yuri walked toward his office, realized it was the one place there would certainly not be anyone, and headed down to the media room. There were others filing down the steps, too. Karl Fletcher was standing in the stairwell, staring up through the glass wall at the softening light. He turned.

"Hey. You're back."

"It's clear today," Yuri said. "Don't know if that's good or bad."

Fletcher snorted softly. "It passed the moon twenty minutes ago." They stood in silence for a moment, looking up at the sky.

"Dr. Fletcher?" Yuri hesitated, then plunged on. "Do you believe in parallel universes?"

"Yeah," the director said. "I do."

"In another universe, would you have made same decision? Not to take that final shot?"

"No," Fletcher said, looking him in the eye. "In another universe I would have chosen to use your version. That's what makes it another universe."

"So if we save ourselves here, do we kill ourselves there? Did we turn Earth into Schrödinger's cat?"

"It's complicated enough the way it is," Fletcher said. "Don't make it harder."

"I just don't like idea of getting smashed in any universe." Yuri nodded to Fletcher and moved on, but he was thinking, *In some universe, I didn't switch the models. In some universe, I was wrong.*

Someone had set up coolers of bottled water outside the media room doors. Yuri grabbed a water as he walked in. He held the bottle under his chin as he struggled into his suit jacket. It was time to put it on.

Time was racing the asteroid. He'd intended to nap briefly, not for hours, and then review his work. Reassure himself that he was right, that the switch he'd made was necessary. Be confident as he went to the media room to watch the intercept. Panic rose in his throat like a red line of mercury. He felt weak, trembling as he walked into the media room. Must be hypoglycemia, he told himself. Couldn't be fear.

He filed into the room with his eyes on the carpet and sat near the back, away from Simons. A cameraman was set up with a camera on a swiveling tripod. There was no TV station logo on the equipment. Must be for posterity's sake, if there was to be a posterity.

The screen was already lit. It was split into two pictures. On the left was a view of the high-flux antimatter accelerator, its fuel contrail nearly lost in the glare of the sun. On the right was the control room that had launched it. Yuri had expected a long room with dozens of people. He had seen video of rejoicing scientists slapping each other on their matching blue polo shirts after the Mars probe landed. This was a smaller room, fewer people.

Yuri glanced around at the scientists seated near him. There were two kinds of people in the room—those who hadn't risked the lives of every living thing on the planet on their own untested theory, and him. Wherever he went, that would always be the case.

He blinked. The asteroid hurtled forward twenty-four kilometers.

Fletcher walked to the front of the room, dropping a cell phone in his pocket, and then the picture from the launch site disappeared, and the president of the United States, seated at his Oval Office desk, filled the right side of the screen.

"Good evening," the president said. "I wanted to thank Director Karl Fletcher for his oversight of this project, and to thank all of you for your work. You know, when Winston Churchill said that never have so many owed so much to so few, he was talking about the fighter pilots fending off Nazi planes over Britain. But you have those boys beat. At no time in the history of the planet have the stakes been this high. At no time have individual decisions and mature judgment mattered this much. Never has the fate of history itself been held in so few hands."

Yuri ran to the garbage can at the back of the room and threw up. His gut spasmed and clenched, and acid burned his throat. He hadn't eaten anything in hours, so his bile was a green slick at the bottom of the wastebasket. Seeing it made his stomach heave again.

"So again, thank you," the president continued. Yuri hoped like hell it was a one-way feed. "And may God bless your work."

The picture cut from the Oval Office back to the accelerator control room. Yuri rinsed his mouth out and spat in the wastebasket, then took his seat again. He didn't look at anyone around him, but the man seated to his right gripped his shoulder and Yuri glanced up. The man was at least seventy, and Yuri recognized him. He was an expert in the fine-structure constant, a brilliant physicist, and Yuri had just thrown up in front of him. Actually, he'd just thrown up in front of a hundred of the greatest minds in the world. And a television camera.

"How do they get that video of flux accelerator?" Yuri said, in order to say something. His throat was raw. The man's keen brown eyes continued to bore into him for a moment, then the old fingers let his shoulder go.

"They swung a space-based telescope around to watch. Not an easy thing to do, but it was worth it. That's why we're meeting down here. Some of us wanted to watch from the parking lot, but it'll happen so fast we wouldn't really know. Here we'll get a replay."

"I still think I'd rather just watch it. See it with my own eyes."

The man smiled.

"Me, too. But this is the most important footage of all time. Not film it? It'll get more hits on YouTube than a moose on water skis." He waved his hand vaguely in the air. "Also, it will be nice to know if we're going to die or not."

"Oh. Yeah."

Black numbers appeared, superimposed over the top of the right picture. A silent countdown, starting at five minutes. What it would take to get a red countdown? Yuri felt dizzy. He looked around the room absently, and pushed his jacket sleeves up. His forearms were so familiar to him. How many hours had he spent with his shirtsleeves rolled up, his forearms propped against the edge of a desk? He loved his arms. Was that weird? He loved *arms*. If there was life somewhere else in the universe, did it have arms? Could it love itself, and hate itself?

A collective gasp rose, and Yuri snapped back to the screen. The BR1019 asteroid was visible behind the accelerator. Of course it was. It was kilometers long.

Yuri had expected the speed, understood it intellectually, but not what it would really be like. It was like watching a bullet the size of Manhattan, except that it was moving many times the speed of a bullet. The ideal would have been to park the equipment alongside the asteroid, keeping common velocity. That wasn't possible here.

The accelerator would fire as soon as the BR1019 was within range. It wouldn't take long. With each pulse there was a danger of the asteroid breaking apart. And the accelerator had to discharge the antimatter without ever coming in contact with it. One touch between the accelerator and its load and both disappeared—which meant the asteroid didn't.

Yuri had calculated the strength of each pulse, and everyone in the room knew it. If he was wrong and shot too much antimatter at one time, the asteroid would break apart and hit Earth with multiple catastrophic impacts. If it cracked, everyone would see it, and they would know whose fault it was. Were they showing this to everyone in the world? Would his mother know, standing in her hospital, watching the television? Would Kryukov? Would his advisor die disappointed in his favorite student?

Or the plan might work, the asteroid hold together as it was reduced bit by bit from the side. It would be reduced in mass, but it might not be pushed far enough away, so it would still hit Los Angeles—smaller, but still a planet-killer.

It was the final scenario of failure that made Yuri's palms slick, and his eyes throb—what if it worked, and the final shot back at Earth missed the asteroid and annihilated the Pacific Rim? What if Fletcher and Simons had been right, and the earlier pulses were enough? If the final shot came and there was no asteroid to stop it, the antimatter would spread out as it traveled back toward Earth. By the time it reached the surface it would be diffuse, weak and spread out, and everything within its limits would simply disappear— people, buildings, trees, mountains, the surface of the Pacific Ocean.

Or, if they missed the asteroid entirely, or the equipment somehow jammed, more than four jillion pounds of iron would hit the Earth at astonishing speed.

Damn shit hell.

"It's different seeing it, isn't it?" The man next to him smiled.

Yuri looked up at the warm brown eyes. "Yes. It is."

Yuri heard a liquid rattle to his left, looked over, and saw a man peeing into his drink cup. Must have needed to go, and couldn't bring himself to leave. Yuri turned away. One of his last sights was going to be some old American's *chlen* sending up a pungent urine-Pepsi mist. Terrific.

The black numbers counted down, below a minute now, hundredths of seconds shearing off. Yuri couldn't breathe. Probably no one could. He wondered what Dovie was doing. The last minute shredded. He tried not to blink.

Five.

Four.

Three.

Two.

One.

The accelerator shot instantly, lobbing a burst of antimatter at an obtuse angle at the approaching asteroid. Yuri hadn't known if they'd be able to tell or not if the antimatter had hit, but the asteroid's shape helped. It looked as though something with an oval mouth—a crocodile, maybe—had taken a bite out of the body.

The physicists gasped, but the accelerator was already shooting another burst, and another. With each pulse there was a danger of the body breaking apart. If it did so, the high-flux accelerator might shoot through gaps without hitting the asteroid. Divots appeared in its surface. The antimatter was hitting, annihilating itself and the material it touched. That much was clear. It was impossible to tell, though, if it was pushing the asteroid farther out.

The accelerator was turning as it fired, shooting at the asteroid first as it approached, then as it passed by. It swiveled, like a gunfighter turning, and shot again as the asteroid moved past its position, hurtling on toward Earth. Another piece of the asteroid simply disappeared.

Yuri leaned forward, his hands clasped in front of his mouth. Had it moved? Had the asteroid been pushed sideways?

Fletcher stood, still staring at the screen. The accelerator shot again, at a long, acute angle down the side of the asteroid. The scientists could see into the barrel.

It was pointed at them.

Another burst of antimatter came, scraping down the iron side as the asteroid rocketed toward Earth. There was a collective roar as the scientists suddenly understood. Fletcher turned, eyes searching for Yuri. Then he looked back toward the screen in time to see the final, massive burst of antimatter as the accelerator released an enormous amount of energy. And blew up.

It looked like a firework, exploding up and then trailing down in graceful arcs of debris.

The asteroid's side disappeared, all the way to the end of the body. Which meant that there was no end limit for the antimatter— the angle was so tight that it had shaved the side and continued on, down toward Earth.

Yuri tried to focus, tried to think if they would be hit first by the asteroid or by the antimatter. Because he'd switched the data in order to get the final shots back toward Earth, especially the final, huge pulse. Which had overshot.

He'd been wrong.

He had killed the world. He had killed life. He was the asteroid.

His eyes burned as he stared at the screen, the visible evidence of his atrocity. He had committed the single most arrogant act in the history of the world. Hands down. No second place. He was the most arrogant person ever. A mass murderer. Stalin had nothing on him.

Damn. Hell. Shit.

Fuck.

He began to collapse inward, to rock. His eyes filled, blurring the black shape that expanded outward across the screen, blocking the light as it spread out toward the corners.

The edge of the planet became visible in the picture, and a groan rose in the room. The asteroid was too close. It was going to punch through the atmosphere and slam Earth. It was a matter of seconds.

How many breaths did he have left? Four? Three? Yuri wanted that last breath, but he couldn't make his rib cage expand. He would die with a high concentration of carbon dioxide, and then realized that would be his last thought, and it seemed unfathomably sad. His mind scrambled for something to hold on to, anything, and he saw Dovie lying among crushed cabbage leaves, her eyes on him, smiling softly. *That.*

The BR1019's scarred iron side, flattened from the antimatter bursts, shuddered as it hit the atmosphere and sliced through the stratosphere. The room vibrated, then was absolutely still.

The screen was empty.

The people in the media room gasped again and stood as one, staring at the ceiling. Had it worked?

Fletcher jumped on his seat, his cell phone to his ear, and just before he spoke Yuri understood.

"The telescope is telling us," Fletcher said, pausing. "They can't give us results . . ."

A loud groan escaped from the room at large.

". . . because it can't swing fast enough to follow what's left of the BR1019 asteroid as it moves away from us."

He shouted, "It just kissed us as it went by," but no one was listening anymore. People were crying, grabbing shoulders, and thumping each other's backs. A planetary motion specialist in front of Yuri turned and kissed him on the mouth, and he laughed out loud.

The soft-eyed man beside him seized fistfuls of his shirt, and Yuri hugged him. They sank together to the floor, crying, Yuri's hair in his eyes. The old man mumbled some words in Hebrew, and Yuri repeated them, two atheists trying to pray in a language that one couldn't remember, and the other had never known.

Yuri didn't know how long they were like that, crying and hugging, beating on each other's backs, but at some point someone wheeled in champagne and they sprayed it around the room like hockey players who'd just won the Stanley Cup. The room stank of unwashed bodies and grapes, and someone poured a bottle down Yuri's back, the chilled glass neck touching his neck, the champagne gushing cold down his spine.

He didn't see who grabbed him, but he felt himself hoisted unevenly in the air, and for a moment the astrophysicists passed him around overhead, champagne dripping off his shirt. It was an exhilarating moment—better than matching shirts would have been—and scary when he thought about the age and bone density of the people holding him up. And then he was down, lowered awkwardly with one leg on a chair, and he wondered if Dovie knew yet. They were safe. He had saved her.

He left the media room, pausing a moment at the door to look back. They'd trashed the place. He grinned.

In his office, Yuri packed his book bag. He stuck in the papers scrawled with his angular handwriting, the ones he'd waved in frustration in Mike Ellenberg's face. The Americans might take the notes, or the Russians might. They could wind up in a museum somewhere, but he wanted to frame and hang them in his office— let Fyodor Laskov see them as often as possible. Besides, Yuri had the feeling he'd be reading them by moonlight on many sleepless nights.

There wasn't really much to pack. He looked around this small, spare office in which he'd spent the most intense moments of his life. It was someone else's space. Someone else's books were on the bookshelves. Time to give the place back. He sat on the cot for a moment, then lay down, staring at the ceiling. It was strange to know that he didn't really belong here.

He'd never wondered until now who usually used this space. Did the normal occupant keep framed family photos on the desk? Or did he carry an unframed photo of his advisor around in his book bag? Yuri sighed. Not much chance of that.

He imagined beyond the roof the asteroid, one side flattened, hurtling on through space. They would have changed its orbit when they swatted it away from Earth. Maybe now it would bury itself in some far planet, or plunge into the sun. Figuring that out was going to be somebody else's problem.

Then he was asleep.

A hand on his shoulder woke him. It was a guard. He was relieved that it wasn't the one who had brought Lennon back.

"Director Fletcher wants to see you. Now."

Yuri nodded and rose, taking his book bag with him. He glanced quickly around the office, wishing he were alone for his last look. Probably Fletcher was going to tell him now that he was stuck in the United States. Yuri flirted with the idea of telling Fletcher what he'd done—that it was his hand that shielded Earth. Fletcher would gape, then check the computer to see if it was true. Then he'd shake Yuri's hand and have their picture taken together. Send him home in a luxury airplane full of caviar and . . . Dovie.

The guard rapped lightly on Fletcher's office door.

"Come in."

The man opened the door and nodded toward Yuri, then shut it after him. Fletcher was standing with his back to the door. He turned slowly and aimed eyes like flamethrowers at Yuri, who felt himself desiccating under the gaze. They could have used Fletcher's eyes to melt the asteroid. Why hadn't he thought of that?

"The antimatter beam made it the distance it had to travel. It stayed tightly focused. Also, the high-flux accelerator fired rapidly while it rotated, and continued to fire after it pointed at Earth."

"Oh."

In his fatigue he'd forgotten that Fletcher had seen the final shot. That he knew.

"And that was consistent with its behavior if I had entered your models. But I didn't, did I? So the accelerator should have stopped firing when the asteroid flew past it. It should never have shot at us. It should never have *tried such a huge shot that it blew up the goddamn high-flux accelerator of the United States of America.*"

Yuri licked his lips.

"'How could that have happened?' I asked myself. 'It shouldn't behave like that,' I said to myself. So while you were napping, I looked at the models I sent on to the people who programmed the accelerator. And do you know what I found?"

He took a step toward Yuri. Yuri took a step back.

"I found line after line of data," he whispered, "that I never entered."

Yuri glanced behind him at the door.

"You switched the math. On your own, without my permission and against my will."

"Sorry." His voice sounded high, the apology incredibly inadequate.

"There shouldn't even have *been* a second set of code."

"Um . . ."

"You gambled with my children's lives. With *everything*." Yuri stared at the carpet, fingering the rubber piping behind his belt. "Anything you want to say?"

"Sorry."

The asteroid had blown his clothes off after all. He stood naked before the world, exposed for exactly what he was—unfathomably arrogant. Would Gregor Kryukov, his advisor, be ashamed of him? He wanted to cry. He wanted Fletcher to throw an arm over his shoulders and tell him it would be okay, that he'd done right. That it would still be possible to get up every day, knowing what he'd done. But he couldn't say any of it, so he said what he could.

"Did you call me in to apologize for doubting me, or to thank me for saving your life?"

They locked eyes for a long moment, and then Fletcher said, "My God, you've got a pair." He smiled faintly. "Don't do it again."

Yuri turned to go, saw the shadow of the guard in the hall and remembered what he had to do. "About my return home," he said, and saw Fletcher's face change, tighten. Until that moment, he wasn't sure they would detain him. Nothing he'd been through, nothing he'd done, made any difference at all. He took a moment to catch his breath. "I was wondering if I could delay my return."

Fletcher's eyebrows rose.

"There's conference in Detroit that I'd like to attend. They have panel on antimatter."

"Oh. Sure. That makes sense."

"But if you want just to put me on next plane to Moscow, I understand."

"No," Fletcher said, a little too quickly. "We can get you to Detroit. That would work out fine."

The guard hustled him into a NASA car, nosed past a phalanx of reporters gathered around the Jet Propulsion Lab, and drove him to his hotel. Yuri stopped in the little shop off the hotel lobby and bought a prepaid cell phone, which he slipped inside a news-paper. Back in his room, he called Dovie and told her that he was going to the conference in Detroit.

"You know I'm coming, right? For the big escape attempt?"

He crouched down, his head bent forward, and felt an immense sense of gratitude. "You shouldn't. How will you get there?"

"I'll drive. Duh."

"Is very long distance, Dovie. Would take two or three days."

"When does the conference start?"

He hesitated a moment. "In four days."

"Perfect."

"But I don't even know how I'm going to get out."

"You're going over that bridge—the one to Canada. And I'm taking you."

"Your parents won't allow it."

"Allow? You need remedial hippie lessons." She kissed the phone and hung up.

He smiled and thought about Dovie sitting in her car, one wrist on top of the steering wheel, driving across the country. And then he thought about Dovie, in that rattletrap, with one wrist on the steering wheel. Driving across the country. He called her back.

"I'm coming, so shut up. By the way, nice job saving the world." She hung up.

He stared at the phone. No hello, no good-bye. Just "I'm coming."

He took a long, hot shower to wash the dried champagne off. The water steaming over his bare skin had probably been delivered to Earth by an asteroid hundreds of millions of years ago. He was awash in irony.

He rubbed the thin hotel towel over his hair and then flipped it around his waist. He clicked the lights off and walked to the window. A shooting star flashed across the sky beyond the restaurant next door—not a piece of the asteroid, just a regular meteorite. The sky was still there, Earth and the moon. He stood in the dark for an hour, looking at the stars.

He'd saved the world. Now it was time to save himself.

CHAPTER 27

AN EQUATION OF LONELINESS

Five Days to Impact

Yuri spent three days in the hotel room, waiting to be moved for the Detroit conference. He tried not to think of his flash drives in Fyodor Laskov's sausage fingers. Yuri needed to get home.

He wanted to call Dovie, but she was driving, and he was afraid she'd answer. Dovie streaking across the continent might do more damage than the BR1019 had. He caught up on his sleep, and googled himself—just the usual academic references, and a mention that he was part of the asteroid team at JPL. Apparently the extent of his role wasn't public knowledge. Then he watched an American senator on a talk show argue that NASA's budget should be cut now that the danger was past.

The third day he watched TV reports on the convulsive street parties in cities around the world, interrupted by commercials for knockoff NASA merchandise. The most striking footage was of three guys about his age in Paris, dancing in a fountain with a topless girl, her breasts made rectangular by the censor's blurring. The guys were wearing matching shirts with a NASA logo. They got to dance in a fountain with a naked French girl, *and* they got matching shirts? That was incredibly unfair.

He jumped off the hotel mattress, checked his dead bolt, and used a pants hanger to pinch the curtains together so there wasn't a gap. Then he stripped to his underpants and danced with the crazy Parisians, throwing his pale arms over his head. The TV news switched to a celebration in Iowa City involving a scary chicken—the mascot for some local sports team, no doubt. Yuri flapped his arms and clucked and leaped between his bed and the chair. The big chicken shook its tail feathers at the camera, and Yuri turned and shook his butt back at it.

He wasn't sure if he was going stir-crazy, or regular crazy.

He flipped off the TV and flopped on the bed. Dovie and Lennon should be stopped for the night by now. Lennon would have insisted on it—there'd be only so much of her driving that he could take.

Dovie answered on the second ring.

"You're not driving?" he said.

"No. We're in a cheap little motel with no handicapped showers."

He'd never even thought about that. "Is Lennon okay?"

"Oh, he's been screaming a lot." Yuri laughed. "As for the hotel, I just helped him wash up. He's shaving now."

"I got hotel information for Detroit," he said, and told her where he'd be staying. "I've been imagining you driving there, all your rings refracting sunlight."

"Hey, Yuri? Do you dream in color?"

He hesitated for a moment. He didn't usually remember his dreams. "I don't know."

"I dream in color and I remember in color and I hope in color."

"What color is hope?"

"I hope in all the colors," Dovie said. "That's what makes it hope."

"I don't really understand that."

"Nobody does." She was quiet for a moment, but Yuri could hear her breathing. "I feel like I was the whole color wheel as a kid. And growing up means losing some of that."

"Like your art teacher said?" Yuri thought of her cookie jar, *Dreamland*, and the teacher's complaint that it was too vivid.

"Yeah. That's why I wear the rings. I'm trying to hold on to the color, literally and figuratively." Her sigh was soft in his ear. "If you can only keep some, how do you choose?"

"Maybe by expiration date?" Yuri said.

"We're not talking about paint!"

Yuri clutched his head. "I hate words. So unpredictable."

Dovie snorted softly, then said, "I want to keep all of me, and I don't think you get to do that. I think becoming an adult means leaving part of you behind."

He didn't say anything. He didn't know what to say. But he finally understood that they weren't talking about paint.

"I don't know how to be me and be an adult," Dovie said.

Yuri stared at his naked legs. "I don't know how to be kid."

"Yeah, we know," Dovie said. "We picked up on that."

"Hey, do you have computer with you? There's painting I want you to see," Yuri said.

"Seriously?"

"Yes!" He was incredibly proud of himself. "There's copy in building on my campus."

"Len! Give me your phone. Yuri says so." He could hear Lennon's voice but couldn't make out the words. "He's a genius and he wants me to have your stuff. Deal with it."

"Run image search for Kandinsky's painting, *Squares with Concentric Circles.*"

"Got it," Dovie said. "I know this one."

"Kandinsky painted with many colors, and he was adult. You should keep all your colors, Dovie."

"You found an inspirational piece for me. Thank you." He beamed. "Although I want desperately to free the circles."

"No! It's very symmetrical painting. That's why I like it."

"Wow," Dovie said. "Are we arguing about art?"

"Yes," Yuri said. "I am Mr. Versatile."

Dovie laughed. They talked for a couple more minutes, then she handed the phone off and Yuri listened to Lennon's tales of highway woe. Then he wrapped up in the sheet and fell asleep.

The next morning a couple of guards picked him up at his hotel.

"Kevin Decker," the guy said, shaking his hand.

"Azenet Linares," the woman said. "FBI."

Yuri introduced himself, even though it seemed pointless. They knew who he was.

"We're your security detail while you're in Detroit," Decker said. "Dr. Fletcher asked us to stop by JPL before we go to the airport." Yuri shrugged and followed them to their car. They didn't talk on the way in. Clearly neither Decker nor Linares was going to make the Olympic small-talk team.

Karl Fletcher was standing in the JPL parking lot, leaning against his car, arms folded across his chest. Neither of his guards said anything, so Yuri got out and walked over to the NEO director. Fletcher stuck his hand out, and Yuri hesitated a moment, then shook it.

"You know, if you ever want a job here, you've got it."

"I already did my job here. Now I want to go home."

The director shrugged and looked away. "Had to try." He reached in through the open window of his car and picked something up off the seat. "Here, I have a souvenir for you." He handed it to Yuri. Yuri turned it over in his hand for a moment, not placing it. It was a small board with numbers, and some exposed electronic equipment and clipped wires on the back.

"Is this . . ."

"Yeah, it's the keypad from outside my office. Instead of having it reprogrammed, I just took it off and told them to get me a new one." He grinned. "I wanted to get you something you knew how to use."

Yuri laughed. "I'll treasure it. It doubles my souvenir

collection." He turned the keypad over in his hand and shook his head. "I'm sorry I didn't get anything for you."

"Are you kidding me? In addition to the planet, you've given me a case of heartburn that's gonna last for years."

Decker and Linares drove Yuri to the airport, getting him through security with the flash of a badge. He scored a window seat on the plane and spent the flight looking at America turn below him. An asteroid's eye view. The guards hustled him through the Detroit airport, into a rental car, and then to a hotel off the highway ramp.

He wanted to save a clothes-shopping trip as a potential opportunity to break away and head for the Ambassador Bridge that led into Canada. But he was wearing his black suit, which he'd sent to the cleaners while in Pasadena. Everything else was filthy. He had stuffed his champagne-soaked gray suit in the trash.

So they drove him to a department store and stood back while he bought another gray suit and three dress shirts, jeans and a blue T-shirt, socks, and underwear. He bought a pair of black sneakers, too, in case he needed to do any sneaking at night. He'd run over a roof in dress shoes, and never wanted to repeat the experience. He still had cash the Russian government had given him when he flew out of Moscow—but not much. He had money of his own, but he wasn't sure how to access it in America. He'd probably need Decker and Linares's help, and that could prove awkward.

In the hotel, he changed into jeans and the T-shirt, and sat at the edge of the bed for a moment, trying to decide what color socks to wear with black casual shoes. *This is something a normal teenager would know. Or maybe this is something a normal teenager wouldn't care about.* He threw caution to the wind and went with navy.

Decker and Linares were in their own rooms, flanking his. He could hear occasional soft *thunks* as they moved around, pulling chairs out, shutting dresser drawers. He flipped on the television and caught the last period of a hockey game, then ordered dinner from room service and kept the television on, but muted. Not as good as Gregor Kryukov, but still company. He ate at a little round table by the window, the curtains open, looking out at the city, eyes following people on the sidewalks, feeling a faint sense of abandonment when they would disappear behind doors, or into the labyrinth of a parking garage.

After eating, Yuri flipped open his briefcase and tossed a pad of paper on the table. He bent over it, writing a single neat calculation. A billion people lived in the Western Hemisphere. He had two friends: Dovie and Lennon. He wrote it as a ratio on the pad: one in every 500 million people would talk to him. An equation of loneliness. But not a solution. Were there things that couldn't be solved mathematically?

He raked a hand through his hair. He felt like he was cracking up. The intense pressure of the work, of dealing with Simons, of navigating through a strange land with a strange language . . . Hell, *Russian* wasn't even his language. His mother tongue was math.

He craved the Nobel. He'd *earned* it. The asteroid almost took his opportunity away. But his theories had destroyed his competition, and his antimatter had destroyed the asteroid. He had to be a shoo-in with the Nobel committee now.

And in Moscow, Fyodor Laskov was rooting through his flash drives.

When did life get easy?

He traced the ratio he had written, over and over, repetition making the lines bold. He was lonely. He'd always been lonely. Maybe he'd been too busy to notice much before, or maybe he'd just gotten used to it.

"I'm lonely," he said out loud. He told himself because there was no one else to tell.

He turned back to the television and saw Fletcher shaking hands with the American president. He grabbed the remote and tapped the volume up as the camera cut back to a blond anchor and his own face in the upper corner of the screen. It was his staff photo from Moscow State, and for the briefest moment he didn't recognize himself.

"This is the scientist, on loan from Russia, who was solely responsible for a crucial part of the attack on the asteroid."

Yuri stared, stunned.

"Director Karl Fletcher says that without the work of this lone scientist, the asteroid would have hit Los Angeles. No one else at NASA's Near Earth Object Program agreed with Dr. Strelnikov's analysis, but he courageously stood by his work. And get this— he's seventeen years old."

"Incredible story, Caitlyn," the male anchor said as the camera pulled back to a side-by-side shot. They began to banter about being flattened by the asteroid.

No mention of the hacking. Probably Fletcher didn't think that reflected well. Yuri hit the "mute" button, but kept staring at the television. The anchor had presented it in a positive light. Probably that was going to be NEO's official version, and maybe it had to be to prevent an investigation of Fletcher's security procedures. Or maybe it was a threat, that if Yuri fought his detention in America, they would reveal what he'd really done—the hacking, the deceit—the chance he'd taken. Except Fletcher had gone out of his way to highlight it as Yuri's work, as though he was trying to help him.

Why?

Yuri checked his e-mail on his cell phone. There was a message from Gregor Kryukov that had come in hours before. *Yuri, they've retired me. I can't help you. I am so sorry.*

"Damn Laskov," Yuri said in English. Laskov was tying himself to Yuri's star—that was one thing. But bringing down Kryukov for defending Yuri's authorship of his work? Kryukov had a towering intellect and brought wit even to his seminar on quantum phase transitions. He was all brain and eyebrows and kindness—and he had lost his job, a sacrifice to Fyodor Laskov's ambition and political connections. "Damn Laskov," he said again.

Yuri rose abruptly, grabbed his key card, and left the room. He was three feet down the hall when Linares charged out of her room, almost colliding with him.

"Where are you going?"

"Movie."

"Movie? You want to see a movie?"

"There was cinema couple of blocks down. We passed it, yes? I'm going to see movie."

"Which one?" Decker asked behind him.

"Does it matter?" Yuri stuck his chin out fractionally.

Decker and Linares exchanged a look.

"Guess it doesn't. Yeah, we can see a movie."

English first person plural: we.

Yuri stalked to the stairwell, passing the workout room. He thought briefly that he might be better off attacking the treadmill, but the TV above the machines was on, and his picture covered it. Different channel, same photo. Russian boy hero. He wanted to sit in the dark, in the back, among strangers. Because he needed to be with people, and this was as close as he could get.

And then the TV showed a photo of Fyodor Laskov, weasel, and son of the president of the Russian Academy of Sciences. He couldn't hear the audio, but he didn't have to. There was a banner at the bottom that said "Laskov-Strelnikov Theory of Antimatter Containment."

The Russians knew by now that he wasn't coming back—everyone had been told except him. Laskov could make his play. But Yuri *was* going back, and when he got there he would claim his work as his own—he could prove it, because *he* could understand it—and restore Kryukov to his position.

Yuri turned and kicked the wall hard three times. His foot sank through the drywall the third time, and he gave Linares a hard stare. She seemed completely unperturbed by his display of rage, and somehow that made him angrier. He pulled his shoulders up and stalked to the cinema.

It was lit up, brass trim, dark carpet with a vine pattern, a guy his age in the ticket booth, wearing a white shirt and black pants.

Yuri recognized himself—the age, the shock of blond hair, the dress clothes—and laughed out loud. What was this guy's worst dilemma? Which movie to sneak into when his boss wasn't looking?

"Which movie?" the guy asked.

"That one." Yuri pointed at a poster. One of his favorite actors, and it looked like there'd be car chases.

The guy nodded, took his money, and printed a tiny receipt. Linares kept stride with him as Decker stepped up to pay for the guards' tickets.

"I don't need help to watch movie," Yuri said without looking over.

"You want popcorn?" Linares said.

He started to say no, then changed his mind. Why shouldn't he? What if he clogged his arteries and had a heart attack in a week? He'd done his life's work. There was nothing after this. No matter what he did for the next seventy years, his obituary was already written. It was all downhill from here.

"Give me biggest popcorn you have, extra butter, please, and large drink."

The girl at the snacks counter smiled at him and grabbed a red-and-white paper tub big enough to wash a sweater in. He paid and stalked into the theater.

He sat in the back, in a short row tucked behind the door, in the aisle seat so he blocked the other chairs. Decker and Linares hesitated. Yuri swept his arm sarcastically around the room. Half the seats were filled, and more people were filing in. Linares sat on the end of the long back row, the one in the middle, and angled her legs toward the aisle so that she could see him over her left shoulder. Decker sat at the other end of her row. He couldn't see Yuri, but he was next to the far door.

Yuri savagely shoved popcorn in his mouth and wondered how he could need privacy and company at the same time, and so badly.

The theater was three-quarters full when the lights went out and the screen lit up with reminders to turn off cell phones, then commercials featuring attractive young people playing volleyball by open coolers of beer and girls in bikinis washing pickups. By the time trailers for other movies blared, Yuri was tapping his foot on the rope lights along the aisle, thoughts swirling like a star circling a black hole—circling the question he'd been trying to avoid.

Not what he was going to do to Fyodor Laskov. He knew the answer to that.

But what if he had been wrong?

The world would have been destroyed. Dovie and her paint-stained fingers and crazy hair and hippie holidays, but also Moscow, the city where he had been born. The towering banks of lilacs at Gorky Park, the ice cream vendors on the street, wonderful, cantankerous Gregor Kryukov, who had taught him so much, who had started taking him to dinner when he was fourteen, and had treated him as a colleague. Who had taken him to the hockey game where he'd gotten his puck. His mother would be gone. They hadn't been close in years, but still—she was his *mother*. Then again, Fyodor Laskov would have been gone, too. Yuri snorted softly.

He shouldn't have hacked in, even if he was correct. He knew that now. It was too much for one person. Too much responsibility. If the other physicists had agreed, that would be one thing. But the way he did it—it was indefensible. He had blundered. Kant said *Do what is right though the world should perish*. Yuri had done what was wrong, so the world wouldn't perish. Kant had sucker punched him.

In front of him, three teenage girls were leaning in to each other, arguing. One had her cell phone on and was running a search. The glare was distracting. On-screen, Matt Damon was weaving between buildings, avoiding gunshots.

"Shut up! It was Liam Neeson, not Mel Gibson."

"Mel Gibson is *dead*. Isn't he?"

Yuri shifted in his seat.

"Ohmygod, you are so stupid. *Stupid*. It was Indiana Jones."

"Indiana Jones is a character, not a actor. Duh."

"Well you're a whore, Britney. Anyway, it wasn't Indiana Jones, it was Samuel L. Jackson."

"Samuel L. Jackson is black!"

"What, you're a racist?"

Yuri coughed quietly.

"*No*. I'm saying he's black and Indiana Jones is white, and that movie had a *white* guy. Didn't it?"

"If you weren't so *stupid* . . ."

Yuri stuffed his popcorn bucket over the head of the middle girl, the one with the cell phone. She lifted her hands in the air, fingers splayed, elbows tight to her body. He stood up.

"Matt Damon is running in suit. Nobody runs in suit like Matt Damon. I wanted to see this." The whole audience had twisted to look at him. "And you are arguing about some stupid thing, and calling each other names, and *you could have been dead right now*." The girl pulled the bucket off her head and popcorn cascaded over her shoulders.

As he leaned toward them, the girls grabbed each other's forearms and shrank back. "Do you understand that? Giant M-type asteroid was coming at Earth at *seventy-one kilometers per second*. It was going to impact Earth with unimaginable force. You would be dead or dying, choking on dust, freezing." He started down the aisle toward the screen. Linares rose to block his path. He turned back to the girls, their staring eyes white in the dark theater. "And Indiana Jones isn't actor; he's character."

"See," one girl said. "I told you so."

Yuri turned back, saw Linares, and stepped onto an armrest, then ran over seat backs toward the front of the theater.

"You would all be dying! You would be freezing, and crops would shrink. Wither. You," he said, pointing to an overweight man with his hand poised over a popcorn tub, "you would be dead if it weren't for me. I saved your life. I saved your greasy fingers."

Linares exchanged an alarmed look with Decker as the agent trotted down the far aisle.

"I saved your husband! I saved your life! And yours! And yours! I saved *life*." He balanced on the balls of his feet on the front-row seat backs, threw his arms out and laughed, his shadow wide across the screen. "I saved Matt Damon! I saved his suit!"

He laughed again and jumped to the sticky floor, stumbled, then ran out the front exit below the screen.

Behind him, Linares said, "Shit."

"Damn, hell," Yuri shouted, as the door closed behind him.

He ran behind the theater to the block beyond, shouting at startled passersby.

"I saved your life!" *There is no one I will ever meet that I can't say that to: I saved your life, and I shouldn't have.*

People stopped and moved together, grabbing each other's arms, gripping hands. Yuri smiled grimly. He was bringing people together. Maybe he was a people person after all.

He ran into a convenience store. The middle-aged man at the cash register reached under the counter. Yuri banged on the Formica. "I saved your life!" He leaned in toward the man's face and said it again. "I saved your life!" He turned and shouted "I saved your baby!" at a woman holding a stroller handle with one hand and clutching a pack of batteries to her chest. He ran out the door by the restrooms as the front door chimed for Decker and Linares.

A dog was in the alley.

"I saved your paws!"

The dog wagged its tail.

"You're welcome."

Yuri pushed open the door of a bar on the corner and ran in. It was dark and had seating in the front, pool tables in the back, and a television hanging over the bar, which ran down the side of the room. The patrons were men in black leather vests, and a few

women with heavy eyeliner and high-heeled boots. Yuri strode to
the back.

"I saved your life!" he shouted at a giant man in a Harley
T-shirt. The man stroked a forked beard and kept a level gaze
on him. Yuri turned to a man with a face pocked with old acne
scars. "I saved your life!" He looked at the other players. "I saved
your fat ass! I saved your snake tattoo! I saved your ugly
girlfriend!"

"It's that Russian guy," the forked beard said, throwing a
meaty hand toward the television. "The physicist."

"That right?" the man with the ugly girlfriend said with
interest, leaning on his pool cue. "Here?"

"Is right. I'm Russian physicist who saved whole world!" Yuri
shouted, throwing his arms wide. It left him completely unpro-
tected as the man handed the pool cue to his girlfriend and
launched a fist into Yuri's solar plexus.

The universe exploded with pain, a big bang that began in
Yuri's ganglia and expanded forever, launching galaxies of light
behind his eyes. He crumpled to the floor, smelled beer and the
rich iron of blood as he bit his tongue. He struggled to breathe and
asteroids hit his face, over and over, and he thought, that's right—
the period after the creation of the universe had a very high level
of cosmic collisions. And then a woman was yelling, and he could
see high-heeled boots through the stars, and they shuffled backward, and his diaphragm spasmed and he drew a little air into his
lungs.

Decker's face hung over him.

"You all right?"

Yuri sucked in a breath and looked up. The ugly girlfriend was standing behind Decker, fists up like an old pugilist, a smug look below the eyeliner. Pool Cue Guy had floored him, but after that he'd gotten beaten up by a girl.

He nodded, touched his left eye, and winced. Decker grabbed his arm and pulled, and Yuri stood and raised one hand toward the pool players.

"Did I mention that I saved your lives?"

"TV was talking about that," Pool Cue said. "Boy hero. But you don't have a cape."

"Nope," Forked Beard said. "He doesn't have reflexes, either." He chuckled.

Linares was to the side of the door, covering the room with a pistol. No one paid it the slightest attention. By the time Decker pushed him out the door, the crack of pool balls ricocheted through the bar again, and someone was shouting an order to the barkeep.

"That was incredibly stupid," Linares hissed, shoving the pistol into her waistband. "What were you thinking?"

"I was thinking," Yuri said, licking blood from the corner of his mouth, "that since I bothered to save world, people might shut up during movies."

"Yeah," Decker said. "Let's get you home."

"Oh!" Yuri said with exaggerated interest. "Moscow?"

"I meant your room."

Yuri stayed in his room, icing his face periodically, until nine the next morning, when Decker and Linares walked him three blocks to the conference, held in another hotel. Everyone had heard of the late registrant and he got an ovation when he walked into the lobby. He nodded, flushed, and searched for his adhesive name tag.

"You really don't need a name tag, do you?" the woman behind the table said, smiling. He nodded numbly.

He wanted to slip into the first panel discussion, on neutrinoless double beta decay, sit in the back and ignore the proceedings. Figure out how far he was from the Ambassador Bridge, and how he could possibly get to it. But his progress down the hall and into the room was slowed by well-wishers and heralded by applause. And every single person, after introducing him or herself and expressing admiration for his work, had to comment on his bruises and split lip. He told the story over and over of having been assaulted by a deranged man. Decker and Linares, hovering nearby, said nothing, and Yuri didn't admit that the only deranged guy he'd been near the previous night was himself.

He slipped into the conference room, and someone recognized him and started clapping. The rest of the room picked it up, so he raised a hand in acknowledgment but turned to get a cup of tea from the refreshments table. Decker and Linares flanked him, both in dark Windbreakers with "FBI" on the back. When he'd arrived at JPL he was lugging a suitcase, and thought that was embarrassing. Now he was dragging two federal agents around.

He slipped into a seat. The guy behind him reached over Yuri's shoulder to grab his hand and pumped it, even though Yuri was juggling the tea and a notepad. The moderator stepped to the podium and tapped the microphone, blasting sound through the room. Why did people who understood amplification do that? But the room quieted, and people stopped looking at him, and that was a relief.

"I think we'll go ahead and get started," the man said. "We've got Thomas Kroc scheduled to speak, but we also unexpectedly have Yuri Strelnikov here." The guy grinned. "A pleasure, Dr. Strelnikov." Yuri nodded and tried to smile. The moderator swiveled. "Thomas, you don't mind if we get Yuri up here first, do you?"

A tall, red-headed guy waved a hand in agreement. "Could you explain a little about your work?" the moderator said. "We'd love to hear what you guys did at JPL."

Yuri rose, still holding the tea. "Thank you. I don't want to interrupt conference, and anyway I don't have anything prepared."

"We don't care. Off-the-cuff remarks are fine," the moderator said, stepping aside from the podium and throwing an arm toward it.

Yuri hesitated, then trudged to the front, thinking, *This conference was supposed to get me out of sight and close to the Canadian border.* He gripped the edge of the podium, cleared his throat, and stumbled through an explanation of antimatter containment. It was choppy and awkward, partially muffled by his swollen lips, and desperately in need of visual aids.

And he had to repeat it in four subsequent panels.

But a crowd surrounded him at lunch, patting his back and shaking his hand. *So this is what it takes to be the popular kid in the cafeteria.*

Yuri ducked out after dinner, skipping an evening panel on spin-orbit coupling in cold atoms. Decker said, "Well, that was successful," and seemed to mean it. Yuri stared at him.

He walked into the lobby behind Decker, ahead of Linares, and so neither guard saw his gaze bounce across the lobby and stop on a guy in a wheelchair and a girl sitting beside him. The girl rose and stepped toward him. Yuri threw his palm out.

"Sorry, no autographs." He turned to Linares. "This is going to be real pain."

She smiled, and he dropped the key card in his hand into a potted palm and caught Lennon's eye for a moment, making sure he saw it.

"Just, um, moment," Yuri said to Decker and Linares, and he walked to the desk, fifteen feet behind Dovie and Lennon. "I'm afraid I forgot my key to room 410. So I'm locked out of room 410. Is it possible to get another key? I have another in my room—in 410—but I can't get in to get it." He shrugged his shoulders. The woman at the desk smiled.

"No problem, sir."

A moment later he had a replacement card. As he walked to the elevator, he could hear the whisper of Lennon's wheels on the carpet as he went to retrieve the other key.

CHAPTER 28

CALLIMACHUS AND MINT CHIP ICE CREAM

Twelve Hours to Impact

Yuri was pacing in his room when he realized he couldn't possibly have a conversation with the Collums without Decker and Linares being aware of it. If he could hear them shutting dresser drawers, they would certainly hear murmured conversation from his room. He fretted for half an hour, not wanting Dovie and Lennon to show up. Because even if they quietly let themselves in, the guards would surely investigate once they heard him talking to someone. It could make it harder later to escape, to get back to Russia and defend the authorship of his theory. If he didn't get home, Laskov would officially become his co-author. *He* would be *Laskov's* co-author—Laskov's father had that much clout.

There was a knock at the door.

"Pizza."

Yuri checked out the peephole and saw nothing. Lennon. He opened the door as Linares and Decker opened theirs.

"I'm still growing," he said to them, shrugging. "Here, bring it in, please. I need to get my money."

Lennon rolled in, a small pizza box on his lap, face shaded by a baseball cap. He was wearing an "I survived the BR1019 asteroid" T-shirt. Decker and Linares exchanged a glance and retreated to their rooms.

"How much do I owe you?" Yuri said loudly, then whispered, "If you'd showed up with book again, I would have killed you."

"I figured that," Lennon whispered. "Hence the pizza. Besides, eating pizza is a credible teenage activity." He raised his voice. "Twenty-two dollars."

"Twenty-two dollars? For small pizza?"

"Yeah." Lennon whispered, "And the worst part is, I ate it on the way here." He flipped up the lid to show a box empty save for a couple of ridges of cheese and a sauce smear.

"That's outrageous," Yuri said, grinning.

"What happened to you, anyway? Did they beat you up?"

"Here's two twenties," Yuri said. He whispered, "No, I angered bunch of tough guys in bar."

Lennon pulled his head back and squinted sideways at Yuri. "That doesn't sound like you."

"I was stressed."

Lennon tucked the twenties in his jacket.

"My change," Yuri said.

"My tip."

Yuri sighed.

"Dovie was upset at how your face looks," Lennon said.

"I get that from women."

Lennon snorted.

"Can you get to the roof? We thought we'd meet up there, plan your escape."

"This is top floor. I can swing up from balcony if they don't see me."

"Jeez, man, that's stupid. Those things don't always work out okay."

Yuri looked at him, then glanced down. Lennon was right, and he had the wheels to prove it.

"You take my chair down the hall, they'll think it's me. Just hike it up onto the roof with you so no one sees it."

"Damn, shit, hell, Lennon. You're brilliant."

"True," Lennon conceded. "Completely true. I'll stay in your room for a couple of minutes, in case the zookeepers are paying attention. I'll switch TV channels, flush once—refine your theory of antimatter if there's a pen around here."

Yuri grinned, then thought of something. "How will you get up there?"

"Dovie's commandeered a maid's cart. She's dumping the stuff underneath—like the Windex and crap. She'll just stop by and get me."

"That might actually work."

He waited for Lennon to get out of the wheelchair, then realized he couldn't. "Um, how do we . . ."

"You're gonna have to put me on the toilet."

"On—what?"

"The toilet, damn it. On the lid, so I can flush. How do you think I'm going to get in there to do it?"

Yuri nodded. Lennon put his arms up and Yuri bear-hugged him, and lifted him onto the toilet. He handed him the remote, and angled the TV so Lennon could see it through the open bathroom door.

"Thanks," Yuri whispered, and took the baseball cap Lennon handed him. He pushed aside the NASA restraint Lennon still had on the chair, and sat. It felt weirdly intimate. He twisted the doorknob, then realized one wheel was in the door's arc. He backed up, lost his grip on the knob, and had to try again. Lennon just shook his head. *It's one thing to know he has to deal with this every minute. It's another to have to do it yourself.*

"Thanks for the tip, man," Lennon called as Yuri wheeled himself past Decker's door and down to the elevator. The door swung shut and clicked behind him.

The elevator opened to the roof, but when it stopped the doors wouldn't slide open. The hotel probably didn't want guests diving off—bad for business. Yuri groaned in frustration and slammed the control panel with the side of his fist. A barrette crusted with lime-green sparkles fell to the carpet. He retrieved it and stuck it in the lock beside the button for roof access. The doors swung open and he put the barrette back on the control panel. It was shaped like a peace sign—it had to be Dovie's, and she was going to need it.

He wheeled out onto the flat roof of the hotel and immediately stepped out of Lennon's wheelchair. It was too personal—not like wearing someone else's jacket. Like wearing their underwear. He looked out over Detroit's evening skyline until he heard the elevator doors hiss open, and turned.

"You don't sign autographs?" Dovie said, shoving the maid's cart aside. From inside, Lennon yelled, "Hey!"

Yuri smiled and pushed Lennon's chair over to the cart and locked the brakes. Dovie reached under and lifted her brother's legs out, then heaved him into his seat as he grabbed the hand rests.

"*I* want an autograph," Lennon said, grinning and fishing a Sharpie out of the bag on his chair. He tapped his shoulder, and Yuri leaned down and signed the T-shirt. "It's in Russian," Lennon said, peering sideways. "You signed in Russian."

"I didn't think about it. Does it matter?"

"You might have written, 'Lennon smells like hamster farts.' I mean, how do I know?"

Yuri grinned. "I said 'guinea pig,' but you were very close."

Dovie sighed and ran a finger across Yuri's swollen left eye. "We know what you did. We heard on the radio on the drive up here. They said it was all you."

"No, not all me. We had hundred people, and we needed every one."

"They said it would have hit if it weren't for you."

He hesitated and looked at the roofline while he told her. "I hacked their computer and changed important data. I made it send one extra, huge antimatter pulse. It scraped off side of asteroid and gave it final push away. It was also aimed directly at us."

She stared at him for a long moment.

"Jeez, Yuri."

"Yeah."

Finally she said, "I brought ice cream. It's probably half-melted."

She retrieved it from the cart and they sat on the tar paper with a brick of mint chocolate chip between them, three wooden spoons sticking up like antennas.

"It was this or little plastic spoons, and they would have broken," Dovie said.

"This is good."

They ate, the ice cream cold and sweet. Above them, stars began to glimmer.

"It's really pretty," Dovie said. She turned to Yuri. "Do you find beauty in it?"

Yuri looked at her, startled, then at the sky. "Yes, I guess I do."

"What's beautiful about it?" Dovie asked.

Yuri struggled, trying to find the words. "Its precision. And imprecision. And our struggle to know."

"Whoa there," Lennon said. "You almost expressed yourself."

They ate in silence for a few minutes.

"I'm sorry," Yuri said.

"For saving our lives," Lennon said, "or for almost being articulate for a moment?"

"For my arrogance. I was trying to do what was right. Like Kant said."

"I think you did," Dovie said, sweeping a spoon up toward the sky.

"But is doing right thing issue of process or content?"

"You lost me there, big guy," Lennon said, wiggling his spoon. Yuri held the carton up so he could reach it.

"Should I have done things right way—by best process—even though result would have been bad?"

"No," Lennon said. "No, you shouldn't have."

"Or should I have produced right result, by using wrong process?"

"I already answered that," Lennon said. "Saving my ass is always the right thing to do."

"This was really hard on you, wasn't it?" Dovie said.

"Yeah."

And then he was crying, hugging his knees, and Dovie threw her arms around him and held him and Lennon put a hand on the back of his head. When he was done crying, and just making embarrassing little gasps, Lennon said, "You remember the story of Callimachus? From ancient Greece?"

"Of course not," Yuri said. "Do I look like historian?"

"No, historians don't generally have snot running down their chins. They're a dignified people."

Yuri swiped at his face with his sleeve.

"The Persians invaded Greece. They had like a hundred eighty thousand men, and the Greeks had maybe five thousand gathered on the shore, watching the Persians getting off their ships. And there were like a million of them."

"Their forces just increased almost five hundred percent."

"Do not," Lennon said, "do a statistical analysis of my story." Yuri shrugged. "So anyway, being Greek, their generals voted on whether to stay and fight, or run like hell. There were ten generals, and the vote was five to five. So the head general turned to Callimachus, and . . ."

"He was this official," Dovie said. "He had the tie-breaking vote, but nobody thought he'd ever have to use it—certainly not with Western civilization hanging in the balance."

"Thank you for telling my story, Dovie."

"Welcome."

"So anyway, he turns to him and says, 'With you it rests, Callimachus.'"

"And Callimachus voted to run as hell?"

"No, he voted to fight, and inexplicably they beat the Persians and saved democracy. That was the Battle of Marathon, dude."

"Never heard of it."

Lennon bugged his eyes out.

"You know, if I'd spent my time studying history, your frozen blue ass would be orbiting Pluto about now."

"Fair point," Lennon said. His eye held Yuri's. "I always thought that was the most pressure anybody's ever been under. I mean, the Persians were *getting off the boats*. They were *right there*. But now there's you."

They ate.

"You believe in God, yes?" Yuri said.

Lennon and Dovie exchanged a glance.

"Yeah," Dovie said. "I guess."

"If God exists, why didn't he stop asteroid?" Yuri said.

"Maybe he did," Lennon said. "Maybe you're the tool he used. Not that you're a tool."

"You'd think being atheist would have gotten me out of that," Yuri said. "Anyway, I was thinking more like giant medieval shield. Would have made great eclipse."

"If it had hit, would that have been Armageddon?" Dovie said. "Do you think there'd have been a Second Coming of Christ?"

"Oh, great," Yuri said. "That's just what I need. Jesus was on Earth and I screwed up his plans. There'll be like fifteen-foot-tall pissed-off Jesus coming after me."

"Don't forget his death-ray eyes," Dovie said.

They passed the ice cream around.

"Do you think there will be a Second Coming?" Dovie said.

Yuri licked the back of his spoon. "Maybe there already was. What if he came again in 1943? They'd have put him in Dachau. Maybe they threw him in cattle car, made him wear striped pajamas, and finally gassed him in shower."

They stared at him.

Yuri shrugged. "What? It's kind of thing that would happen to him."

"That's the most depressing thing I've ever heard," Dovie said.

"You know, he's gonna be really pissed if this was his second attempt at a Second Coming," Lennon said. "That, and what happened to his relatives."

"Watch out for Godzilla Jesus," Dovie said. "Better look both ways before you cross the street."

"You live in such three-dimensional world," Yuri said.

"Um, yes. Yes, I do."

"Hand me the ice cream again before Jezilla shows up, would you?" Lennon said.

Yuri held the carton up while Lennon carved out a gigantic scoop.

"So anyway, we have an escape plan for you," Lennon said, then put the spoon in his mouth.

"Yeah? What is it?"

"We weren't sure we should get you out," Lennon said around the mouthful of mint chip. "Might be unpatriotic."

"We wanted to help," Dovie said apologetically. "We just had to think whether we should."

"You didn't learn anything here that would help the Russians invade or anything, right?" Lennon said.

"Actually, yes. If we can cut off your pizza supply, we can bring you to your knees."

"Sounds about right," Lennon said. "But I don't think that was a secret. Anyway, since you saved our lives, and also, you know, America, it seemed wrong not to help."

"Where I live is my decision," Yuri said. He ran his spoon around the edge of the carton, where the mint chip had melted to a pale green liquid. "So what are we going to do?"

Lennon explained. Yuri frowned, listening, making occasional objections. When Lennon was done, Yuri tapped the wooden neck of his spoon on the toe of his shoe.

"This isn't great plan."

"No," Dovie said. "Can you think of a better one?"

Yuri sighed.

"If it doesn't work, they'll know I'm trying to get out. They'll probably give me more guards. A second attempt would be harder."

"That's going to be true no matter what we try," Dovie said. "It needs to work the first time."

CHAPTER 29

I AM NOT A GNOME-KISSER

Ten Hours to Impact

They left the ice cream carton on the roof, three spoons plunged in like Greek spears in the sand.

"I wish I had better idea if this would work," Yuri said as he walked to the elevator. "I'd like to calculate probabilities."

"Some things aren't mathematically calculable," Lennon said.

"Not things worth knowing."

"Do you want to know what I feel like pressed against you?" Dovie said.

"Um. Yes, please."

"But you can't calculate that."

"Actually, I could. If I knew the density of your tissue, and the force with which it was applied to my mechanoreceptors . . ."

"Yuri, this is where you shut up and take me in your arms."

"Okay. That's another way to do it. It's just I'm more theoretical than experimental."

"Time to hit the lab, Science Boy."

"Right." He cleared his throat and put his arms around her.

"Shouldn't there be a control?" Lennon said, hitting the elevator button. "You should hug me, too."

"Can you calculate the force with which I'm going to slap him?" Dovie said.

"Gonna be damn lot of Newtons per square centimeter," Yuri said.

"You shoulda gone with 'hell' in that situation, but you're improving," Lennon said.

"Ignore him, and apply your lips to my mechanoreceptors. Or something like that," Dovie said.

So Yuri kissed her.

"First there was my tragic accident," Lennon said. "Now I see this."

The elevator stopped on the fourth floor, and Lennon pressed a thumb on the door's "open" button.

"By the way, the government might not pay for the porn flicks you ordered, so you may get stuck with the tab."

Yuri stared at him.

"I left your TV on. Figured if your zookeepers heard the luscious groans of *Bambi and the Firefighters*, they'd be more likely to leave you alone. Especially now that you have a documented history of self-gratification," Lennon said, miming opening a book.

"See you at five," Dovie said. She tented her fingers on Yuri's chest and gently pushed him out of the elevator, and the doors closed while he was still staring at Lennon.

Yuri took his pen from his jacket pocket and rolled it down the hall. It stopped between his door and Decker's. He ran low, below the level of the peepholes, gently inserted his key card, and clicked his door open. He slipped inside and was facing out from his room, reaching for the pen, by the time Decker cracked his door open.

"Found it." Yuri held up the pen and smiled, and slipped back into the room.

A moment later he heard Decker's bolt click shut again. He stood with his back to the door and exhaled.

Three Hours to Impact

Yuri's watch alarm beeped at 4:30 a.m. He hit it instantly, then lay still for five minutes in case the sound had carried into one of the guards' rooms. He got up, dressed in the new suit, and collected the belongings he'd packed the night before: a single suitcase and his book bag.

He had slept without the chain on the door, but had thrown the dead bolt by habit of residence in one of the world's largest cities. He eased it back now, slowly, and it clicked as it returned to its housing. He stood silently for another five minutes, looking out the peephole. Finally he rotated the doorknob, grateful that it wasn't a lever style. He opted for smooth and steady, and when the tongue was completely retracted, he slipped a stock card advertisement for a local restaurant between the tongue and its groove. He pushed his suitcase into the hall with his foot and shut the door behind him. The tongue hit the card and didn't snap home. No noise.

Yuri picked up his suitcase and ducked under Linares's peephole, just in case, then walked down the hall with what he hoped was the confident stride of a typical American teenage physicist checking out of a hotel at 4:45 a.m. He trotted down the stairwell closest to the lobby, thinking that if he had awakened a guard, that's the last point of egress they'd check. He left the hotel through the pool room, the chlorine stench sharp, the concrete still damp from the previous evening's swimmers. He felt alive, his stomach and fingertips tingling with adrenaline. He was free, and ready to fight to stay that way.

And then he was outside and alone.

The sky was lightening in the east as he made his way to the rendezvous point, a gas station a block down. Dovie's green-and-yellow car was waiting, parked facing the building. Yuri tossed his bags in the backseat next to Lennon, then stood with his hand on the door.

"I'm going to run in and use toilet. I'll be right back."

"We've got to go," Dovie said. "Get in here."

"You shoulda gone before you left, man," Lennon said.

"I couldn't flush. It might have awakened guard."

"Yeah, but you coulda *gone*," Lennon said.

"And not flush?" Yuri looked horrified.

"Sure. Given the circum—"

"Listen, I didn't save world so people can go around not

flushing." He swung the door shut and disappeared into the gas station.

"Unbelievable," Lennon said.

Three minutes later, Dovie herded the car onto the road away from the hotel. Fifteen minutes after that, they swung through an exit and were on the highway, heading for the Ambassador Bridge and beyond it, Canada. Yuri sat hunched forward, peering through the windshield. He was anxious, but he was moving, and there was something exhilarating about it.

"Mom sent some muffins," Dovie said. "Pass them up, Lennon."

Lennon handed a box forward.

Yuri popped the lid and looked inside. He lifted a muffin.

"Chocolate?"

"Carbon," Dovie said.

"Even I can't save these." He put the box on the seat. "Tell your mother 'thank you.'"

The route from the hotel to the bridge covered eighteen miles of strip malls and fast-food joints. Detroit's cityscape was like a dementia patient's brain—there were places where connections were needed, but there was nothing but a burned hole. Rain began to fall, lightly but steadily, and Dovie fishtailed twice.

"I think my tires are bald," Dovie said.

"You should buy her new tires," Lennon said. "And some counseling for me. We drove all the way from Pasadena, man. Do you know what it's like to ride with Dovie all the way from Pasadena?"

"It was good driving experience," Dovie said. "I think I might be ready to test for my license."

Yuri rubbed his forehead, and then decided to change the subject.

"So we just drive over bridge? And when we get to checkpoint at far end, we explain I need to go to Russian embassy, that it's emergency?"

"Yep," Dovie said.

"And what if they don't let us drive on through?"

"They probably won't," Dovie said. "You'll probably have to go forward on your own."

Yuri looked out the rain-streaked window.

"I'll miss you both."

"Yeah. You better."

"There's a pretty reasonable chance they'll take you off and question you for a while," Lennon said. "Just keep demanding to speak to the Russian ambassador. He should be in Ottawa, which isn't very far. Shouldn't be too difficult." Yuri nodded. "The important thing is that you'll be on Canadian soil."

Yuri pulled a folded conference schedule from his jacket pocket and wrote his address and phone numbers and e-mail on it. He handed Lennon the paper and pen, and Lennon wrote the Collums' contact information, and then ripped the paper in half. Yuri gave him a thin smile and shoved the folded paper in his pants pocket.

"'Yuri' means 'George,' right?" Lennon said, looking at the paper.

"No, 'George' means 'Yuri.'"

Lennon smiled.

"Is there a nickname?" Dovie said. "For 'Yuri'?"

"Yura."

"You're a?" Lennon said.

"Yura." He shrugged. "But most people call me Yuri."

"Yura? Seriously?" Lennon laughed. "Yura nut. Yura gorilla. Ha! It lends itself to so much."

A horn blared as Dovie strayed into the adjacent lane.

"Sorry," she muttered under her breath.

"Traffic's really getting heavy," Dovie said. "I thought people would still be asleep, that we'd at least beat rush hour, but I guess it starts early."

She bumped around a curve and they saw a stretch of highway before them, traffic crawling. And they saw the bridge.

The Ambassador Bridge stretched for almost two miles across the Detroit River. It was a suspension bridge with two towers made of crossed blue beams, each stacked three high: XXX marks the spot. The highway became impossibly complex, with exit and entrance ramps shunting traffic on and off, and a major curl of highway veering off to the right as it neared the bridge, as though it had seen Canada, and thought better of it.

Dovie sped along, water hissing under her tires.

"There's a checkpoint on this side," Yuri said. "On *this* side, Lennon."

"Huh. Well, it shouldn't be any trouble. I mean, Canada will want papers to get in, but you don't need papers to get out of a country."

Yuri swiveled to look back at him.

"I do. I need papers to get out."

"But they don't know who you are."

"*That's why they'll want papers.* To make sure they're not letting people out who are supposed to stay in. We talked about this."

"I think he's got a point, Len."

"I didn't see it on the search, okay? I had limited time." Lennon tapped his fingers on the window glass. "We just go through like there's no problem. Act confident. This is one of your strengths."

"And if that doesn't work?"

"Jump out of the car and run like hell for Canada," Lennon said.

Yuri threw his head back and exhaled. "That big loop, it's maybe kilometer from bridge. And bridge is another two kilometers easily. You want me to run three, four kilometers into Canada?"

"Look, the rain's letting up," Lennon said. "You might not even get wet."

Dovie took a curve and the line of booths was lost to sight.

"When will they notice you're gone, anyway?" she asked.

"Probably around six thirty. Maybe seven if I'm lucky."

"Six thirty?" Dovie turned to look at him, and another horn blared. "Jeez. This is really backed up."

"They'll expect shower noise, probably. And I left piece of paper in door. If they look carefully, they'll see it."

"It's already seven," Dovie said.

Yuri glanced at his watch.

"They won't know where I am, though. They'll search all over hotel, then at conference—maybe think I went in early. Russian ambassador might have me on airplane to Moscow by time they broaden search out this far."

"Not if we can't get through all these cars," Dovie said.

Yuri looked out at the clogged artery leading to the bridge.

"Next time I save world, I'm omitting Detroit."

"I was shocked you didn't do it this time, man," Lennon said.

A helicopter flew in, then hovered over the bridge intake with a *whap whap whap* of rotors. They crawled forward, then stopped again. Yuri rolled down the window and sat on the door, craning to see if there was an accident ahead. The rain had dissolved into a fine mist that hung suspended in the air, wetting his face. He flopped back onto the seat, springs creaking in protest beneath him.

"There's police cars ahead, but I don't see ambulance. Maybe is not bad accident."

Dovie bit her lip, concentrating on driving, her hands gripping the top of the steering wheel. The sun broke out and spilled over her, colored reflections scattering off her rings.

Yuri lowered his head and peered through the windshield. A rainbow arched above them. He wiggled his toes. If the Canadians demanded a physical exam before they let him in the country, he was not taking his socks off.

"Oh. I got you both something."

Yuri bent down to his bag and pulled a book out. He handed it to Lennon. "It's volume of Pushkin—collected works. I got one for myself, too, to read on plane home. That's part of gift."

Lennon looked up and caught his eye. "Seriously? You're going to read Pushkin?"

"I'm going to try."

Lennon flipped open the front cover. He read the inscription out loud. "I am not gnome-kisser. Yuri Strelnikov. P.S. I saved your life." He caught Yuri's eye. "'He stood, and dreamt a mighty dream.' You're still a gnome-kisser till you find that line."

Yuri smiled. "Challenge accepted." He fumbled in his bag for a moment, and turned to Dovie. She accelerated, moved forward a car length, then rocked to a stop on the clogged highway. She blew out in frustration, then turned to him.

Yuri opened his hand to reveal a small rock hammer.

"Wow," Lennon said. "You are such a romantic."

"Shut up, Len."

"Yes'm."

"It's to help you break out of rectangles," Yuri said. "Keep it in your locker. Remember there's life after high school. Things to paint, people to visit."

Dovie grabbed it off his palm and threw her arms around him.

"Thank you," she whispered in his ear. "It's exactly what I needed."

Her foot slipped off the brake and they jerked forward. She pulled away and slammed her foot down, and they jerked to a stop inches from the bumper of the car ahead of them.

"Something just occurred to me," Lennon said. "That pair guarding you?"

"Yeah?" Yuri said.

"So what if you're not the only one good at your job?"

"Whaddya mean?" Dovie said.

"What if they realized he was gone and simply called it in?" Lennon said. "I think that's a roadblock ahead."

CHAPTER 30

IMPACT

Yuri bent forward, staring ahead as Dovie drove them through the tangle of highways. A strand of road curled off to the right like frayed wire, taking some of the traffic with it. Dovie took a curve, following signs for the bridge. Blue and red light washed over the hood and was reflected in the wet asphalt. A hundred yards ahead was a line of seven guard booths at the base of a ramp. The guard stood beside it, behind the drip line coming off the booth's overhang. A uniformed police officer stood next to him. Three police cars sat nearby, one parked, the others idling on the right side of the road, one behind the other.

"We'll mail you your stuff, if you have to make a run for it," Lennon said.

"No way I can beat those cars to bridge," Yuri said.

"Lennon, you idiot. These are just tollbooths," Dovie said, heading for the middle one.

"How does that make me an idiot?" Lennon said.

Dovie shrugged. "Default setting."

"They're tollbooths with lot of police," Yuri said.

There were five vehicles ahead of them.

"They're checking everybody's trunks," Dovie said.

"They must not have a description of us," Lennon said. "They don't know who he's with."

"You should pull off somewhere. I'll go on alone," Yuri said.

"How far do you think you'll get?" Dovie said.

"I don't know, but they'll measure it on Planck scale."

A red hybrid pulled through.

Two vehicles to go.

"We'll tell them you were a hitchhiker," Lennon said.

Yuri snorted.

"As soon as I talk, they'll hear accent."

"Lennon, is your chair strapped in?" Dovie asked.

"It's wedged in the foot well."

"Strap it."

A frazzled woman in a red van was having trouble finding her money. The police officer looked around while they waited for her, taking in the bottleneck at the seven booths, the decreased congestion on the road beyond. Lennon clicked the seat belt around his chair. The woman finally handed over a bill and the cashier took it, handed back change, and waved her on.

One.

A black Camry pulled in. Dovie took a deep breath and rolled her shoulders, then bounced her palms on the top of the wheel.

The Camry driver handed exact change over, and a moment later he was pulling through onto the road ahead, cleared to cross the bridge.

Dovie rolled forward.

She handed the cashier a five-dollar bill. The police officer stepped forward and bent down, peering into the car. He looked at Yuri and with his hand on the car roof, he motioned another cop over from his cruiser on the right margin.

"How did you get that shiner, sir?"

Yuri stared straight ahead. An American border guard was staring at his face from a hand span away. Yuri wondered suddenly if an escape attempt was the kind of thing he could go to jail for. They wouldn't do that, would they? But what if it was illegal? He felt a surge of panic, and an intense desire to move. He tensed, but stayed still. *Röntgen, Lorentz, Zeeman, Becquerel, Curie, Curie, Rayleigh, von Lenard, Thomson . . .*

"Oh, he's deaf," Dovie said. "He's our deaf cousin."

"I'm going to ask you to step out of the car, sir," the officer said to Yuri.

The approaching cop was weaving his way past the right three tollbooths, heading for Yuri's door.

Dovie stomped on the gas pedal.

Yuri ducked, throwing his hands over his head, as the red-and-white barrier bar shattered the windshield.

"Jesus, Dovie!" Lennon shouted.

. . . Michelson, Lippmann, Marconi, Braun . . .

Round nuggets of glass cascaded into the car and scattered

over the asphalt. Dovie wove around the black Camry, then floored the accelerator. For a moment it didn't respond, then the engine shrugged and clanged and they rocketed past two police cars at the side of the road. The one in front flipped its siren on and nosed out, falling in behind them. The helicopter tilted and swooped around to follow.

Yuri held tight to the door handle.

"I think I'm gonna have to tell them you had a gun to my head," Dovie said, weaving around a pickup. "So be sure you make it across the bridge."

He stared at her.

"Oh, boy," she said, jerking right on the wheel.

. . . *van der Waals, Wien, Compton* . . .

They were on the giant loop of highway, which wrapped around a duty-free shop and a gas station before rising for a second pass on pylons, then stretching out straight to the stacked blue Xs of the Ambassador Bridge.

Yuri sank his head in his hands. "We are going to die," he said.

The tires squealed in agreement.

"Yeah," Dovie said. "But not today. You're gonna be okay, Science Boy."

"You need to pull off."

They flew past the duty-free shop, Dovie keeping the wheel jacked to the right to make the loop. The helicopter centered itself in the circle within the road, its rotors beating a steady *whap whap whap*, the battered car pulsating with the rhythm. Yuri could feel his blood rushing in his ears, and it seemed to synchronize with the helicopter. Ahead of them, two parked police cars flicked on lights and sirens and nosed onto the road ahead of them, right before it rose on the pylons.

"We're almost there," Dovie said as the car began to rise, its empty window frame vibrating.

The police cars drove abreast, slowing, forcing them to reduce speed.

"They're gonna make us stop," Dovie said. "Unless . . ."

She eased up on the wheel, letting the car straighten from the big right curve and whip to the left. She passed on the left shoulder, a line of sparks flying between the cars where she scraped the police car in passing. The officer looked over at Yuri, his face contorted with rage, their heads a foot apart. He mouthed, "Pull over." Yuri raised his hands in a helpless gesture. There was no way to explain that this was pretty normal driving for Dovie.

They nudged past one squad car, but the other stayed even with them, finishing the rising curve and keeping pace as they hit the straightaway. The Ambassador Bridge lay ahead. Yuri felt a surge of exhilaration, and beat his fist on the dashboard. It was going to work.

. . . Dalén, Onnes, von Laue, Bragg, Bragg . . .

Dovie wove through traffic. One moment the bridge was directly ahead of them, and then they were on it. Lennon pumped his fist and shouted, and Yuri turned to grin at him. One of the towers with the crossed blue beams flashed by. Two flags hung at the center of the bridge, one American and the other Canadian. They were maybe a third of a mile away. The police car slowed beside them, boxing them in behind a dark blue sedan. Dovie pulled left and sped around the car.

"This is for other direction!" Yuri shouted. "Is not lane for passing!"

"Yeah, but hardly anybody was coming," Dovie said, cutting in tight in front of the blue car.

The cruiser sped up, opening space between them, then braked hard and pulled sideways, blocking the road ahead. A semi chugged in the left lane of oncoming traffic, an SUV was to their right. No place to go. Dovie slammed her brake and yanked the wheel left, spinning the car, bald tires grabbing at wet asphalt. For a moment the semi's huge tires rolled by, filling the window, then the truck was past and they crashed sideways into the police car and rocked to a stop.

Yuri stared for a moment at Dovie.

"Go, go!" she yelled, making a motion with her hand. "We're fine. Go!" He opened the door, but there wasn't space to get out. The officer was scrambling across his seat, exiting through his passenger door. Yuri launched himself over the seat into the back, landed on Lennon's folded wheelchair, and kicked the door open. There was just room to squeeze out. He caught a glimpse of Lennon's smile, his thumbs up, and then Yuri's soles hit the pavement above the Great Lakes and he ran, dodging past the police officer, arms pumping, lungs already burning. He wasn't afraid of anything. He was running, and he was free.

"Strelnikov," he whispered, skipping all the winners since 1915. *Strelnikov.*

The main cable dipped down between the towers, below the edge of the railing, and as Yuri ran past the Canadian flag the cable began to soar upward again, a reverse rainbow. He was more than halfway across the bridge. He was in Canada.

He'd made it.

He would go home and protect his work. Laskov couldn't claim authorship if he was there to defend it. Yuri would win the Nobel Prize in physics, the ninth winner from Moscow State University. He would make Gregor Kryukov proud. He would make his father immortal.

Brakes squealed and metal ground on metal, electrons shearing. Yuri looked over his shoulder and saw the dark blue sedan bounce away from Dovie's car and settle at an angle, the hoods in close as though the cars were whispering. Yuri stopped, his features as crumpled as the cars. The driver wouldn't have been going too fast, would have seen the first wreck unfolding ahead. Surely.

Was Dovie okay?

A woman stumbled out of the sedan, walked around the tangled fronts of the cars and leaned down to talk to Dovie through her passenger window.

He needed to run *now* while the police officer chasing him was watching the wreck. Yuri needed to run, but he stood, waiting to see if Dovie emerged from the car.

Something was going on in the back of the green car; then she popped out the back door, stumbling around the wheelchair. Probably she hadn't been able to get the driver's door open. She made a shooing motion behind her back. Yuri grinned and started to turn, but something caught his eye.

The back door of the blue sedan opened. A little boy slid out, maybe two years old. He was fine. His mother would have checked on him first, before talking to the other driver. But he wanted his mother and she was talking to Dovie and the police officer on the far side of the crumpled green car. And he was running, arms outstretched, to get to her, and the only way to do it was to run into the right lane.

Traffic was still moving in the right lane.

The police officer turned, saw Yuri, and began to run at him.

The boy ran with the inefficient movement of a toddler, his arms flung out, crying for his mother. Around the crumpled cars, to where there was space. A bus was coming, one of those charters retired people take to waterfalls and casinos, but it was a ways off. It would probably see him and stop in time. Yuri took a couple of steps backward, deeper into Canada.

The exhaust from the bus rose and in his mind turned to steam rising off a bowl of borscht in front of Gregor Kryukov's face, toward his eyebrows, and Kryukov smiled a little sadly, and then the steam obscured his face and he was gone.

The boy's mother didn't see him. Dovie didn't see him.

The child was low to the ground, but the bus driver would notice and would stop. Surely.

And if not, what was Yuri supposed to do about it? He'd already saved his life once. The kid was on his own from here on out.

Yuri blinked at the savagery of the thought.

Something moved behind Dovie's tires. It was Lennon, pulling himself on his hands, useless legs dragging behind him, his feet bumping awkwardly. Trying to reach the boy.

Yuri had never really noticed Lennon's legs before. They were thin and oddly long, and they didn't match the rest of him, like some kind of animal you'd find in Australia. There was something grotesque in his desperation, horrible to watch, impossible to turn away from.

Lennon was out of his chair after all.

Then Lennon grabbed the boy, and the child shrieked and Yuri thought now, now someone else will fix this, but Dovie and the woman were talking and the police officer was running at him and the bus driver's eyes flicked for the first time from the wreckage to the people down low in the lane before him. He hadn't seen. He hadn't slowed. Yuri saw the man's face the moment his eyes started to widen.

Distances, angles, forces, velocity. Yuri knew this stuff. He ran forward, toward the United States, and the policeman slowed for a moment, confused, then recovered and dived sideways but missed Yuri as he ran back toward the wreck.

Lennon rolled onto his hip for leverage and tossed the child to the edge of the bridge by the railing, and for a mad second Yuri thought the boy would fall through. But he bumped against the barrier, sat down hard, and wailed. His mother turned and screamed.

The bus's brakes screeched.

Yuri ran toward Lennon, who had swiveled to pull himself

back to the shelter of the tangle of cars. Lennon realized he wasn't going to make it and spun in panic back toward the railing. He threw his hands out as though he were swimming, clawing the pavement with his fingers, dragging himself toward the edge of the bridge. In front of the bus.

The bus started a long, hard slide, pale faces staring out the black-glass windows, mouths opening into Os. Maybe three seconds to impact.

Yuri leaned down, grabbing Lennon under the armpits.

Two seconds.

He jerked up, pulling Lennon's chest out of the big tires' path. The bus driver threw his hands up, crossing his arms over his face.

Yuri heaved and Lennon's hips cleared the lane.

One second to impact.

Lennon's legs followed easily, his mass unequally distributed, and they fell backward, Yuri scraping his cheek on the roadway, the toddler screaming in general outrage, the bus tires squealing past, leaving rubber on the pavement and lingering, acrid, in the air.

Yuri lay, holding Lennon, the sky clearing above him. Rainwater soaked through his suit jacket, and he didn't care.

The boy's mother reached them, grabbed her child up and rocked him back and forth, weeping. Dovie appeared above him, panting, her bangs standing at attention. The police officer ran up, breathless, and then settled for resting the heels of his hands on his belt as he waited for the other squad cars to wind through traffic to the wreck at the first blue tower.

"People are gonna get the wrong idea about us," Lennon said.

Yuri threw a hand up and Dovie grabbed it, helping him sit up. Lennon's butt rested on the road, his legs stretched out, but Yuri kept an arm wrapped around Lennon's chest.

"We're not lovers," Lennon told the cop. "I don't go for blonds."

"That was close," Yuri said, his eyes suddenly wet. "That was really close."

Lennon *thunk*ed him awkwardly on the back with his fist.

"You would have made it if it wasn't for me," Lennon said.

"Thank you," Dovie said to Yuri, stroking her brother's hair. She began to cry.

"Don't let him eat those muffins," Yuri said. "I don't want my sacrifice to be wasted."

Dovie laughed and wiped her eyes, then sat down and leaned against him, her purple Keds tapping the wet asphalt.

Two more police cars pulled up and their officers spilled out, rushed over, and consulted with the cop securing the scene. One of them began to talk to the boy's mother, another got on his radio. No one approached them.

"I realized something," Dovie said. "The asteroid only landed on you. You're the only one who lost your life. Your old life, I mean."

Yuri nodded. "Ironic, isn't it? And maybe is fair."

She looked at him. "You know, Kant would be proud of you."

"He better be," Yuri said. "My world just perished."

"He lives to impress dead Germans," Lennon explained to the police officer standing a few feet away.

Dovie kissed Yuri's neck.

"Rebuild," she whispered.

Yuri looked over, saw Decker and Linares getting out of their car, wearing matching black Windbreakers and walking fast.

Dovie blinked back tears. "You didn't carve your name on the sash."

"No," he said. "It was more important to do good work than to get honor for it. I learned that." She nodded. "It would be beautiful day to hang in air over Great Lakes, under rainbow, kissing girl with green bangs."

"Hmm," Dovie said. She leaned forward and kissed him on the lips.

"Help!" Lennon called. "Officer, this is cruel and unusual."

The police officer threw a strong arm around Lennon's chest and lifted him gently, moving him out of Yuri's arms, then walked to the car to get his wheelchair.

"You know why rainbow is beautiful?" Yuri said. "Because it has all its colors."

Dovie put a palm on the back of his head and kissed him again, chewing gently on his lower lip.

"Keep all your colors, Dovie."

She threw her arms around him, kissing him and knocking him backward, and rode him down to the pavement. She rolled off and they lay side by side, backs on the wet asphalt, holding hands and looking into the sky.

If he was going to live in America, he was going to have to buy a cowboy hat. And a pickup truck. He would play volleyball with a large group of friends in front of an open cooler of beer, and girls in bikinis would wash his truck. He had seen the pictures; he knew how these people lived. And it wouldn't be so bad. But how exactly did you get the girls to do that?

"Dovie, if I buy pickup truck, will you wash it?"

"No. Besides, you don't know how to drive."

"True. Then will you at least tell me where to buy cowboy hat?"

She turned her head to look at him. "Sure thing, Tex."

When Decker and Linares approached, the police backed away, watching. The agents stood looking down at Yuri and Dovie, Windbreakers flapping, blue sky behind their faces.

"Hi," Yuri said.

"Heard what happened," Linares said. "Are you okay?"

"Yeah," Yuri said. "Actually, I am."

Linares crouched beside him.

"I take it you learned that your stay in the United States has been extended?"

"Yeah."

"You know, there will be some exciting opportunities for you here. You'll have your choice of positions."

Dovie sat up, pulling Yuri with her. She hugged him.

"I'm so sorry. I'm so sorry you didn't make it."

"No, it's okay. It was my choice. I chose to come back." He smiled, kissed her lightly on the lips, and rose. Linares stood with him and nodded to the police officer.

"This all looks like an accident, don't you think, officer?"

The cop hesitated for a moment, looking at the wreckage.

"Yeah. Hey, is it true this is the meteor kid?"

Decker nodded.

"Asteroid," Yuri muttered.

Lennon reached a hand up and Yuri shook it, then walked backward between Decker and Linares, back through the blue Xs, with Michigan beyond. He raised a hand to Dovie, then turned and faced the United States.

"Did you see me running in suit, like Matt Damon? Pretty good, huh?"

"Yeah," Decker said. "You did okay."

"Damn, shit, hell, yeah."

AUTHOR'S NOTE

A few disclaimers are in order. First, an asteroid's name begins with the year in which it was discovered. Since the events in this book occurred the year that the BR1019 was found, I named the asteroid differently so as not to date the book. I used my daughter's birth date, because she's the brightest, fastest thing in my sky.

The acronyms get confusing. The Near Earth Object Program (NEO) is housed at the Jet Propulsion Lab (JPL) on the California Institute of Technology (CIT) campus, and is a part of the National Aeronautics and Space Administration (NASA). None of this is my fault.

I'm aware that Strelnikov should be transliterated as Strel'nikov, but it seemed cumbersome, and I didn't want to change Yuri's last name because I liked the meaning. No, I'm not telling you. Learn Russian.

We don't know the size of the Persian force at Marathon, just that the invaders greatly outnumbered the Greeks. Estimates of the Persian force range from about 20,000 to 1.7 million. Lennon is entitled to his own estimate.

Also, Immanuel Kant argued in favor of the maxim, "Do what is right though the world should perish," but he was quoting an earlier, obscure Latin line. We associate the saying with Kant, however, and I thought it was reasonable for Dovie to attribute it to him.

I did a lot of research to write this book, but if you're trying to stop an asteroid, you probably shouldn't use it as a guide.

Finally, if you do notice an incoming asteroid, please give the nearest astrophysicist a heads-up because there really are only about a hundred people in the world looking for them. And it really is a big sky.

ACKNOWLEDGMENTS

One of the best parts of writing a book is getting to acknowledge the people who helped along the way.

This book was greatly improved by Dr. Robert A. August Jr., who explained many things to me, including that the marker would be orange and that you can't stop an asteroid without pizza. Thanks, Bob.

Dr. Pablo Muchnik was both generous and speedy in sharing his expertise on Immanuel Kant.

Larissa Hill and Diana Murray checked my Russian profanity. Much hilarity ensued. *Bol'shoye spasibo!*

Many thanks to Dan Martin, who was thoughtful enough to live in California.

Michael Adam checked my math problems. Bruce Aaron Bilgreen set me straight on high school percussion. Kira Vermond drove the Ambassador Bridge and gave me a full report. I'm grateful to all of them.

Thanks also to Judy Palermo, who read and wanted to know what kind of boy doesn't call his mother to tell her that he landed safely. Fixed it, Judy. Shelley Seely and Amy Jomantas read some late-addition scenes. Dave Wright, Adia Molloy, Jenny Mundy-Castle, Katrina S. Forest, Miriam Spitzer Franklin, and Lindsay Eagar read the first draft, and that can't have been fun. Christine McMahon read on short notice. Thank you all.

Additional thanks to Dr. Katrin Flikschuh, Kristin Stanchina, Megan Miller, and Mary Ellen Kennedy.

I'm indebted to the incredible team of moderators and administrators at the SCBWI Blueboard. Thanks for the sparkles and "research help." Yeah, you know who you are, and you know what I mean. Tell no one.

Kate McKean is the Yuri Strelnikov of agents: she's smart and knows how to take chances. Kate, thanks for taking a chance on Yuri and me.

Thanks also to my editor at Bloomsbury, Sarah Shumway. This book is better because she touched it. Sarah, congratulations on your biggest—also littlest—recent project. Françoise Bui went above and beyond. Linda Minton copyedited the manuscript. The hush money is on the way, Linda.

Thanks to the rest of the team at Bloomsbury for their expertise and support, especially Claire Stetzer, Diane Aronson, Lizzy Mason, Donna Mark, Melissa Kavonic, Catherine Onder, Cindy Loh, and Colleen Andrews.

I don't even know how to go about thanking my family. John Robert McFarland and Helen McFarland taught me about love and stories. What else is there? Mary Beth McFarland shared that journey with me. Patrick Kennedy understands that when I'm sitting in a chair staring into space, I'm working. Thanks, Boogums.

And more thanks than my heart can hold to Brigid Kennedy and Joseph Kennedy, who make life worth living and the world worth saving. I love you.